Wolf Heart

MAEGAN M. SIMPSON

My Lord and Savior Jesus Christ lived the only perfect human life. I have edited this to the best of my ability, but there will undoubtedly be mistakes. Please forgive my lack of perfection. Thank you.

Cover design by MoorBooks Design

Under jacket design by Maegan M. Simpson

Chapter Background artwork by Chicklen Doodle

ISBN: 978-1-966420-00-2

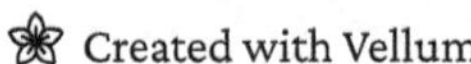

For the young and fierce.
Age doesn't forbid you from making a difference.

CONTENTS

Acknowledgments

I would first like to thank my Heavenly Father for the talent and love for writing that He has given me, and the time and freedom to pursue that talent. The credit and glory for this story goes to Him.

A huge thanks to my beta readers: Lexi, Penny, Liz, and Stormie! Each of you was a tremendous help polishing this book in time for release!

Thank you to all my friends who encourage and support me in many ways. I especially want to thank Sarah, for sticking with me since the beginning of this whole writing thing, and Lexi, for listening to all my fragmented story ideas and encouraging me that they're worth something. And thank you both for being so willing to read my writing and for not laughing at my crazy ideas and moments of inspiration.

Thank you to my professors at Colorado Christian University for teaching me so much and helping me grow, in soul and faith as well as in knowledge. Throughout my time at CCU, you challenged me to think deeply, to always be learning, and to pursue God with all I am. Thank you for pouring into me, and I pray that the lessons I learned from you are visible in my life and my writing.

And finally, thank you to Mom, Dad, and Levi. Your support allows me to pursue these stories as more than a hobby, and your work behind the scenes is why my books are legible and I am still sane. You help me more than you know, and I continually thank God that He gave me *you* as a family. I love you!

CHAPTER ONE

Izzy

Steel glinted in the torchlight as a sword split the air, coming for her neck. Izzy parried the strike, darting in with a thrust that her oldest friend knocked aside with a knife in his off hand. She twisted her sword and struck again, only to have the blade nearly knocked from her grasp. Her opponent was inside her guard before she could recover, a knife tip pressed to the leather armor covering her stomach.

Izzy looked up to see a grinning face more familiar to her than her own reflection. She imagined Collin would say the same about the glare she offered him in reply.

"Care to go again?" he asked, blond hair hanging across his eyes and giving him a roguish look. He wasn't much taller than her, but he made use of every bit of his height as he leaned over her.

She itched to say yes, to knock him on his rear so *she'd* be the one grinning, but a glance around the courtyard revealed that others were arriving. The sky was gray in the east, a sure sign that their time was up.

"Not now," Izzy said, turning to stare up in Collin's golden eyes again. "But tomorrow, you're mine."

His grin only grew. "Perhaps when the sun sets in the north."

Izzy scoffed, shoving his chest. His grin widened as he swayed, then slowly took a single step away from her with an amused light in his eyes. She shook her head, twisting away before she said something she shouldn't. But as they turned toward the armory, Izzy bumped her shoulder against his just for the contact. He elbowed her back

They returned their practice swords to the armory, navigating the narrow paths between racks and racks of glinting weapons with practiced ease despite the dim light. They nodded to the handful of their comrades who were already retrieving their weapons for patrol. Most of those Izzy and Collin passed looked like they'd only woken up minutes before. They were the younger set. The experienced Red Cloaks had risen a while ago and were already eating breakfast. Andred was the one exception, but she always looked half asleep. And anyone who mistook her heavily lidded eyes for apathy soon regretted it.

Izzy had been awake for over an hour. She and Collin always met well before dawn to spar and prepare for the day. Most considered their routine a sign of dedication. To Izzy it was a matter of survival.

Collin handed Izzy a dagger she usually claimed, set apart by the black cord she'd woven into the grip, and she handed him a few of the daggers he preferred. Then he passed her the sword she always chose, nearly indistinguishable from the rest except for the small star she'd scratched into the head of the pommel.

Izzy breathed deeply, letting the scent of leather and oiled steel center her. Soon they were outfitted with half a dozen blades each, their grips familiar beneath Izzy's fingertips. Theoretically the weapons in the armory didn't belong to any individual, but they all had their favorites. Most of the other claimed weapons were already gone, taken by their owners before they went to breakfast.

One of the newer recruits, his brown hair sticking out in all directions, watched their practiced routine with unbridled curiosity. Izzy tried to ignore him. Collin, though, smiled and gestured to the racks of weapons filling the room.

"Choose fast," he said. "You don't want to be caught unarmed when the Commander calls."

The recruit tumbled into motion, tugging on the edge of his red cloak as he poked at some of the short swords. Hopefully he knew not to choose any weapon with a claim mark, like her black cord. Izzy shook her head and followed Collin outside.

"Berke," Collin called low.

A brown-haired man, built like a troll with an impressive beard, lifted his head from where he spoke to a few others.

"Your new robin is in there getting lost," Collin said lightly. "Give the poor kid a hand, will you?"

Berke cursed below his breath. "Should've known not to leave him. Can't seem to make a quick decision to save his life."

"Quick decisions are often rash ones," Alair called after Berke.

"Oh, shut up."

Alair winked at Izzy and Collin before pushing off the wall, entering the chamber ahead of them.

Inside was dim, lit only by candles and the light coming from the door. Commander Rhett already stood at the head of the room, his tall frame dwarfing the wooden podium he stood behind. Only Alair came close to rivaling Rhett's height, though no one would know it by how he slouched as he wove between the men and women crowding the space. She kept her own back straight as the last few filed in and took seats on the worn benches scattered around the room.

There were only two dozen or so on duty today. Most were still placed on night shift, though the wolf moon had passed three weeks ago. The waning of the moon didn't seem to have an effect these past months: more beasts were coming out of the forest than ever, making the Red Cloaks' task of protecting Kedar a constant responsibility. The only relief they had were nights when the moon stayed hidden or kept its path to daylight hours. Recently even the day brought danger.

Izzy and Collin chose seats near the wall halfway up the room, as always. A short and broadly built man was already sitting there, his legs stretched along the bench and crossed at the ankles. Izzy kicked the wooden legs.

"Bright and cheerful as ever, Izzy," Dal said, slipping his feet onto the floor.

"Who says I'm never cheerful?" Izzy muttered, taking her seat with Collin.

Collin snorted, and she thrust her elbow back, catching him in the ribs.

"You'll notice I didn't say that," Dal replied.

Izzy rolled her eyes, shifting her cloak out of the way of Eldon as he sat between her and Dal.

"How's Abby?" Collin asked quietly, as the room filled around them.

"Tired," Eldon replied. "Maizy has an ear infection again."

Collin made a sympathetic sound in the back of his throat but said nothing more. Izzy held her silence, though when Eldon grinned and tweaked her braid, she smiled in return.

Eldon was one of the few Red Cloaks with a spouse. He was sworn in before Izzy was born, under the old vows. Only the Commander had served longer than him. There had been a few others under the old vows when Izzy and Collin had joined, but most were gone now: either retired or killed in duty. The lamp light glinted on the handful of gray hairs peppered across his head and beard. Not many Red Cloaks made it past forty years, and those who did usually took it as a sign to leave the order. But here Eldon and Rhett were, four years later and still two of the most highly skilled Red Cloaks who lived. Izzy dreaded the day that would change.

If Commander Rhett was the stern father over the Red Cloaks, Eldon was the indulgent but unpredictable uncle. No one could be sure which side he'd take until he'd already made his decision...and those decisions were final. Izzy had spent months living with him and Abby before taking her vows, and to her he was family.

"Berke to the east quarter," Commander Rhett called with no preamble. He didn't need any: his deep voice easily carried through the room, silencing everyone as he stared at them with stern and deep-set eyes. "Eldon and Dal to the south fields. Moonrise today is midmorning, and we can't afford any interruptions to the harvest."

Each man nodded sharply at their orders, as a solemn mood settled over the room. There wasn't much harvest left after the Horde's attack this past moon. But they had to salvage all that they could. The rest held their silence as Commander Rhett read out lists of who would go with each captain. Izzy listened closely, but her own name wasn't called. Neither was Collin's.

Izzy kept her gaze carefully ahead toward the Commander, though energy jolted around inside her like lightning searching for its place to strike. She and Collin had been off night duty for a week, but they had yet to leave the city walls. Today that would change. And, dangerous or not, she was ready to begin their work again.

As their comrades filtered out to their different areas, Izzy followed Collin to the front of the room where Commander Rhett still stood. Tay and Farren were already there. Two days ago they'd been sent to clear the lands surrounding the southern road in preparation for a few caravans expected in the next moon cycle. They must've found something larger than usual if Rhett had decided they needed aid.

"Go South," Commander Rhett said, eyeing each of them. "Collin, Izzy: stay with Tay and Farren for today. They have a den to eradicate."

Izzy stood a little taller when his eyes landed on her, aware that Collin did the same. The sisters didn't react.

"We'll begin immediately," Tay said, bowing her head before she and Farren turned away.

Izzy also nodded, keeping her expression carefully schooled as she turned away. Collin wasn't so cautious, turning to grin at her as they followed Tay and Farren out of the chamber and deeper into the main building. The room where they kept maps and reports was upstairs, a windowless room that was full of dust no matter how much it was cleaned, but oil lamps on the walls lit their way.

"Finally," he muttered.

Izzy agreed. From halfmoon to halfmoon they'd scoured the forest for pockets of adversaries only to be pulled back to the city as soon as they felt like they were getting somewhere. It was a cycle that had repeated for years: they would go out, clearing dens of goblins and their moonstruck pets that had strayed too close to Kedar, and searching for whatever hideaway the ogres and trolls had found to hide from the sun. But no matter how much they searched and fought, the horde that assailed them each night never grew smaller.

That didn't change their determination to keep fighting. Better to strike out into the wilds and eliminate those who dared to attack during the day than wait within the walls for night to fall. Collin in particular had been itching to get back out there ever since the moon began to wane. The fact that Rhett had kept them in the city, running patrols in tandem with the Watch along certain streets of the city, had made them both stir crazy. Izzy hated when Rhett used her and Collin as the face of the Red Cloaks.

Tay and Farren were already spreading maps on the dark, wooden table when Izzy and Collin entered, making Izzy wonder if they also were eager to be back among the trees. It was hard to tell what the two women thought...they were more stoic than Rhett was. That combined with their nearly identical looks—long noses, straight dark hair, and pale blue eyes—made them intimidating at the best of times.

"There's a depression in the land here," Farren said, pointing to the map. "The far end has a cluster of stones, with a cave hidden among them. A well-worn trail leads within. With all luck, it's still there."

Izzy frowned as she stared at the location Farren marked on the map. What she described was nothing like the carefully hidden dens they were used to...nor did it sound like the elusive center of command they'd searched for over the years.

"With all luck, the mosquitos won't devour us before we reach it," Collin replied.

"Afraid of the buzzing, are you?" Tay remarked dryly, glancing up at Collin with the closest to a smile she ever wore.

"Hardly. I just don't want to deal with Izzy's complaining when the itching starts."

"As if you're any better," Izzy muttered.

"My bad moods can't hold a candle to yours."

"The frost should've killed them out," Farren said, glancing at Collin as she rolled up the map. "Your precious blood is safe."

"Good to hear."

Tay slid the last map back into its place and turned to face Collin and Izzy with her hands on her hips. She stared for a moment, unspeaking.

"We're ready when you are," Collin said.

With a nod, Tay turned for the door where Farren already stood. Izzy glanced up at Collin. He shrugged, a crooked smile on his lips, before following the sisters back into the hall. Izzy stayed close to his side.

Collin

Collin kept a close watch on the path behind them as he and Izzy followed Tay and Farren south. They'd already left the wide road to plunge into the wild forest. Here it was thick and wet, full of tangled trees, dripping moss, and bogs that blocked their path more and more as they drew close to the river. Most of the trees were tinged brown, with fallen leaves already thick on the ground among mushrooms and frostbitten grass. Those leaves made it nearly impossible to tell solid soil from spongy marsh. It wasn't an area he enjoyed spending time in. He'd take rough mountainsides over wet boots any day.

Looking over, Collin caught Izzy's eyes and smiled. Her green eyes were warm, though her lips hardly shifted from their serious set. A strand of pale hair had escaped her tight braid to hang beside her face.

The crack of a branch in the distance made her turn away, west of their path. Reluctantly, Collin returned his attention to the east. Tay and Farren walked side by side a few steps ahead, eerily silent as usual. Neither sister had spoken a word since they left the map room, and it was starting to grate on his nerves. He liked the sisters well enough...but he preferred people he could tease into actually conversing, like Izzy. Whenever Collin had tried prodding them into conversation in the past, Tay and Farren stared at him like he was wearing a flowerpot on his head.

He knew if he said anything now, one of them would turn around and glare at him until he shut up. The last time he'd opened his mouth was greeting the two Watchmen at the gate. He sighed, and when he glanced at Izzy again she was rolling her eyes. Mouth tilted in a smile, Collin almost broke the silence just so she'd turn toward him again. But just as he was wondering what whispered words would draw the best reaction, the forest around them shifted.

Thus far on their walk, they'd been surrounded by enough noise to cover their passage. Bird song, rustling leaves from fleeing squirrels...normal, comforting sounds. Now the air around them was as silent as Tay and Farren. That put him on his guard.

Collin angled himself away from Izzy. She did the same, letting Tay and Farren guard the front while they watched their sides. It was a familiar formation. Izzy bumped her shoulders against his, and that brief contact steadied his mind.

Tay and Farren continued on as if nothing had changed, but Collin knew better. They expected this. It was probably their first indication that something was off. He was more inclined to agree with them hearing even the birds fall silent.

They stopped. After one more glance around the forest at their backs, he and Izzy turned to see what the sisters had brought them to. He began to whistle and bit it off, glancing at Izzy to see her staring at the interrupted forest with narrowed eyes. It was more impressive than they'd described.

Before them, the ground plunged down over a man's height. The banks were steep, but covered in moss and grass. It wasn't a recent change, or it wasn't supposed to look like one. But there was no question the depression wasn't natural...it was in a perfect circle, clear of all trees and underbrush. Toward the far end, rocks were stacked in a replica of Mount Talith with a dark hole marking its base. The ground near the cave was packed and bare. Something, or lots of somethings, were inside. But it took a minute for Collin to pinpoint why the sight of the place made him uneasy...it was shaped like an arena.

It looked nothing like the carefully hidden dens they rooted out. More like a carefully set snare.

"Looks perfect for an ambush," Izzy whispered, echoing Collin's thoughts.

"That's why we wanted you two here before we went into it," Tay said, glancing back at them with sharp eyes. "We enter, you watch our backs?"

Collin didn't like the idea of sitting around waiting for everything to fall into chaos, but he nodded. They had their orders: follow Tay and Farren's lead.

Farren slipped down the slope first, standing at attention with a bare sword in her hand while Tay followed. Collin reached to his side, loosening his sword in its scabbard, as Tay and Farren creeped across the open space. Even watching them sent a shiver across his back.

Izzy shifted beside him, drawing her sword slowly. In the eerie silence, the hissing scrape nearly made him wince. Collin looked around the edge of the depression to ensure they were the only ones watching while Izzy checked behind them. But the stillness matched the silence as Tay and Farren approached the mouth of the cave. Collin heard Izzy pull in a deep breath and hold it as the sisters disappeared into the shadow.

Wind tossed the branches, scattering brown and gold mottled leaves through the empty air. Collin stared beyond them and wished his vision could pierce that darkness. Whatever was in there...

A deep growl rose, shaking the ground beneath Collin's feet. Before he could do more than draw his sword, creatures spilled out of the cave mouth, blocking all else from sight. He thought he heard Farren shout above the turmoil.

Izzy slid down the bank in a flurry of dust and leaves. Collin was only a heartbeat behind her, hitting the ground in a run and reaching Izzy's side in a bound. They were hardly halfway across the open ground when the fight began.

Moon-struck animals snarled, stopping their flight to turn and attack them. Using his sword to block a deer trying to gore him, Collin glanced around to see how bad off they were. There were dozens of animals, some of which were already fleeing into the trees. Among them were a handful of tall goblins wrapped in thick cloaks to shield themselves from the sun, cursing and whipping the creatures toward Izzy and Collin, but no trolls or ogres.

Collin and Izzy fought back-to-back, creeping forward as they battled normally peaceful forest creatures salivating for their blood. The goblins hung back, letting their pets do their dirty work, but Collin could understand enough of their shouting to know that they didn't intend to let anyone leave alive.

From the cave, he could hear strained voices, punctuated by crashing rock and strange, strangled cries that were *definitely* not human. Not troll, either.

The attacks slowed as they neared the cave's mouth, as if animal and goblin alike wanted to leave a separation between themselves and whatever was inside. Collin spotted Farren's back.

"Farren!" he called.

She didn't turn around, dodging a thick arm that looked like *mud*. Collin twisted, facing their attackers while Izzy faced the cave. There was a look in the goblins' eyes he didn't like, but it wasn't until Izzy cried out and jerked into Collin's back that he wondered how thorough this trap was.

"There's a barrier across the entrance," Izzy said.

Collin thrust his sword through the chest of a badger trying to rip out his kneecaps before he had time to consider that. *Sorcery*.

But what that meant for the horde's attacks on Kedar would have to come later. For now, it meant that Tay and Farren were trapped... and Collin and Izzy had to figure out a way to get them out.

"It won't be anchored in the ground," Collin said, blocking the swipe of a bear's paw. It was a black bear, hardly as tall as he was on its hind legs, but it was still a *bear*. He jumped back to avoid its next swipe of a paw, thrusting his sword into its chest. The blade glanced off bone.

"I'm going up," Izzy said, before her presence at his back disappeared. The sound of shifting rock above his head told him where she was.

"You couldn't wait a minute?" Collin muttered, risking a glance toward the goblins and nearly losing his throat for his trouble. They were watching Izzy, but he didn't see a bowman among them.

The bear growled, revealing yellowed teeth. Collin drew himself up to his full height and growled back. It didn't intimidate the bear, drunk as it was on bloodlust. But Collin followed the act by lunging forward to sink his sword through its throat. Blood poured down the blade, and Collin kicked the bear backward. It pinned badger to the ground.

Collin turned, glancing up to where Izzy was perched on the stacked boulders, searching every crevice for whatever the barrier spell was anchored in. None of the animals were paying any attention to her, but Collin spotted a goblin crawling over the crest of the pile.

"Left!" he shouted, leaping onto a boulder to scramble to Izzy's side.

The following screech didn't come from Izzy.

Collin straightened, searching for any other goblins who might try taking them by surprise. No others were climbing the rocks, yet. Some grimaced as the moon-struck animals tore into their comrade's body where it lay at the base of the rocks. Others whipped the backs of mountain rams and deer, wanting them to climb the rocks. They were more interested in the spilled blood from those Collin and Izzy had already killed. One goblin glared at Collin with potent hatred, twisting his fingers in an obscene gesture Collin had seen plenty of times before when he fought at Kedar's gates. Collin lifted an eyebrow and kept his sword raised.

"Found it," Izzy said, plunging her hand into a dark space between stones. She pulled out an obsidian orb, faceted with carved stars and runes. Izzy set it on a flat stone, bringing her sword's pommel down on the orb.

It shattered, and oily shadows spilled out from the shards, darkening Collin's sight for a heart-pounding moment. It drove the animals wild.

Those still alive turned and fled toward the banks, heedless to the goblins' cries and whips. And as another rumbling cry came from the cave, the goblins followed their pets.

"It's open!" Collin shouted, climbing to stand above the cave's mouth.

Red flashed below him, as Tay and Farren left the cave. Dread flooded his limbs when he realized not all of that red was from their cloaks. Farren was half carrying, half dragging Tay into the open ground. From his vantage point, he couldn't tell if she was still alive or not.

But a grating growl turned Collin's focus back to the opening below his feet, as a creature shuffled out into the daylight. Collin held his sword hilt with both hands, ready to leap down and end whatever enemy was stalking their comrades. But when the creature came into sight, he paused.

He'd never seen a creature like this before. It was tall as an ogre, but it looked like it was made of sunbaked clay. Collin could see gouges where Tay and Farren had attacked it: there was no blood, no flesh. Only dirt pouring from the cracks.

"Its neck," Izzy whispered.

Collin spotted it: an obsidian stone set into the clay where the top of the spine should be. Already the creature was a few steps away from the cave's mouth, and Collin judged the distance with a wary eye.

"Now?" Izzy said, shifting into stance beside him, daggers in her hands rather than her sword.

"Now."

They jumped together, each sinking their blades into the creature's back. It gave like a crust covering softened soil, and Collin's sword went in to the hilt. The creature roared, shaking its shoulders as it turned to see what was on its back. One large, stone-clad hand reached back to pluck them off, and Collin twisted to avoid it. Izzy was already bringing the back of her dagger onto the obsidian. The glass shattered, and the creature froze. The sound of cracking stone filled the silence.

Collin looked over at Izzy, seeing his own realization mirrored in her eyes. The creature dissolved into sand.

He landed on the bear's wiry hide, his sword and dagger clattering to the ground. Collin winced as he stood, plucking his weapons from the ground as he turned to find Izzy. She was already sheathing her knives. Their eyes met for a heartbeat before they ran toward Tay and Farren.

Farren had her sister laid out, pressing a corner of her sister's cloak to the wound in her side. Blood dripped down Tay's face from a cut on her head, her eyes were closed...but she was still alive. Tay winced as Izzy helped Farren tie the pad of cloth to the wound using Farren's belt.

Collin knelt to lift Tay into his arms.

"Careful," Farren said, supporting Tay's head.

"I've got her," Collin said gently, cradling an unconscious Tay to his chest. He stood, and Izzy rested a hand on Farren's shoulder. Farren flinched.

"I'll lead," Izzy said. "You help Collin."

Farren nodded, tears running down her face though her expression was blank. Was she in shock?

Almighty, help us, Collin prayed, as Izzy led them to the easiest path out of the depression. He didn't know how long they had to get Tay to Kedar before it would be too late. If Farren was going into shock... *Help us reach Kedar in time. Please, clear the path before us.*

CHAPTER
TWO

Izzy

Izzy nearly wept at the sight of Kedar's gates. She glanced over her shoulder, meeting Collin's eyes and finding weary relief. Tay still breathed. They all picked up their pace as they entered the open fields dividing Kedar from the forest. Two watchmen ran out to meet them as they approached.

The first rushed to Collin's side, taking Tay from his arms.

"Any enemies approaching?" asked the second, his hand on his sword hilt.

"We weren't followed," Izzy said.

The watchman nodded, but he still watched the edge of the forest as they moved as a group toward the open gate. Izzy let him guard their backs and turned her focus to Tay and Farren.

"I'm fine," Farren snapped.

Collin backed away from her side with his hands raised, twisting to look at Izzy. Worry pinched his expression, but he didn't interfere again. Farren's eyes never left her sister, even as people on the street stopped to watch them pass. Their expressions were grim but resigned. Every soul in Kedar, to the smallest child, had seen a similar sight. They'd lost a Red Cloak and six watchmen during the past wolf moon alone.

We won't lose another, Izzy silently vowed, slipping ahead to clear the path before them. Their trip through the city felt nearly as long as their journey through the trees, though the Watchman half ran through the streets with Tay in his arms.

There was a flurry of activity once they reached the estate, and Izzy stood against the wall to stay out of the way. She had one sight of Tay being laid on the white bedding, bloody and still, before nurses blocked her view. But still Izzy stared, her eyes drawn to Farren's red cloak as she stood at her sister's side. Tears ran down her face.

Collin stopped at her side, their shoulders brushing as they watched together, listening for any sign that Tay would survive. Izzy leaned closer, just enough that her arm pressed against Collin's, and wished that would ease some of the heaviness in her heart.

The watchman stepped back from the fray, still breathing heavily as he moved to the door. He paused before Izzy and Collin.

"Thank you," Collin said warmly.

"Glad to help," he said, nodding. "I hope..."

"Yes," Izzy said when the man didn't finish.

For a moment they stood in awkward silence, all watching the nurses and physician tending to Tay. One of them set up a screen around the bed, blocking their sight.

"I should return to my post," the watchman said. But as he shifted backward, he paused and glanced at Izzy and Collin.

"What's her name?"

"Tay," Izzy whispered.

"I'll keep her in my prayers."

"What's your name, Watchman?" Collin asked, as he began to turn away.

"Brenner, at your service."

"Collin. And this is Izzy," Collin said, gesturing to her. "I hope we cross paths again."

"I as well."

He nodded to each of them before leaving the room. And after another heavy moment, straining to hear what the nurses said without much success, Izzy and Collin followed him.

Collin turned toward Commander Rhett's office, and Izzy followed half a step behind. She wished he'd walk slower. She knew they needed to tell Rhett what had happened, to share every detail they had of the trap they'd walked into. But dread was a heavy weight in her chest, stealing her breath as they stepped over the threshold. Inside was dim, the only light from two flickering lamps mounted on the wall. They entered to find him standing beside his desk, staring at the moon map hanging on the wall.

"How badly is Tay injured?" he asked, as they took their places standing before his massive desk.

"We're not sure," Collin said. "She wasn't conscious on our way back."

Rhett nodded. He turned toward them, his face set in the same steady, stoic expression he wore when he gave out orders this morning. She swallowed back the ache as Rhett's attention focused again.

"Farren?"

"Shaken, but uninjured as far as we can tell," Izzy said. "She didn't want to leave Tay's side."

"We walked into a ambush," Collin said. "As soon as they entered the cave, a spell activated that trapped them within with a creature I've never seen before."

Rhett's eyes narrowed, and he leaned forward in his chair.

"A spell? You're sure?"

Izzy reached into her pockets and pulled out the shards of obsidian she'd taken from the site. Even with the magic broken, they seemed to draw all light away from where they laid on Rhett's desk.

"Two spells," Izzy said. "One to trap them within, and another to animate a creature of mud."

"I think it was a golem," Collin said, glancing at Izzy.

She nodded in agreement, recognizing the name for their studies years ago, before turning back to Rhett. He was staring at the shards of the holding stone, a haunted set to his face that Izzy hadn't seen before. Had he seen something like this before?

"Ogres don't use holding stones in their magic," Collin said. "This proves that there's a human sorcerer behind this."

"Not necessarily human," Rhett said. "But a sorcerer, yes."

Izzy narrowed her eyes. He sounded...off. What sort of being was he thinking of if not a human? Faeries? Moon folk?

"I'd like to request that Izzy and I return to our own search tomorrow," Collin said, gesturing to the obsidian. "This might give us more answers than we've found in years. If we can find this sorcerer..."

"Do not engage," Rhett ordered, his gaze piercing Izzy to the marrow. "A sorcerer capable of raising a golem cannot be taken on by two warriors, no matter how high ranked."

"Understood," Izzy said.

"We'll be cautious," Collin added.

He held their eyes for a moment longer before leaning back with a sigh.

"Then I'll send you out tomorrow. Get some rest."

Izzy bowed in unison with Collin. But when she reached the door she paused, looking back over her shoulder. Rhett was still staring at those obsidian pieces, a look in his eyes that spoke of old wounds. A chill settled deep within her, wrapping around her heart. It was the first time Izzy had ever seen him look afraid.

Izzy was glad when morning assignments were finished, slipping between people to leave the crowded room before the rush could slow her escape. Collin squeezed out behind her with a huff, but he didn't speak until they were alone. Izzy was staring at two maps, one divided into quadrants with initials and brief notes scribbled within, when Collin planted his hands on the table and leaned toward her.

"She's still alive," he murmured.

Izzy took a slow breath. She knew that. She and Collin had gone to check on Tay and Farren before their sparring. Farren was awake, but red eyed and unresponsive. Tay hadn't woken up since arriving in the infirmary. It was a nurse who'd explained that they'd done all they could, that now it relied on Tay to fight and heal. It was better than Izzy had feared as she tossed and turned during the night...but less than she'd hoped for.

"I just...need out of this city for a while," Izzy murmured, glancing up at Collin.

He nodded, and the understanding in his gaze made Izzy's throat tighten. She looked away quickly, running her finger over the quadrants. Most of those to the south had dates showing they'd been searched and cleared within the past few weeks, but in the west the recent marks were all near the city or the roads. She paused over a square where she'd scratched her initial beside Collin's. A glance at the better map showed it was on Mount Talith, the easternmost peak of the Pitch Mountains.

What did we find there? She couldn't remember. Several of the quadrants around it also bore their customary "C I," but none of the marks looked recent. Why hadn't they searched there recently? She doubted it was a lack of enemies.

"The mountain again?" Collin asked.

"When was the last time we cleared it?"

"Two years ago," he said. "I remember lots of climbing and taking three days to search one quadrant because of all the rockslides and steep little canyons. I thought Rhett told us to stick to the base after that."

"Right," Izzy sighed, with hazy memories matching Collin's description flowing through her mind's eye.

"What about here?" she asked, pointing to a square further north. "It's sticks to the mountain's base to preserve your poor lungs."

Collin raised one eyebrow. "And far enough from the city to give us some quiet."

Izzy allowed her smile to be her answer. Most wouldn't consider a day of rooting out goblins in the deep woods to be quiet. But then, most didn't venture into the deep woods at all these days. She and Collin had good reason for their twisted definitions of peace and quiet: neither was something they found much of in their lives.

"West it is, then," Collin said, scribbling their initials and the date in the square with a charcoal pencil. Izzy was already rolling up the second map, returning it to its place on the shelf.

There was new energy in her steps as she and Collin left the cramped room, passing beneath the open gates that separated the Red Cloak's command center from the rest of Kedar. The red wool of her cloak sat heavily on her shoulders, a comforting weight as she and Collin walked side by side through the streets. Dawn had come while they looked at maps, bright light crawling down the walls of the buildings and leaving the streets they walked in shadow. But the air still bore a chill that quickened Izzy's step, revealing her breath in a puff of fog. It wasn't biting, not like it would be in a few moon cycles. This morning it was a brisk reminder that she was alive.

The city was already wide awake. Many people ignored Izzy and Collin as they passed, and Izzy was satisfied to ignore them in return. Others looked and paled, ducking their heads when Izzy's eyes fell on them. She'd grown up in the west quarter, but even men and women Izzy had known since she was a small child wouldn't hold her gaze. But she was long past being hurt over that fact. What the Red Cloaks were trained to do...well, she remembered being afraid of them herself when she was little. It must be strange for them to see how she and Collin had changed. There was few similarities between the two children who scampered after each other and the assured warriors they now appeared to be: Collin broad-shouldered and effortlessly confident, Izzy lithe and quiet.

But a few, just a few, stopped what they were doing as Collin and Izzy approached. A few met her eyes, offering a shallow bow with hands pressed over their heart. Izzy returned the gesture with a nod, knowing that beside her Collin replied with a benevolent smile that could light up a room. She'd tried to smile like Collin did, years ago... until Dal asked why she grimaced whenever citizens offered their silent gratitude. Izzy had made do with nodding ever since. Let Collin smile for her...he was better at it.

But no one bowed when they turned down Blackwood Street. Few people were outside at all, especially near the large house bedecked in wreaths of cypress and willow: a house in mourning. The wolfsbane twisted amid the branches spoke clearly enough why this house mourned, even if Izzy hadn't already known.

Izzy only knew a few details of the curse's most recent victims. The werewolf had grown up in the southern quarter, the son of one of the wealthier families. His parents had begged to bury their son in their family tomb rather than the crypt on the northern edge where the rest of those touched by the curse were laid. They'd been refused.

His foil had lived here on narrow Blackwood Street, the second born daughter of the large family that dwelt in that house. A seamstress. The dark magic that plagued their city didn't discriminate between classes and backgrounds: Izzy and Collin had watched both their coffins being carried underground.

It wasn't always that way: while the werewolves were locked in the Tower of the Cursed long before sunset, the foils were always given a choice. Safety outside the tower walls, or death within. But most chose to enter alongside the werewolf. Whether out of a belief they could overcome the curse or a desire to kill the werewolf themselves, their choice to step within the tower was always a death sentence.

Slowing her steps as they passed the house, Izzy bowed low with her fist held to her chest. Collin copied her. No one was visible to accept their gesture of sympathies, but Izzy didn't care. She knew the grief this curse wrought. Her comrades could whisper all they wanted about her cold heart, but she would have *this* family know that she mourned with them.

Her cloak hung a little heavier as they continued down the street, the clasp digging into the skin at her throat. She wouldn't be wearing it if not for the curse. Most days she gave little thought to who she would be now if the werewolf hadn't taken her family, but some days were more difficult than others.

She and Collin turned north, walking a few streets out of their way by silent agreement. Sometimes Izzy did walk past the narrow building she once called home, reliving happy childhood days and taking in how everything had changed, but not today. Not with far darker memories clawing their way to the surface.

They were silent through the city, reaching the western gate as the sun chased the final vestiges of night from the streets. Izzy nodded to the watchmen, squinting in the glare off their armor. They nodded in return, lowering their eyes as they passed.

The Watch of Kedar was separate from the Red Cloaks, though Izzy had heard that many in the Watch hoped to earn a place in the more elite order. Izzy didn't even know the names of these men, though they likely knew hers. She felt their eyes on her back as she and Collin walked the road leading west from the city wall. She stood tall, shoulders thrown back. She was hyperaware of Collin at her side, the edges of his cloak fluttering against her hand.

They left the road when it cut north, walking beneath the trees. Near the city the trees were far apart and well groomed, the ground clear of underbrush. On a clear night, those defending Kedar could see beasts coming long before they left the forest. It gave them more time to prepare for their attacks on the wall.

The people of Kedar still ventured this far often, foraging and hunting. Woodcutters slowly increased the groomed area, but most of their work was further north where the terrain was easier to traverse. The horde hadn't yet grown so bold to encamp this close to the city, and they set a fast pace. It was a while more before they reached the edge of wilder woods, where ancient trees and tangled underbrush made their passage more difficult. There the shadows were darker, the sunlight weaker. Izzy could search a thousand years and never finish uncovering its secrets.

Collin turned right, stepping behind a tree wider than three men. And as Izzy followed, she reached for the clasp at her throat, tugging the red cloak free from her shoulders to hang on a broken branch just within her reach. Collin did the same. For a heartbeat Izzy stared at the blood red fabric, a beacon against the subtle browns and greens of the wood. Then she turned to Collin.

His lips split in a grin, eyes bright as he stared down at her. Izzy felt her own mouth spread wide in a smile...her first *true* smile in days. All her pains and fears seemed to flow down, spilling onto the ground and leaving her light and free, with a wildness filling her veins that set her senses on fire. Collin snatched her hand from her side, raising it to his lips as he tugged her away from the tree, toward the mountain. There was a dare in his gaze, and Izzy followed after him with a reckless grin.

Izzy couldn't begrudge the forest its secrets, not when it so faithfully kept her own.

The entirety of Kedar knew that Izzy and Collin were inseparable. From dawn's breath to moon's final song they could be found at each other's side, and stars help the soul that came between them. But as long as those red cloaks hung from their shoulders, a wall stood between them: those who wore the red cloak belonged to Kedar, never to join themselves to another. So said the new vows Izzy and Collin had each sworn when they were fourteen.

But the forest didn't abide by rules written by man. For that alone, Izzy would never tire of wandering beneath those trees no matter how many goblins head among them.

They path they took meant walking through several quadrants that had been cleared since the wolf moon before they reached their goal, giving them time to themselves. Time for a taste of peace before the day's battle began.

Collin helped her over a fallen tree, leading them to an open stretch filled with frostbitten fern and the first fallen leaves. He threw his arm around her shoulders, pulling her close to press his face to her hair. Izzy wrapped her arm around his waist to hold him even closer. And she tried to ignore the ache, the piercing longing that never left her even when she pressed herself against his side.

"The kid with the wild brown hair, Berke's cousin," Collin said, releasing her so they could walk single file between two thick pines. "The one who watches us all the time. What's his name?"

"Isley. And he's a year older than we are."

Collin shrugged and took her hand again. "You think he's going to complain about what I call him?"

"Not everyone holds us in awe."

"But he does."

Izzy shook her head, leaning to avoid catching leaves in her hair.

"Let him catch you talking in your sleep one time, and that'll change."

Collin glanced down at her, eyes bright though his lips were turned in a frown.

"I don't talk in my sleep."

"Dal and Alair say otherwise."

"You'll take their word over mine?"

"You did," Izzy said, turning to examine the ground as they passed.

"That was *years* ago, Izzy," Collin replied with an exasperated huff. "How long must I atone for my mistake?"

Izzy bumped her hip against his, fighting against the smile tugging at her lips.

"Back to Isley," Collin said.

"You're certainly interested in him."

"I wonder why Rhett let him in. He seems...nervous."

"He'll adjust," Izzy said, though her smile dimmed as she

pictured the young man, who at a year older than her was still only twenty-one. Collin was right.

"He better not be put on gate duty."

"Mmm," Izzy said in agreement, letting Collin lift her onto a rock shelf.

Gate duty during a full moon meant the fiercest fighting. She and Collin were usually put on the ground during those nights, and they'd both seen what happened to those whose nerves broke under the strain. They didn't usually see the sunrise.

"Dal is up to something," Izzy said, wanting a lighter topic to suit the bright morning.

Collin huffed. "He always is."

"Something with the laundry."

Collin eyed Izzy. "What makes you think so?"

"He's doing his own washing, for once."

Collin's laughter was sudden and bright, silencing the birdsong around them. They were still in safe territory or else he never would've dared to be so loud.

"Maybe he ran out of people to do it for him."

But when Collin glanced at her, Izzy knew he agreed with her. Dal's pranks were notorious and ceaseless, no matter how many times the Commander had instituted creative punishments in retribution for his mischief.

"If he drags us into it, I'd say it's time for a tournament," Izzy said.

She'd like the chance to teach him some humility.

Collin gave her a sideways glance. "I'd say it's time even if he leaves us out of his mischief."

"Wanting a little revenge, are we?"

"Not against Dal."

Izzy watched Collin, silent and waiting. They were nearing the base of the mountain now, and they'd scrambled across fallen rocks and through a narrow gully before his silence broke.

"I caught Mercer and his circle talking about us."

Izzy's heart faltered, fear sending a chill through her chest. *Were we not careful enough?* But though Collin was staring ahead, she caught a glimpse of his face and calmed.

"Talking about me," she corrected, seeing the fury tightening his expression.

Collin's hand tightened to a fist, and Izzy knew she was right.

"More of the same?" she asked lightly.

"In a sense. And not just you."

Izzy wasn't surprised. Commander Rhett hand-chose his Red Cloaks for skill, not personality. There would always be some boys among them who thought women were placed there for their enjoyment. But the women of the Red Cloaks were also chosen for their skill, and any man foolish enough to act on his twisted desires quickly regretted it. The few Izzy knew who had attempted anything had left the Red Cloaks with a less skin than they entered. Talk, though, was harder to stomp out completely.

"In that case," Izzy said. "We should suggest it to Eldon."

"They'd love to go up against either of us," Collin said. "They've convinced themselves that we have our rank because we're Rhett's favorites."

"They'll know better by the end of it."

Izzy and Collin were young for their rank, but it was earned. Not that explaining that would convince any of the young men Collin spoke of: they'd come from the Watch half a year ago, after several Red Cloaks were killed during the wolf moon. They were still arrogant and itching to prove themselves.

Mercer in particular was used to being the golden child of the Watch, and it seemed that he had expected the same to be true in the Red Cloaks. He'd made it clear over the past few months that he blamed Izzy and Collin for his lack of recognition.

They'd reached the base of the mountain. Izzy and Collin quieted as their path turned up, their attention now trained on their surroundings. This was land that had been left in peace for months, meaning that there would likely be a dozen or so small pockets of adversaries to deal with. They didn't want to draw attention to their passage, not until they were ready for a fight.

Despite his earlier complaints, Collin scrambled up the steepest slopes without issue. Izzy accepted his hand whenever he turned back to assist her, though they both knew she could make it fine on her own. It was another excuse to stay closer than they could in the city.

They'd passed signs of animals all along their walk, but now they slowed to take a closer look. There were several kinds of beasts that regularly attacked Kedar, all larger and fiercer than they should have been. Most thought the bears were the most unnerving, with hair matted into thick armor that arrows couldn't pierce and a malicious glint in their eyes, but Izzy thought the elk were worse. Grazers weren't supposed to attack predators, nor were they supposed to devour those they gored to death.

Truthfully, the twisted forest creatures weren't the true horror. It was the ogres and other creatures of legend that truly posed a threat to Kedar's safety. Bear and elk could be held back with walls and fire. Trolls possessed enough intelligence to rip gates from their hinges, to climb walls and hold their silence until they were among the darkened streets. Ogres could use black magic to weave shields and blast stone with the power of a cannon.

They always attacked when the moon was high, and they always disappeared before dawn. Until the past spring, when they'd begun launching smaller attacks when the moon and sun shone in the sky together.

Izzy stooped to examine torn earth, looking up to the grove of trees beyond and narrowing her eyes. There were likely goblins within, fast asleep now that the sun was high enough to reach through the thick trees. She glanced at Collin, tilting her head toward the grove. He gestured to the trail he still stood beside. Izzy straightened to follow him, her steps silent as she moved across the bracken. They'd check it on their way back, then.

The trail Collin had gestured to bore footprints that were too large and wide to belong to goblins. A troll, most likely. Certainly worth following.

When Izzy and Collin were young, a few Red Cloaks were sent to follow the creatures and find where their leaders hid during the day. None ever returned, though a few creatures wore their torn cloaks when they returned the next full moon. Many others had been sent into the forest since, but they'd only discovered the scattered dens where the foot soldiers of the horde hid. No sign of the ogres who commanded them, or the trolls who proved so deadly to Kedar's defenders.

Commander Rhett had increased the searches during the past spring when the horde began attacking even after the moon had waned. Kedar's defenders were hard pressed to keep up a constant vigilance, and increasing their ranks would only postpone their doom. But Collin and Izzy had been searching for years. They had a talent for avoiding detection, and they'd spent enough time in the wild forest to know it better than most.

Izzy's father had been a trapper and hunter. It was half her lifetime ago since those early mornings and long summer days wandering the woods with him, learning his trade with Collin at her side. But the skills he'd cultivated in them had only sharpened with the passing years.

While Collin knelt for a closer look at blood spotting a low bush, Izzy searched for another of the wide footprints they'd been following. Whatever creatures made the trail had passed through last night. There was a fair chance they'd find at least one den by following the trails to whatever hollow they'd laid up in, even if they didn't discover the troll.

Izzy and Collin walked with their shoulders and elbows occasionally brushing each other, turned outward to catch any movement from the forest around them. Following the trail was child's work: whatever made it obviously hadn't been interested in subtlety.

The trail split off in all directions, but Izzy and Collin followed the troll prints and blood spatters. It took them higher up the broken mountainside, and their progress was slow. Izzy saw the body ahead at the same time as Collin, and a squeeze of hands was all the acknowledgement they shared. This might be another trap, albeit a less sophisticated one, and they knew to keep a close eye on their surroundings as they approached.

The corpse was so bloodied and torn that Izzy couldn't identify it until they were standing over it. Then she caught sight of the worn hooves and brown pelt. An elk, its elongated fangs proving it was a part of the horde. It must've been wounded attacking the city and fell there, only to be devoured by the creatures it had fought beside.

"They split again," Izzy whispered, looking at the many trails. Though they searched for what felt like an hour, they didn't find sign of the troll again.

Collin sighed, choosing a trail with deeper prints and continuing on. This wasn't the first time they'd come across this strange pattern. The trail would continue splitting until it was hardly there at all, all signs of the higher ranked fighters disappearing as they went. It made it simpler for their own purposes: smaller groups were easier to eradicate, especially when it was just the two of them. But seeing how *many* trails there were, and extrapolating that across the whole forest, always proved to overwhelm her. The same secrecy she treasured worked in favor of their enemies: they could send out a thousand Red Cloaks and still the horde would come.

They'd suggested to Rhett that they should focus on searching for the leaders rather than spending their daylight hours fighting scattered adversaries who knew nothing more than to gather at the moon's rising. He'd sent them out for that purpose a few times in the past months, but it had never amounted to anything. Wherever the ogres and trolls hid was either too far away for humans to reach or shielded by more than rock and leaf. After seeing power held within the obsidian spell stones, Izzy now suspected the latter.

Collin stopped, and Izzy with him. But as she searched for the threat, for the subtle signs that they weren't alone, he took her hand and tugged her until she turned toward him. She followed his gaze to a thinning in the trees, where the ground dipped into a ravine. On the other side, smoke rose through the trees in a small plume. If she followed that trail toward the ground, she could see the pattern of stone set in a wall.

No one human lived this deep in the forest...did they? Not now, not completely vulnerable to all that dwelt in the darkness. But she couldn't imagine goblins taking over such an obvious structure for their use. They preferred hollow oak, caves, or thick groves of birch where they'd be easily camouflaged.

But even if none of that was true, the smoke still gave away this dwelling as something entirely new and sinister. It rose from the chimney in thick puffs of greenish gray, and every branch near its path was dead and blackened. Sorcery or not, nothing good came from such a fire. But Izzy didn't doubt it was sorcery.

A strange feeling came over Izzy as she watched that smoke rise toward the scattered clouds, a shadow that she couldn't trace. She turned to Collin and found his expression mirrored hers. He stared at the smoke, brows low over his eyes and mouth in a considering scowl, and his hand tightened around hers.

Thought of obsidian runes and a golem's roar was icy water dripping down her back. Rhett told them not to engage. But they needed to know more. They needed to be sure this was worth reporting back. No one could afford to waste resources on nothing.

"We should investigate," she whispered.

"Not today," Collin replied, taking a step back. "Not alone."

A chill swept through Izzy. Collin never backed down from anything, threat or challenge. She let him tug her back, into the shelter of the trees from where they'd come. They'd passed the ravaged carcass before she dared speak.

"You believe it's the sorcerer," she said, still whispering.

"I don't know," he said, glancing at her with a haunted look. "But I don't want to risk it."

Izzy didn't argue. When they were children, she'd learned through painful experience that Collin had a strange premonition when it came to trouble. Perhaps it was that he caused so much trouble himself that he knew how to spot the signs before it began. That's what Berke and others insisted, but Izzy wasn't so sure. This time it was more than instinct...this time Izzy felt it too. And as much as she was tempted to defy that creeping sense of danger, there was a part of her that was glad Collin made the decision for them.

They'd come too high up the mountain. Now they headed back down to their quadrant, quiet and grim as they searched the land around them for signs of the horde.

Izzy held tightly to Collin's hand. Though there was little chance that whoever dwelt there knew they'd come that close, it was a long time before that shadow fell away from Izzy's heart. And longer still before she and Collin stopped looking over their shoulders, searching for that eerie plume against the sky.

Collin

THEY RETURNED to Kedar in early afternoon, as the sun began its long descent toward Mount Talith. They both walked slowly and heavily, worn from the dozen or so skirmishes that had filled their morning. Usually, they wouldn't return for several hours yet, but they'd found more pockets of goblins than usual today. It seemed they'd grown comfortable close to the mountain, packing tighter than they did nearer to the city. Normally he and Izzy could eliminate one den without disturbing another, but even the heaviest of sleepers tended to wake up when their comrades were screeching obscenities a few steps away. It had resulted in a few fights that were closer than Collin was comfortable with.

Collin nodded to the gate sentries with a smile, keeping his hand *firmly* on his sword hilt so he wouldn't reach out and take Izzy's hand.

She'd gone distant again. She always did when others were watching, raising walls around her heart so thick he doubted anyone could break them down. Those walls never stopped *him*: he happened to have the key. But he still hated it.

If they kept living like this, one day those walls wouldn't come down.

But he couldn't take her in his arms and smooth away the furrows between her brows here where anyone might see. The most he could do was try to tease away the worst of it and smile enough for the both of them.

Walking down the streets, Collin watched the people around them. Children played in the street, heedless of the danger that would come when night fell. That had been Collin and Izzy when they were young, except they'd stayed out until the stars winked above their heads.

That was before the beasts of the Pitch Mountains assailed Kedar so regularly. Now, the Watch wandered the streets to find citizens out after moonrise lest any creature who slipped past the Red Cloaks on the wall find them alone. By sunset the streets would be abandoned.

Collin glanced up as they stepped through the arch that led to the Red Cloaks center of command. Words were etched into the stone: *The Almighty bless these halls.* He didn't think many people paid attention to them, but Collin always felt a little more at home when he stepped beneath them. Though they weren't written there for the Red Cloaks.

The arch was one of the few remnants from when the estate belonged to the governor of Kedar. But the governor fled long before Collin had been born, and the Red Cloaks had taken it over to dedicate to the city's defense.

It was in the center of the city, offering quick paths to reach any quarter of Kedar at a moment's notice, and the architecture was halfway between a lavish estate and a fortress. The intricate carving around the gate was only one example of the artistry that remained.

Every addition since the Red Cloaks moved in was a stark contrast to the careful stonework, blank and utilitarian. He understood that artistry wasn't a priority the Order could afford, but he still preferred the areas where the original architecture prevailed.

Voices already spoke in Commander Rhett's study. As they approached the cracked door, Collin recognized the gravely voice of Hendrick, the oldest Red Cloak next to Rhett and Eldon. He could be a captain by now, but rumor had it that he'd refused each time the position was offered to him. Alair asked him why a few years back, but the only reply Hendrick gave was a warning to stay out of his affairs.

Collin knocked on the frame of the door and stepped back, listening to the voices abruptly cut off. Shifting chairs covered a few hushed words. If it was someone other than Hendrick, he might try to eavesdrop a little. Not that Izzy would approve.

"Come in," Rhett said.

Collin let Izzy go first, following close enough behind to catch a whiff of the oils she brushed through her hair. That subtle scent teased him as they stood before Rhett's desk, enticing and mocking him all at once. He clasped his hands behind his back and turned his focus on his commander.

Rhett stared at them, his black eyes narrowed and shrewd. Collin stood still beneath his inspection, meeting his gaze steadily and trying not to guess what he saw. He never had shaken the sense of discomfort when Rhett stared at him like that. For years it had stemmed from a desire to be enough in his eyes, to measure up to the lofty expectations Rhett held for them. But events of the past few years had left that desire somewhat...tainted. Still, no matter what was said, Collin couldn't shake the need to see that subtle approval in his eyes.

Rhett dismissed Hendrick. He left without question, eyeing Collin and Izzy as he passed. He shut the door behind him.

"You found something," Rhett said, leaning forward to lean his elbows on his desk.

"Yes," Collin said. "Someone living on the mountain."

Rhett frowned, and Izzy took up the report.

"There was a plume of poisonous smoke coming from a stone building," she explained. "And a sense to the place that...wasn't right. Not quite like the ogres, but too similar."

Rhett stared at Izzy, leaning back in his seat while he thought. Collin knew it wasn't much to go on. They should've gotten a closer look. They should have...and yet Collin didn't regret turning around. The entire situation had felt familiar in a way he couldn't pinpoint, and he'd rather not take risks so far from Kedar. Not knowing that there was a sorcerer at large. Physical attacks they could handle, but Collin knew enough of black magic to not like their chances fighting it head on.

But Commander Rhett knew they didn't scare easily...not usually, anyway. He considered their report long enough that Collin began to wonder if he knew more than they did.

"Take Andred and Viron to investigate it," he said. "But not tomorrow."

"Sir?" Izzy asked, brows furrowed.

"Declan is sick, and Liam was wounded last night. Both were supposed to be on the north wall tonight. I could send Isley and Kyne, but..."

"We'll go," Izzy said quickly.

Rhett turned to Collin. And though the idea of delaying answers *yet again* made him weary, he nodded. There wasn't much he could say. He agreed with Izzy. The new recruits weren't ready for the wall, not this close to a full moon. Hopefully whoever was living on Mount Talith would stay put while they spent another night battling ogres and their armies.

"Thank you. You'll be on the northeastern breech. Report before sunset."

Collin resisted the urge to frown, keeping his expression carefully schooled. It wasn't that the northeastern breech was less dangerous —he wasn't arrogant enough to be offended by being assigned a night of *less* risk—but rather what the northeastern breech was close to. He never enjoyed spending time near the Tower of the Cursed, wolf moon or not. A place which saw so much death and heartbreak had a presence. And it was difficult to ignore.

"Yes, sir," Collin said.

Commander Rhett leaned further back in his worn chair, pressing his fingertips to his closed eyes with a sigh. He looked tired in a way sleep wouldn't heal. Collin supposed holding the fate of all Kedar in his hands would do that.

"That's all," Rhett said without opening his eyes. "Get some rest while you can."

"Yes sir," Collin said, backing toward the door with Izzy. When he pulled the door shut behind them, Rhett was sifting through papers on his desk.

They didn't speak as they returned their weapons to the armory, despite the few hours between them and another battle, and walked to the barracks. When the path split between men's and women's, Collin turned to Izzy with a smile that sat heavy on his lips.

"Don't oversleep," he said, tugging on the braid slung over her shoulder.

She batted his hand away, a smile flickering on her face. But she said nothing as they parted ways, each to snatch what rest they could before sunlight abandoned them completely.

When Collin emerged, the stone floor of the courtyard laid in shadow, sunlight slowly crawling up the eastern wall. Izzy silently joined him, stretching her arms and shoulders as they left the dim hall.

Eldon was standing outside. His face broke into a smile when he saw them coming.

"I hope you didn't have any clothes being washed today."

The weighty atmosphere melted away, and Collin felt his shoulders sag. He grinned down at Izzy.

"That was fast."

Eldon's expression sharpened in warning. "Did you two have anything to do with this?"

"No," Izzy said easily. "I just noticed Dal has been more helpful than usual with the laundry."

Eldon huffed, relaxing again. His lips twitched with a smile. "Well, Dal is now responsible for cleaning up his mess. Make sure no one helps him, no matter what he offers or threatens."

"Happily," Izzy said, with the smallest suggestion of laughter in her voice. Collin would listen to it all day if he could.

Collin swept his cloak over one shoulder, leaning against the wall beside Eldon. "What exactly did Dal *do*?"

"He slipped red dye into the washing water. The clothes soaking in the basins sat for several hours before anyone noticed, and they're now...fairly pink."

Eldon explained in a detached tone that didn't match the laughter in his eyes. Collin pressed his lips together to hide his amusement. *Dal, what were you thinking?* He didn't need to look at Izzy to know that she was holding back laughter as well.

"As Dal's pranks go, this is one of his better ones," Collin said.

Collin caught Izzy's grin, there and gone in a flash.

"He managed to dye his own clothing with the rest, which is some consolation," Eldon said, shaking his head with a weary smile.

"I'm assuming he won't be issued any new clothes," Izzy said drily.

"No," Eldon replied. "He will not."

There was a twinkle in his eyes Collin didn't see often these days. For a moment, they stood in a companionable silence, and Collin relaxed. Better yet, he felt *Izzy* relax. But too soon, Eldon waved them off.

"Go. Get dinner before it's gone."

Collin pushed off the wall, never one to argue about food.

"Headed home?" Izzy asked.

"Yes," Eldon said, stepping away from them. Some of his good humor faded as he looked them over, showing more of his age as worry overtook his gaze. "Almighty be with you tonight."

"Thank you," Collin said more quietly, echoed by Izzy.

Eldon left without another word.

As Eldon turned away, Collin itched to take Izzy's hand and pull her close. He'd whisper something in her ear to make her laugh, and she'd shake her head at him even as a smile softened her face. But red wool settled heavy on his shoulders. And they were far from alone.

Sometimes he cursed his vows.

If all he was risking was being stripped of his cloak, Collin might've cast it away himself years ago. But stripping a Red Cloak never ended there. He might have been willing to play fast and easy with his own life, but not Izzy's. Never Izzy's.

The rules seemed simple enough to follow when they were fourteen and desperate to belong somewhere, when staying together was all Collin cared about. Now it was nothing more than a cruel joke. For as much time as he spent with Izzy, they were always being pulled apart. Never more than five steps away from each other... never free to close that final distance.

Collin stifled a sigh as he held open the door for Izzy, conversation spilling out in a flood. As much as he loved their hours of solitude, it was always harder to maintain the balance when they returned.

At least Dal had started some chaos. It would give him something else to think about. As he and Izzy walked toward the counter to grab their meal, Collin looked around to gauge the mood of the room. He could tell easily enough who was angry over Dal's trick and who, whether they admitted it or not, thought it was amusing. Mercer and the other Watch brats were solidly in the first category. Little surprise there.

Alair and Berke had already taken one end of a table, the seats around them mostly empty. Someone, likely under Keita's guidance, had placed bowls of chrysanthemums in the center of each table. The bundles of flowers were a bright contrast to dim surroundings, and Collin smiled as he wondered what outsiders would think of garden flowers decorating warriors' tables.

He took a seat beside Izzy, exchanging a grin with Alair. Berke was glaring at the table, plunging his fork into his potatoes with more vigor than necessary.

"Cheer up," Collin said. "Pink will go well with your beard."

Berke grimaced and shoved a piece of potato in his mouth.

"Did your clothes escape?" Izzy asked Alair.

"No," Alair said. "Most of my uniform shirts have pink splotches, now."

"Decide to embrace it, have you?" Collin said, cutting into his meat.

"Hardly. I'll just steal some of your shirts while you're sleeping."

"You will *not*," Collin said, leveling a glare at Alair. He could see Izzy smiling from the corner of his eye.

"You still owe me," Alair said, jabbing his fork in Collin's direction. "Or do you want me to tell Commander Rhett that *you* were the one who rigged those bags of moldy grain to spill in the Watch barracks?"

"Say that louder, why don't you," Collin replied lazily, looking up to check if Mercer and his cohorts heard. They were still cursing Dal, so he assumed not.

"How did I miss that one?" Andred asked quietly as she set her plate down a few chairs away.

"The Commander had reason to believe a few kids were responsible and let it drop," Izzy explained quietly.

Collin was still holding Alair's glare, waiting for him to break. He didn't.

"Fine," Collin said, leaning back. "You can have two of my spare shirts, if you replace them. I don't care what color I'm wearing on wall duty."

Their uniform shirts were a pale brown that they covered up with armor, anyway.

"The Watch will never let us hear the end of this," Berke muttered.

"Let them talk," Collin said. "If they get too haughty, we'll get Dal to do it to *them*."

A new plate slammed onto the table on Collin's empty side. "I'm not *touching* dye for at least a decade."

Collin turned, looking up to meet Dal's glare. He was damp, his skin tinged red from the elbows down. The fierce look to his eyes was ruined by the smudges of red on his chin and forehead.

"Why not?" Collin asked with a careless smile. "I'm sure we could convince Commander Rhett that it wasn't you."

"You say that now."

Dal fell into his seat with a sigh, still glaring at Collin. But then he leaned forward, peering at Izzy on Collin's other side.

"Is that a *smile* I see on our Iron Girl? I see where your loyalty lies."

"Izzy smiles plenty when your rotten personality isn't stinking up the room," Collin said. His tone was too sharp, and his smile came too late to soften his words. Dal raised an eyebrow, and Collin offered an apologetic shrug.

"Was pink the color you were aiming for?" Izzy asked, elbowing Collin as she leaned to see Dal.

"No," Dal said, the tension broken as his voice twisted in outrage. "The merchant who sold it to me swore it would be *crimson*."

"Did he know how much you were trying to dye at once?" Berke asked. The vast disconnect between his bear-like frame and the sulking tone of his voice made Collin chuckle.

"Well, I didn't tell him my entire plan, but yes. I thought I made it clear."

"It takes more than a few hours to dye cloth as deep a color as our cloaks," Andred said. "And there's more to the process."

"And yet it's dyeing my skin just fine," Dal said, glaring at the back of his hand. “How am I supposed to convince people to take me seriously when I look like I bathed in beet juice?”

Collin wasn’t the only one who laughed at that. No one who saw Dal now would guess he was eleven years older than Collin, nor that he was a *captain* among Kedar’s fiercest protectors.

Alair shrugged. “Should’ve thought of that before.”

“Grow a beard,” Izzy suggested.

“How’d you slip the dye in, anyway?” Collin asked. “I didn’t think anything was soaking when you left for patrol.”

A familiar cunning light entered Dal’s eyes. “I’ll explain once *you* share your way into the Watch barracks.”

“So you can get caught and ruin it? I’ll live with the mystery.”

With a roll of his eyes, Dal turned his attention to his plate.

“Find anything in the woods, today?” Alair asked.

Izzy glanced at him, just briefly. She wanted him to answer. Fair enough...he was the one who balked at the sight of a house.

“We might have,” Collin said. “Have you heard of anyone living on Mount Talith?”

Berke sat up, glancing at Andred. There was a lot in that look Collin didn’t catch, but it set him on his guard.

“Used to,” Alair said. “Didn’t think there were any more, though.”

“Who were they?” Izzy asked.

“Moon folk, mostly.”

Dal scoffed. “Don’t get started on those old tales.”

“Dal,” Collin said, turning to face him with narrowed eyes. “You regularly slay ogres, trolls, *and* goblins. Last winter a ghoul nearly slit you open from your breastbone to your navel. But you’re drawing the line at moon folk?”

Dal shuddered at the reminder of the ghoul but held his ground. “Yes.”

Collin glanced toward Alair and Berke. Alair had his arms crossed over his chest, wearing a grin that Collin knew well. Collin turned back to Dal.

“Why?”

Dal stabbed his fork into his roast and left it standing there while he gestured at Collin.

"Because every faery or legend creature we deal with wants to kill and eat us, *not* always in that order. All those stories say most of the moon folk were peaceful, and I don't buy it."

"The wolf curse supposedly originated among the moon folk," Berke said with a narrow look. "But they were able to control it."

"Supposedly. But it seems to affect us easily enough."

"So you doubt the existence of magical creatures that don't want to eat you," Izzy said, leaning around Collin.

He should've leaned back, but he didn't. The excuse to have her close was too perfect.

"That's right," Dal said.

"I'll tell the fairies you said so."

Dal balked. "Sure they don't want to eat us, but fairies want humans as exotic pets. That's hardly what I'd call benevolent."

"That's one fate you don't have to fear," Alair said, tossing a piece of bread at Dal's head. "I can't imagine any of them wanting you."

Dal picked the bread off his plate and threw it back. "Good."

"They might not want him as a pet," Izzy said. "But that doesn't mean they wouldn't want him. They have hunts too, you know."

Collin grinned, elbowing Dal. "Stay away from mushrooms."

Dal rolled his eyes and shoved a bite into his mouth as Collin leaned back in his chair, grinning at Izzy. Her return smile was smaller, but no less genuine.

Andred muttered *something* that had Alair turning toward her with wide eyes, and Berke huffing.

"What did she say?" Dal asked.

"You don't want to know," Alair said, still looking disturbed.

Except Collin could see Andred's smirk as she stared down at her plate, and that Berke wasn't so sullen as he was a moment ago. *I'd give my pinky for better hearing.* But listening to Dal try to figure out what she said about him was entertainment enough, he supposed.

Collin turned his attention back to his cooling food, holding in laughter as Dal and Alair went back and forth.

"How is Tay?" Izzy asked during a lull.

The table sobered immediately.

"She woke up for a while," Alair said. "But they're afraid a fever is setting in."

Collin set down his fork, a dark and familiar weight settling over his shoulders. If infection settled into a wound as deep as Tay's, hope of her recovery plummeted. He'd seen it too many times.

The rest of their meal was quieter, the conversation more subdued. Death was all too common for Red Cloaks. It was a reality they were all painfully familiar with, especially as the Horde's attacks came more frequently. But no one wanted to lose another comrade.

Collin and Izzy finished at the same time, rising together to return their plates to the kitchen.

"Where are you two headed?" Alair asked.

"To see if the faeries will take Dal and save us from his snoring," Collin said with a lazy smile.

Izzy rolled her eyes. "We're filling in on the north wall."

"Ah," Berke said, leaning back. "The Almighty go with you."

Collin accepted the blessing with a bow of his head. Alair nodded soberly when Collin glanced his way. The air around them was stifling, and Collin kicked the leg of Dal's chair to lighten things up.

"Clean up duty isn't looking so bad, is it?"

Dal scoffed. "Want to switch?"

"I'll take the goblins, thanks."

Dal's smile didn't reach his eyes. Everything felt too close tonight. He supposed there was no teasing them out of this one. Collin's gaze fell on Izzy, who offered him a small shrug as she turned away. Collin followed close behind.

The courtyard was empty, or seemed to be. The armory was empty, and as they paused before the racks of weapons Izzy twisted to face him. Her lips parted, a wild look in her eyes that Collin's heart echoed. The temptation took him to close that careful distance between them, to kiss away the worry lines between Izzy's eyes. He stepped backwards instead, reaching out to grab the first sword hilt that came to hand.

"We should get moving," he said.

Her face smoothed and she nodded, turning away to the assorted knives before her. Collin heart pounded as if he'd run to Mount Talith and back. Strange how the battle tonight felt like the least of his worries.

CHAPTER THREE

Izzy

Izzy checked her weapons once more, ensuring each was in its place. The last rays of sunlight cut across the sky, making the scattered clouds glow from within. The moon was already tipping toward the horizon. If it was still summer, they might not have a battle tonight at all. But with the harvest came longer nights....more hours for the moon to cast its light down on them all.

She switched to checking the buckles on her armor, trying *not* to look at the tower interrupting the the twilight sky on her left. She knew from Alair that this breech was close enough to the tower that warriors defending the wall could hear the werewolf and foil fight... could hear them die. She'd reminded herself thrice already that the tower was empty tonight, but her stomach still twisted every time she caught sight of it.

Different hands took over, untwisting the strap on the back of her shoulder. Even the scarce brush of his knuckles against her shoulder blade made her shiver.

"Nervous?" Collin asked.

"Only that I'll have to save your reckless hide. Again."

His hands left her shoulder, and Izzy twisted to see him staring down at her with that small smirk he reserved just for her. The tension drained from her shoulders, though her hand still tensed around the grip of her sword.

"Are we keeping score, now?" Collin asked quietly, his voice low and throaty. "Because I think I still have you beat on that one."

Izzy scoffed.

The land plunged into shadow, taking Izzy's good cheer with it. She turned to look at the forest's edge. Already creatures filled the gaps between the scattered trees, heads tilted back to stare at the moon's silver glow. They would stand there for a while, gathering strength, before surging forward to the walls of Kedar.

A few boys ran along their length of the wall, handing out recurve bows and belt quivers fully stocked with arrows to each of the warriors manning the breech. There were a dozen others watching this breech tonight, all watchmen. They were quiet and grim as they took up their positions.

Kedar had always been a target for the wilder inhabitants of the Pitch Mountains. Their histories said the wall was the first part of the city built: thrice a man's height, as wide as a cart, crafted with stone blocks so expertly fit that a blade of grass couldn't fit between them. For centuries that had been enough. It was only in Izzy and Collin's lifetime that the Horde managed to breech sections of the wall, damaging it in ways that the citizens of Kedar couldn't repair. Not in the few short weeks between full moons. Certainly not in the scattered nights of relief they had now.

There were four gates into Kedar: four weak points for the Horde to target. When they were on duty during the full moon, she and Collin were usually stationed on the ground at the gates where the fiercest fighting would be. But now there were also five places where the wall was broken down enough to need guarding. The north-eastern breech was more recent, and less vulnerable, but there was still no question that they would see bloodshed tonight. The ogres took advantage of every weakness they could discern, and their soldiers were happy to follow orders when it meant tearing into human flesh.

The horde was growing restless. She could see them shifting in the growing darkness, venturing a few paces into the open before their leaders ordered them back. The open land between, empty fields and beaten-down pastures, was washed gray under the moonlight. The wooden scaffolding they stood on creaked as the warriors around them shifted, waiting for the inevitable moment.

Izzy lifted her eyes, staring at the gibbous moon hanging above the trees. The silver glow spread like ripples across the sky, turning the darkness to a blue gray that seemed to reach on forever. And she thought that she *must* be callous. She would have to be to think the moon beautiful after all the horrors she'd seen beneath its light. But there was something about that subtle light, the purity of it as it filled the sky, that she couldn't resist.

A rough call broke the silence, echoed by a dozen voices down the line of trees. Though in a language Izzy didn't speak, she'd heard that order enough times to know what it meant. The horde was moving.

"If we die tonight," Collin murmured, "we go to the Almighty."

Izzy pulled in a slow breath, her own voice a whisper as she completed the prayer. "If we survive, we thank the Almighty."

It was an old tradition, one Collin had found early in their studies among the Red Cloaks that they'd chosen to take up themselves. But the familiar words settled deep inside her and calmed the last of the fear flickering in her ribcage.

The horde spilled from the forest in a flood, covering the fields in an ever-shifting mass that was impossible to make sense of in this gray light. But Izzy didn't need to pick out a single enemy, not when they were packed so tight together. She drew back her bow, breathing slowly in. She released with an exhale, another arrow nocked in a heartbeat. Beside them, she heard the watch leader barking orders, telling his men when to shoot so their arrows rained down on the approaching horde at once. Izzy tuned them out as she and Collin took their own shots.

They were close enough now that Izzy took aim at the tallest among them, trying to take down the leading trolls before they were near enough to act as ladders for their allies. One tumbled, an arrow through his neck. Another roared, ripping an arrow from his leg without even breaking stride. Too soon, Izzy's quiver was empty and the horde was against the wall.

She passed the bow and quiver to the boy waiting behind them. He scrambled down the wall after his companions, his part over. He and the others would hide in a secure barracks for the rest of the battle.

Izzy drew her sword and dagger, assailed by the sounds of battle at the gate to their right. An ogre drew his arm back, throwing something at the wall. A wild snarl was all the warning Izzy had before a moon-struck lynx hit the wood before her feet. It leaped toward her, slashing at her throat with razor claws. She knocked its paw away with her sword, kicking it backward. The lynx hissed, its eyes glowing with unhinged malice. Izzy braced herself.

It leaped again. Izzy stepped forward and slid her sword between its ribs, then dumped its dying body off the wall where goblins and trolls were gathered. Harsh curses rose to meet her, and she backed away from the edge quickly. The clash of metal and goblin curses marked where Collin fought at her back.

Further down the breech, the watchmen battled a troll climbing over the edge with goblins clinging to its back. One of them leaped over the watchmen, landing in a crouch a few paces from Izzy facing the city below. Izzy lunged forward.

He saw her coming, lifting his longsword to thrust at her stomach. Izzy twisted his blade away and kept coming, sinking her sword into his gut and her dagger in his throat. He sneered as he choked, jerking backward off of her sword. She saw his other hand moving, his knife glinting in the moonlight, and knew her defense would be a moment too late.

Collin was at her side, knocking the goblin's arm away and shoving him backward. He fell to the stone street below with a final, strangled curse.

Izzy met Collin's eyes for a heartbeat, feeling ages pass in that single moment. But too soon she was turning to the next battle, taking on a smaller troll thinking to sneak past while the watchmen were distracted.

Settling into her battle rhythm, all fears and complex thoughts faded to the back of her mind in favor of the *immediate*: fight. Watch Collin's back. Don't let them into Kedar. The battle lulled and swelled, but time passed quickly in a blur of her sword sinking through flesh, aching muscles, and the earsplitting cries of her foes. They lost one watchman to a pair of goblins at his back. The grief-stricken battle cry of his comrades still echoed in Izzy's ears as the moon disappeared, shielding the retreating horde from sight.

Adrenaline left with the horde, and Izzy swayed as the shifting shadows disappeared among the trees. Collin stepped closer to steady her, and Izzy tipped her head back to meet his gaze. She'd give anything to lay her head on his chest and let it all fade away. The sorcerer's trap, Tay's life hanging in the balance, the endless battle that was never won... She couldn't do this every moonrise for the rest of her life. None of them could.

Her eyes threatened to stray to the fallen watchman surrounded by his brothers in arms. Collin shifted, pulling her attention back to him as their fingers brushed against each other beneath their cloaks. His face was tight, fine lines around his eyes that Izzy longed to smooth away. She seized his hand, holding on as if her life depended on it. They survived another night.

But footsteps coming toward them marked an end to their moment of privacy. Collin squeezed her hand, heavy reluctance in his gaze as he twisted away to address their fellow Red Cloak.

Collin

The shuffle of feet and trunks falling shut dragged Collin from sleep. Nobody talked above a whisper, conscious of those who spent half the night on the wall, but it didn't matter. Sound traveled. And Collin had always been a light sleeper.

He had the day off, and part of him longed to let sleep claim him again, to wake up to bright sunlight for once. But Izzy would let him have it if he was late.

With a groan, Collin sat up in his bunk. He was wiping the crust from his eyes when Alair dropped to the floor with a *thunk*. Dal shot him a glare, and Alair glanced down at Collin apologetically. Collin shrugged. He was used to Alair's heavy feet in the morning.

Sometimes there was nothing louder than a group of half asleep men trying to be quiet. Or women. Izzy claimed the women's barracks wasn't much different, despite the threat of Andred's wrath if she was woken up earlier than usual.

Collin's mouth moved silently as he pulled a shirt over his head, going through his morning prayers. He wondered at times if he sounded like one of those music boxes the richer caravans sold in the markets, playing a few lines of the same song over and over again. His prayers didn't change much: safety for Izzy and the rest of the Red Cloaks, wisdom to face the day...an end to Kedar's peril.

Many in Kedar had given up beseeching the Almighty, claiming that He had abandoned Kedar when the curse came. But the fact that he and Izzy were still alive, still together, was more than enough reason for Collin to hold to his faith. He'd watched too many good men and women fall to think he and Izzy weren't at risk, no matter how skilled they were.

Collin paused with his leather gaiter half buckled around his calf. Now that they knew a sorcerer stood behind their enemies, their lives were more at risk than ever. Red Cloaks trained to face all manners of magic, that which was inherent to beings outside humanity and powers derived from darker sources. Which meant Collin knew what they were up against.

Numbers weren't going to be enough.

Collin shook himself, finishing his silent prayers as he was buckling his cloak around his throat. The barracks had nearly emptied while he was caught in his thoughts, and he jogged down the hall. While most were already in the mess hall for breakfast, Collin's goal was the courtyard.

Izzy was already waiting for him, her head tilted back to watch the stars fading from sight. But she didn't accuse him of being late. She hardly moved when he took up a place at her side, watching her face rather than the sky. Her lips were pressed tight, eyebrows drawn together in thought. Her hands clawed at the stone behind her.

"What are you thinking?" He asked.

"This can't go on forever," she whispered. "Either we find a way to end this madness, or one night Kedar will fall."

"We're not broken yet."

Izzy lowered her head, piercing him with an incredulous stare. There were dark circles beneath her eyes testifying of a restless night. A bitter smile tugged at the corner of his mouth.

"I know," he said. "I see it too."

Kedar's strength was fracturing, stone and people alike. Their enemies knew it. It wasn't enough to hold back their attack and pick at them during the day...they had to break the pattern. But the longer he and Izzy searched for answers, the less possible it seemed.

"We underestimated them," Collin said, staring at the stone arch above the courtyard's entrance. "The golem..."

"Why haven't we seen anything like it before?" Izzy murmured. "If there's a sorcerer in their ranks capable of *two* potent spells at once, why hasn't he sent them after Kedar's walls? Whatever was in that smoke could surely kill."

"That's the question, isn't it? Why change methods now?"

"Maybe because we've found something that could threaten them."

"Or they're tired of us harassing and killing their soldiers," Collin suggested.

Izzy gave him a flat look. Collin elbowed her side.

"Enough talking. Or are you afraid to lose again?"

That broke her free of her contemplation. Izzy pushed away from the wall, her eyes flashing as she picked up two practice swords laying beside her. Collin grinned as he took one from her.

He backed into place and raised the blunt blade. When Izzy was in place, he raised his eyebrow, inviting her to attack first. She didn't hesitate.

Collin gave up ground, deflecting her sword and stepping into an attack of his own in a single fluid movement. Izzy was ready for him.

They settled into the ritual, and Collin could finally breathe. It was instinct by now. The skills he and Izzy had spent so many hours drilling through under Rhett and Eldon's watchful eyes were now automatic.

But with Izzy it was more than skill and practice. He knew what Izzy intended before she was fully into the movement, familiar with the slightest shift in weight or angle of blade. He knew she could say the same for him. The rhythm of it, their long bouts that so often ended in an impasse while they both gasped for breath, centered him. There was no one who knew him as well as Izzy. Nothing would ever change that.

Collin faltered, a single wrong step, and Izzy slid her practice sword alongside his neck. Her smug smile, the savage glint in her eyes as her chest heaved, nearly undid him. He leaned forward, ignoring the press of metal against his throat. A smile twitched on his lips that made Izzy's breath hitch.

Movement from the shadows saved him. He backed up, lifting his head to identify their watcher. If it was Rhett, they were sunk. But the thin figure didn't match their commander's stature. *Isley.*

Izzy must've seen the change in his expression. She lowered the sword, smile disappearing as she spun to face Isley.

He stepped forward, into the light of the torches. The rueful smile on his face didn't set Collin at ease.

"I apologize," he said, bowing his head. "I was passing through, and...I couldn't help but watch. You look like the sword dancers from the southwest."

"I've seen them," Collin said, his voice gruffer than usual. Hopefully Isley took it as the early hour. "Can't say we've ever fought with fire, though."

Izzy glanced back in confusion, and Collin remembered that she hadn't seen the dancers that Isley spoke of. They came to Kedar after her family was killed. The stern headmaster at the orphanage refused to let Izzy go with him to see their performance.

"Their blades are torches," he explained. "They use rings lit on fire, as well."

"Sounds like something Alair would want to try," she replied drily.

A chuckle built in the back of his throat.

"It does."

"I'll...leave now," Isley said, backing toward the corridor. Collin watched until he was sure Isley was gone.

He'd forgotten the fire dancers. That was the last time he and Izzy had asked permission to see each other. After that night, they found ways to meet away from the eyes of any adults who might try to stop them.

Collin supposed secrecy had always played a part in their relationship.

With Isley gone, Collin turned back to Izzy. She was already watching him. Collin raised his eyebrows.

"Dancers, huh?"

"Hardly a typical dance."

He knew he should let it drop there. But he couldn't help himself.

"We're hardly a typical couple," he murmured.

A smile flickered across her lips, there and gone as quick as a shooting star. She stepped back before he could be tempted to draw out that smile again, raising her weapon.

"Care to go again? Or do you need a rest first?"

Collin huffed, taking another step back as he shifted into the correct stance. For this time at least, secrets didn't matter.

Izzy

Izzy's steps were near silent as she and Collin walked through the forest, so close together that their hands brushed. They were nearing the deep woods, and her heart longed to run ahead. She was tired of eyes constantly following them.

They didn't have to come out today. In fact, Rhett didn't know they *were* in the forest. They had the day off because of their battle last night, but she couldn't sit around the headquarters polishing weapons and washing laundry. Collin only made a show of argument when she suggested they search the woods for a while.

Seeing the edge of the wilds ahead of them, she reached out to take Collin's hand properly. Only as their fingers brushed did she spot the figure walking toward them, a few dead fox slung over his shoulder.

Izzy didn't jerk away. That would arouse suspicion. But she did wrap her hand in the edge of the cloak, her shoulders stiff as the trapper passed them.

"Fruitful morning?" Collin asked.

"Good enough," he replied.

His tone was distant, walking the cold edge between respect and contempt. Collin didn't say anything else as the man continued his march toward the city. Izzy waited until the orange fur draped over his back disappeared completely before relaxing.

He didn't see anything odd enough to share. She doubted he'd even mention their presence in the forest, unless it was to wonder what mischief they were up to. She doubted he'd be offering any Red Cloak a sign of reverence.

It was odd to see him this far south. The moonstruck creatures of the horde had driven most of the ordinary animals out of the forest south and west of Kedar. There wasn't much prey for him here unless the trapper was targeting moonstruck animals. It was his right, Izzy supposed. If there were a handful fewer animals to attack them when night next came, she wouldn't complain.

Izzy tried to relax as they stepped into the deep woods, but it took longer than usual. Even as they left their cloaks hanging on their tree, she was stiff and wary. A glimpse of Collin's eyes told her that the same memories swirling in her mind were plaguing him.

They were growing too bold. And they both knew the consequences of being caught.

They were punished for their closeness once before, when they were sixteen. Rhett had been merciful: he'd merely separated them. But those three months were still a torture she would never forget.

Of course, their forced separation hadn't lasted past the next wolf moon. Izzy was nearly killed by a troll when, in the heat of that battle, she'd forgotten she didn't have Collin watching her back. By the time she was well enough to leave the infirmary, Collin was back at her side.

Izzy glanced up at Collin as they walked, taking in the thoughtful set to his face before lowering her eyes to their clasped hands.

Their friends had told her that Collin stormed into Rhett's office the morning after she was injured, and that their argument could be heard across the courtyard. But he'd never told her what was said, only that he'd promised Rhett that they'd keep their vows as long as they wore the symbol of their order.

They couldn't afford to fail. The consequences of being found out *now* would be far worse than being forced to watch Collin from across a room. They'd seen more whippings in their time than she liked to remember. She didn't want to be the one tied to the post.

The thought of seeing Collin's face twisted in agony, red lines crisscrossed on his back as the whip fell again and again... her hand tightened in Collin's grip.

He glanced down at her, and she made an effort to smile.

"Where are we headed?" she asked, keeping her voice hushed.

Collin shrugged. "Somewhere that's been cleared recently. Or... near it. I don't want to come across any secrets when no one knows we're out here."

Izzy took a closer look at their surroundings, matching landmarks to her many memories. Only vague impressions met her.

"The waterfall?" she asked.

Collin smiled down at her. "It's a bit cool for a swim, but it'll be nice to sit by a while."

The thought of the cool mist drifting over her skin put a skip of anticipation in her step, despite the lingering chill to the air. Perhaps the sound of the water crashing down against the stone would drown out her worries for a while, until she could take them up again without so much strain.

Collin matched her quickened pace, a smile teasing at his lips as they wove between brown fern littered with fallen leaves and tall, evergreen pine. When they met the narrow river, her blood began to sing. They could hear the waterfall before it was in sight.

When Izzy glimpsed the cascade of white water between the trees, the child in her wanted to run ahead, to race Collin to the water's edge. Part of her excitement withered in her chest as years of training won out.

There was a reason they could trust that they were the only citizens of Kedar out here. She couldn't afford to forget that somewhere their enemies lurked in shadow, that even on a pleasure visit they might be required to fight.

Half a dozen steps more, and her wariness was more than training. There was a feel to the air around them, like a high-pitched whine she couldn't fully hear. It set her nerves on edge; she'd felt this before.

She released Collin's hand to grip her sword, her eyes flying to his. He felt it too. He loosened his sword from its sheath.

They moved forward facing away from each other, their shoulders pressed together as they scanned their surroundings for whatever being had soured the late morning air. She desperately wished she could remember more of the landscape than a vague image of white water falling in white sheets, veiled in mist. *Why* couldn't she remember?

A growl on Collin's side interrupted her thoughts. They drew their weapons in unison. Though a voice demanded she turn and face their enemy, especially as another growl sent spiders down her back, she kept her eyes on her own side in search of other threats. Only once she was sure they were alone did she turn.

Once her eyes caught on what threatened them, her heart thundered in her ears. *Wyvern.*

A small one, if the stories could be trusted. It was about the length of a horse, with a wingspan twice that and teeth as long as her hand. It held its head low to the ground, staring at them with a cold and malicious stare. It's tongue flicked out of its mouth as it growled, tasting the air.

They'd never fought a wyvern. A few had attacked with the horde over the years, but it was a rare event...and a dreaded possibility. She'd never heard of two people surviving a wyvern attack on their own. Izzy wasn't arrogant enough to think that they could be the first.

"It can't fly."

Izzy flicked her eyes up to Collin, then back to the wyvern. He was right: its left wing was bent, a bad break that hadn't healed properly. Perhaps they did have a chance of escape, if the creature didn't coat them in acid before they could get out of reach.

As if guessing their thoughts, the wyvern growled again and took a single step toward them, wrapping a clawed wing around a young tree for balance.

"Bruin!"

The voice came from behind the wyvern. More words followed, but in a language Izzy didn't understand. She and Collin kept their weapons raised, even as the wyvern slowly lowered itself back to the ground. Another sharp order in that voice, closer now, and the wyvern turned his head away from them.

It wasn't a relief. Whoever was giving orders to this creature could just as easily tell it to attack them if he proved to be an enemy. Izzy wondered if there was any hope he wouldn't know what they were without their cloaks.

A figure stepped around the wyvern, and Izzy was surprised to see that age had bent his back and whitened his hair. His voice certainly didn't betray it.

Nor did his pale

gaze belong to the old man he appeared to be. There was cunning there. Was Izzy imagining that the high whine grew a little louder as he approached? Izzy edged a little closer to Collin, her weapon still raised.

"I apologize for startling you," he said, resting a hand on the wyvern's bent wing. "Bruin has little use for manners."

"This creature is yours?" Collin asked cautiously.

The old man smiled, as if amused by something only he knew.

"In a way. I found him injured at the base of a mountain side. He's been my companion ever since."

He turned to face the wyvern, who had returned to glaring at Izzy and Collin. The old man whispered another incomprehensible order, and the wyvern reluctantly backed away, offering them a final glare before disappearing in the direction of the waterfall. Izzy would've preferred to have the creature where she could watch it.

Collin slowly sheathed his sword, glancing down at Izzy as he did. Stifling a sigh, Izzy did the same. She felt better with a blade between her and this stranger. But she was afraid her sword wouldn't do her much good here, not if her suspicions about this man were correct.

The old man watched their actions in silence, his amusement still in place.

"Suspicious pair, aren't you?" he said. "Why are you so deep in the forest? Come to visit grandfather?"

His laughter scraped against the air like dry branches, and Izzy felt Collin step a little closer to her side.

"We remembered the waterfall," Collin said with an ease that made Izzy envious.

"A bit cold for swimming."

"It's a nice place for some solitude."

He didn't believe them. Did he somehow know of their scattered skirmishes in these woods? Had he seen them when they came out last? Izzy had no doubt that he was the one dwelling in the rock house higher up the mountain.

They should've stayed in the city.

"It's strange finding others out here," Collin said. "Do you live by yourself?"

The old man's face flashed, with fury or pain Izzy couldn't tell. His voice was missing some of that friendliness as he answered.

"I do."

"I suppose with a wyvern companion, you're safer than most."

His expression shifted back to secretive amusement with a terrifying ease.

"I take it by your many weapons that you could say the same."

Izzy didn't like the way he said that. He sounded contemptuous, as if their weapons were useless. She fought to stand her ground and not reach for the hilt of her sword again. She had a sinking feeling that they were outmatched by more than the wyvern.

"We didn't mean to disturb you," Collin said, taking a step backward. "We'll return to enjoy the water another day."

"I should think not."

Izzy grabbed Collin's arm, reaching for her sword as the man lifted his empty hand toward them. But she'd barely touched the worn leather when fog enveloped them, shielding sight and sound alike in a wash of empty gray.

"Collin," she whispered, voiceless.

She could barely feel his arm beneath her fingertips. Her feet were swept out from beneath her, everything spinning and fading as Collin was ripped from her grasp. She couldn't find her voice to scream his name.

Afternoon sunlight was sharp in Izzy's eyes, burning away a strange film blurring the world around her. She blinked, raising her hand to shade her vision and finding that her arm was strangely heavy. Collin sat up slowly beside her. He was rubbing at his eyes, his other hand grasping for hers.

"We must've fallen asleep," he said groggily, looking around.

Izzy examined their surroundings with him, trying to pinpoint where they were. A small stream wandered near their feet, its quiet murmuring calling to something on the very edge of her mind. A louder river, a growl...

It slipped away before she could grasp it. Izzy looked down at their intwined fingers, frowning as she tried to recall how they ended up here. She remembered the sound of the water soothing her mind. And something...unexpected. Did she dream it all?

The more she tried to remember, the more her head pounded. She shook her head and glanced upward at the sun that woke her. How long were they asleep?

"We should get back," she said.

"Alair is going to let us have it," Collin replied, pushing to his feet. "He wanted to check out the caravan in the eastern quarter before it heads north, and I asked him to wait until we could join him."

Izzy accepted Collin's help off the ground. Where were their cloaks in relation to this place? They must be close: there was too much sunlight above them for the deepest forest.

Collin leaped across the stream, and Izzy followed. She shook her head again, trying to clear her mind. She hadn't realized how tired she was. They should've stayed in Kedar; the forest wasn't a safe place to rest. They were blessed no goblin or moonstruck creature came upon them and decided to add more lives to their collection of bloody trophies.

They found their cloaks easily enough, but Izzy was slow to don hers. She stared at the fabric in her hands, still trying to grasp the dream that filled her with so much dread. How had they slept *that* deeply on the forest floor? It was purely the Almighty's mercy that they were alive, exposed and vulnerable as they were. Never in her life had she let her guard down in enemy territory like that. She couldn't help but wonder if there was something else, something beyond exhaustion, that had caused it.

Collin laid his hand over her arm, and when she looked up she found some of the same muddled questions mirrored in his eyes. She opened her mouth to ask if he had troubled dreams as well…but the words wouldn't come.

He dropped his hand, and Izzy donned her cloak. It felt heavier than it usually did. Perhaps that was due to the fatigue still laying close to her bones.

The walk back to Kedar's gates felt longer than usual. She fought to hold her head high as they passed the sentries. The noise of the streets beyond pierced through the fog around her head, and keeping her eyes open was a little easier as they wove their way toward estate.

"Where'd you disappear to?"

Izzy spun, hand on her knife before she recognized Alair.

"Looking for some quiet," Collin replied.

"Ooo, grouchy much?" Dal asked.

"You should've slept in," Alair said

Izzy agreed with him. If they'd set aside their morning ritual for one day, they wouldn't have been so tired they fell asleep in the middle of enemy territory.

"Did you already go to the market?" Collin asked.

"No."

"You aren't the only ones who got distracted," Dal said, standing on his toes to throw an arm over Alair's shoulder. Alair shrugged him off.

"It doesn't matter. You two coming?"

Collin glanced down at Izzy, letting her decide.

"Let's go," she said.

Some time wandering the city might help her shake the heavy feeling hunching her shoulders.

"Good," Alair said with a grin. "Dal wants to ask the dye merchant how to get his skin back to normal."

"Not enjoying the fruits of your labor?" Collin asked.

Dal cast a glare in Collin's direction that was ruined by the smile twitching on his mouth.

"Are you going to tell him what you used it for?" Izzy asked.

"Not if I can help it."

Alair and Dal were already moving again, and Izzy was envious of the carefree way they walked down the street. She followed half a step behind Collin, listening to them discuss the likelihood that Dal would keep his pink tinge through the full moon.

As they stepped into the market, Izzy's gaze was drawn to the sky where the swollen moon hung. Its missing sliver was barely discernable. The foreboding that spread through her limbs at the sight was familiar. Less familiar was the way the sight seemed to weigh on her mind, making her eyelids droop. Shaking her head, she ran to catch up with Collin and their friends.

CHAPTER FOUR

Izzy

Izzy threw a card onto the pile, staring at the black markings until they blurred before her eyes. Collin sighed as he laid down his own cards, revealing his losing hand.

"She win again?" Dal asked without looking up from the book he was reading.

"Yes," Collin groaned. "I swear she's stacking the deck."

"Cards was your idea," Izzy murmured, gathering the cards together to shuffle while Collin shifted some of his wooden chips to her side of the board. Gambling was forbidden among the Red Cloaks, and she understood why after hearing stories of the fights in the Watch barracks over card games. They got around the rule by using scraps of wood and leather that held no value. There was little competitiveness to the game for Izzy: it was merely a way to pass the hours.

Tonight it wasn't proving distraction enough. No matter how she tried, she couldn't forget the battle that waged all around them. The men and women risking their lives while they sat there like it was just a normal night...

She understood the rotation, and after the wolf moon they had last month she should be grateful for the reprieve. But not tonight, not with scraps of moonlight slipping past the shutters behind Collin's chair.

"Alright," Dal said, closing his book with a snap. "Deal me in. We'll see if Izzy's luck holds when there's three of us."

"Four," Berke said, closing the door softly behind him.

"Thought you were going to bed," Collin said, taking the cards from Izzy's hands.

"Not yet." Berke sat with a groan. "It feels brighter than usual."

Izzy agreed. Her eyes strayed again to the sliver of moonlight behind Collin. It was still deep twilight. They had hours left before the moon would disappear behind the horizon and leave them in peace.

"Heard you went to the scribes today," Collin said, quickly dealing out new hands for all of them. "Did they say anything about the spell stones?"

Izzy ripped her eyes from the moonlight to watch Berke. She couldn't tell if his scowl was due to his visit with the scribes or his cards.

"They did, but it was as cryptic as everything else they share," Berke said, rearranging his hand.

"Well?" Alair prompted.

Berke laid his cards face down on the table before answering.

"The runes are an old language spoken before Kedar existed, now mostly used by other beings. Moon folk, faeries, ogres...you get the point."

"What do they say?" Izzy asked quietly.

"They're calling on the moon to power the spell."

Dal snorted. "I thought that was obvious."

"Rhett say anything about it when you told him?" Collin asked.

Berke shook his head.

Izzy exchanged a glance with Collin. Did this mean the sorcerer behind it wasn't human? Or that he had access to knowledge that most didn't?

Perhaps she should go to the scribes. They wouldn't tell her anything more than what they told Berke, but maybe she could gain more information in other ways. Most of the chronicles the scribes guarded were accessible to the public. And as a Red Cloak, she had access to some of the collection they kept locked away. She could find the runes' significance on her own.

It would mean giving up her few hours of liberty locked away in the dark archival rooms, struggling to comprehend language that had been archaic when Collin's grandmother was a child. But if there was even a chance they could find a weakness in this sorcerer's work, it would be worth however many evenings it took. Izzy wanted every advantage they could find before meeting this sorcerer face to face.

Izzy's lips pulled down as she stared at the cards in her hand, not truly seeing the markings on their faces. There was something on the edge of her mind, something that she knew instinctively she shouldn't forget. If she could grasp it...

"We've got her this time," Dal said, leaning back in his chair with a grin. "See, you just needed a little help."

"Sure," Collin said flatly.

That scrap of memory disappeared entirely, leaving Izzy with a strange hollow feeling. She purposefully rearranged her cards. But as she opened her mouth to inform Dal not to count his victory just yet, a commotion broke through the shuttered windows.

All four of them were on their feet in an instant, but it was Collin who reached the door first. Izzy slipped out on his heels to find a stranger in the courtyard, shouting in a panic.

"The wolf is *here,*" he said, grasping at the Red Cloak who stood before him.

Dread washed over Izzy with the icy, condemning moonlight.

"It isn't a wolf moon," someone protested.

Izzy was already running for the armory. The man's words

echoed in her head, drowning out his frenzied explanation. *The wolf is here.* The count of the moons, the pattern of the curse, none of it mattered. Izzy had witnessed firsthand what the werewolf could do set loose in the city. She could feel the blood on her hands.

But even as her mind ran wild with old fears and vivid memories, her hands were steady. She knew already which blades to take. She knew without looking where to place them. Too many years stood between her and those memories to overcome her now.

Collin was right beside her, strapping on knives while she buckled her belt. There was no time to retrieve her armor. Even without it, she stood a far better chance against the wolf than the families he would tear apart. She swallowed hard at the thought of what they might find. No one was prepared.

As they left the armory, Berke tossed two cloaks their way. Izzy threw it around her shoulders in a numb, practiced movement.

"West quarter," Dal said. "North side of Birch Street."

"Wait for us," Viron said, slipping past Collin and Izzy to reach the armory.

Izzy was already running for the gate, one hand on the hilt of her sword. Wait? For the wolf to slaughter more families? For the poor girl he was searching for to bleed out at the werewolf's feet?

The streets were empty, and soon enough the sound from the courtyard had faded beneath the steady pounding of their feet, side by side. The silver moon hung above their heads, flooding the streets with a shallow light, gray and lifeless. Izzy would've sworn it dimmed as they heard the first screams.

They rounded a corner to a massive wolf ramming its head into an already splintered door. Screams came from within, but Izzy locked away the part of her heart that quailed at the sound. The wolf snarled, forcing its shoulders through the doorway. Izzy prayed that the piercing shriek that followed was purely terror.

She glanced at Colin, waiting for his nod. They moved forward as one.

The wolf heard them coming, pulling free of the broken door to spin on them. Jaws snapped beside Izzy's head, spittle hitting her cheek as she slipped beneath the wolf's neck and thrust a dagger into his throat.

It caught on fur, as she knew it would. Cloth also came away with her knife. The walls around her heart wavered seeing the scrap of clothing, the only sign that the creature before her was *human*. Or used to be. But she kept moving, slicing her sword across the wolf's front shoulder while Collin attacked its rear. The wolf snapped and howled, unsure which enemy to bleed first. His eyes locked on Izzy, reflecting moonlight. She threw her cloak over her shoulder, taking a step back to hold his attention. It worked. The wolf's head dropped, a low growl emanating from his throat as he took a slow step forward.

She knew the moment he would spring, knew what angle to hold her sword so it would pierce hide and muscle. She knew Collin would be there to aid her, ensuring those teeth missed their mark. She knew how the blood that poured over her hands would never wash away.

The wolf shifted, and Izzy braced. She couldn't help but notice the scraps of clothing still hanging around his neck. But the sight of the destruction already surrounding her tempered her resolve.

"Thane."

The voice was faint, high and reedy with fear. But the wolf paused as if the world hung on that single word. Something changed in his eyes as he twisted to face the source of that voice, something so ephemeral Izzy wondered if she imagined it.

A crossbow bolt sprouted from his neck.

The wolf jerked, a wild snarl splitting the chilled air. His eyes were wild again, searching the street for his enemy. Once more his eyes focused on Izzy. But more bolts sank into his side with dull thuds. His last, defiant cry pierced to her soul.

Izzy stepped back as the wolf fell, twisting away. But it was too late. He was already shrinking, the monster stripped away to leave behind the body of a boy covered in his own blood. Once she saw it, she couldn't look away. Not even when the foil rushed forward, falling to her knees with wild sobs. Izzy squeezed her eyes shut as those cries split her heart in two.

The foil would've died if they hadn't intervened. *All* of these people would've died, soaking the street in blood. The werewolf wouldn't have stopped his rampage until he had the foil within reach...and after he'd killed her, after his one desire was fulfilled, his madness would only have grown worse. The werewolf would've torn through the city, slaughtering everyone he could reach. She *knew* that. And yet...

A hand rested on her shoulder. She was leaning back against Collin before she realized it, letting him take most of her weight.

"Berke," Collin said quietly.

Izzy pried her eyes open, taking a small step away from Collin as she remembered they weren't alone.

More people were out in the street. Some gathered around the dead boy...the werewolf she'd been prepared to kill. Others watched from a distance. Izzy couldn't read their thoughts in the wan light. She wished her own identity was so shielded.

"Get out of here," Berke replied, closer than Izzy was prepared for. "We'll handle the rest of this."

His voice was heavy, and Izzy wished desperately that she wasn't familiar with his tone. It was the grief of a warrior who'd already seen too many fall. It was the grief of one who couldn't afford to let sorrow break him. The emotion filling Izzy at that moment was far more volatile.

But she bit back every hint of tears, cleaning her sword blade on her pants with as much dignity as she could summon. She kept her eyes far away from anyone standing around them. And when Collin tugged her away, she went without argument and without a backward glance at the grieving family now gathered on the bloody street.

It seemed every Red Cloak not on the wall was awake and outside when Collin and Izzy returned, but none of them asked questions. The light on in Rhett's study warned Izzy that their night was far from over.

But Collin steered her away from Rhett and their comrades, into shadowed halls empty of another living soul. Further and further he tugged her, until they were in a crowded linen closet with the door shut behind them. Collin's arms slipped around her back in the darkness.

"Collin," Izzy protested, trying to slip free. "We can't. If someone..."

"I don't care," Collin growled.

He pulled one hand away, and a moment later she heard heavy cloth falling to the floor. Then the clasp around her throat was undone. Collin had her against his chest before the cloak hit the floor. She stayed stiff, knowing she should pull back again, that she *needed* to step away. This wasn't worth the risk. It *wasn't*. And yet, as Collin's steady warmth soaked through her clothes the last of her composure crumbled away.

She slipped her arms around his waist, tears already spilling over onto her cheeks as she melted against him. He held her a little tighter as the first sob shook her body.

"Collin," she whispered.

"Don't," Collin whispered. "I know."

Izzy choked on her tears, twisting her face to press against the hollow of his throat. Eyes open or closed, all she could see was the lifeless boy laid out on the street. *Thane*. He was so young. Just like...

Rhone. She could still see his face, alive and smiling as he slipped Izzy a hard candy on his way to greet her sister, Mariel. She could still see his empty eyes staring up in the street. The carnage that surrounded him, the blood of her *family*...

Collin had held her that night, too. Though they were only children, though he knew every person laying dead in the street just as well as she did, he'd stayed strong for her. Vow or no vow, she needed him just as much now as she had then.

Her fingers twisted around his shirt, arms trembling as she held him with every scrap of strength she had. It was such a sharp contrast to how he held her, with that steady gentleness that had been her pillar ever since that night.

He was stroking her hair, calloused skin catching on her braid. She could hardly understand the words he whispered in her ear. But though the sound of his voice gave her something to cling to, it didn't erase the torrent of grief and guilt tearing her apart.

Rhett argued that killing in protection of Kedar absolved them of their guilt, that they were only doing their duty. Most believed him. Some days Izzy did too. But his words meant nothing now, not when she'd helped take one of the lives she was supposed to protect.

"He was a *kid*." The words were dragged from her lips, shaking and ragged. "We...we killed him. Collin, how much blood is on my hands?"

"It's on my hands too."

She must be a wretched person, because those words gave her ground to stand on. She may be broken and bloodstained, worthless except for the blades she wielded. But she wasn't alone.

"We're the same," Collin whispered. "I'm not letting you go."

She shuddered, and a dangerous desperation took hold of her.

"I love you," she whispered.

Izzy felt Collin sigh, and she pressed her face into his shoulder again lest any other words slip from her lips. She shouldn't have said it. He knew already, and speaking those words *here*, in the depths of Kedar, was treacherous. And yet...and yet if their story among the Red Cloaks ended the same way it began, soaked in blood, she couldn't stand the thought of never *saying* it. She would've given anything to say those words to her family one last time.

Collin's arms tightened around her, and he shifted his head closer to hers. Rather than say anything, he pressed his lips against her temple. Lightning spread through her skin, and Izzy couldn't say if it was exhilaration or fear.

How many nights had she dreamed of what kissing him would feel like? How many times had she reminded her weak and selfish heart that it was a line they could never cross? *This isn't the same,* she told herself. But she couldn't shake the thought that they'd taken fire in their bare hands.

If they were condemned already, why not give in entirely? All it would take is turning her head and lifting her face to his. She could almost convince herself that the breathless pressure in her chest was anticipation.

Someone knocked on the door.

Izzy jerked backwards, hitting her head against a wooden shelf. For a heavy moment she and Collin stared at each other in the near darkness, their heavy breathing the only sound. Then light flooded their small bit of sanctuary.

"Rhett wants you."

The voice was stilted, and it took Izzy a moment to recognize Isley. He was staring at the ground, his hand white-knuckled on the edge of the door. Every warm and pleasant feeling drained out the soles of Izzy's feet. If he told anyone what he saw right now, they would be blessed if a turn at the whipping post was all they received.

How many lashes would Rhett give them? Six? Twenty? The most Izzy had ever witnessed was thirty-nine. They'd had to drag the man away afterward.

"Thank you, Isley," Colin said, and only Izzy could've recognized the fear at the edges of his voice.

He stooped to pick their cloaks off the floor, handing Izzy hers before striding out of the small closet as if everything were normal. Izzy watched Isley closely as she walked past him. He was careful to avoid her gaze, and as soon as they were in the hall he shut the door and walked off. Collin didn't follow immediately.

As she refastened the heavy cloak around her throat, she forced her eyes up to Collin's face. The regret in his eyes was a dart in her chest, even if she felt it too. They stepped too far. What had possessed her to lower her guard so completely? They'd left their fate completely in Isley's hands, and that was a kind of vulnerability she despised.

"He didn't see anything," Collin whispered.

"We were alone," she replied, dropping her gaze to the floor. "That might be enough."

Collin didn't reply. As they walked down the hall side by side, Izzy squeezed her eyes shut. The ache in her chest was almost worse than before. But more than anything, she was *tired.* She'd rather spar in the courtyard until she collapsed than face Rhett right now.

But she marched forward anyway. And when they reached the open door to his office, she didn't allow herself to hesitate before stepping into the lamp light. Collin entered at her back.

Rhett was standing behind his desk, listening to Berke give the names of the wolf and foil and what information he could pry from the neighbors and family members. Izzy wished he'd let such matters wait. To question them *now,* in the midst of the shock of losing their loved one to the curse, seemed cruel. They'd waited until the next morning to question *her.*

Izzy clasped her hands behind her back as they waited for Berke to finish. She learned the foil's name, Carolin, and that her family had no immediate connection to the wolf's. He didn't say whether the foil and the wolf knew one another. They knew the answer to that already: the wolves and foils *always* knew one another. Whether by chance or by long proximity, they were always connected.

Izzy had her suspicions about what tied each of them together, but she'd only shared it with Collin. She didn't want Rhett to begin searching for star-crossed lovers as targets for the curse. Besides, she could be wrong. She only knew her Mariel's secret, not every foil to fall to the curse.

Perhaps that was the cruelest piece of the curse: it took a couple who'd give anything to be together and twisted them into enemies. The wolf would always seek and kill the foil. The foil would always be the wolf's greatest weakness.

Rhett dismissed Berke. He gave them a concerned look as he left the office, closing the door behind him. Izzy reluctantly turned her head to face their commander.

"You ran off without support and against orders."

Izzy winced. She carefully schooled her expression again, though she knew Rhett had caught her reaction. She stood tall and forced herself to match his stoic expression, despite the wriggling feeling of being scolded.

"There wasn't time to wait," Collin said. "We knew the wolf would be slaughtering people every moment we weren't there. By running ahead, we were able to distract the werewolf until reinforcements arrived."

"And what would you have done if the wolf had proven too strong for you? Do you believe yourselves invincible?"

Invincible? Hardly. How could they when the proof of their mortality surrounded them every day? Izzy raised her eyes to Rhett's gaze.

"We've offered our entire lives to this city's protection," she said steadily. "How is risking our lives before a werewolf different from risking them in the gates?"

Rhett stared back at her, and for all the years she'd known him she still couldn't discern the thoughts behind that gaze.

"Well done."

Izzy inhaled sharply. Beside her, Collin stiffened.

Those words were meant to reassure them, and perhaps they should. Rhett approved of their actions. But all Izzy could think of was the wolf twisting in agony, his form shrinking to the body of the teenage boy he truly was. For a moment she struggled to breathe, choking on the horror of being praised for taking part in the death of a young man she was meant to protect. Their vows to guard the people of Kedar shouldn't fall void so easily.

But Izzy clenched her jaw and nodded, lowering her eyes to the floor to hide her mutinous thoughts. The temptation to glance at Collin was deafening, but she bit her tongue and kept her face forward.

"What will we do now that the cycle is broken?" Collin asked.

Rhett sank into his chair with a weary sigh, staring at the wall where the moon map hung.

"We'll search the populace at each full moon from now on."

Even the thought filled her with weariness. The people of Kedar were uneasy with the searches, uneasy with the Red Cloaks' heavy-handed actions regarding the curse. To stoke those embers with every full moon, in the midst of the fierce battles each night, wouldn't be sustainable for long. Surely not through the long winter that approached.

"Finding the sorcerer responsible for the spells we've encountered might provide an end to the curse," Izzy said carefully.

Rhett watched them, a new look in his eyes she didn't understand. He tapped his fingers on his desk, deep in thought. What was he considering so carefully? Did he know something about the obsidian stones that he hadn't told them?

"Perhaps," Rhett replied at last. "But the curse isn't your first priority. The wolves can be contained. The horde cannot."

Contained. How she hated that word. Locking the werewolf and foil in a tower until dawn was hardly the solution Izzy wanted. Perhaps the foil *was* the key to breaking the werewolf curse, as so many in Kedar believed. But that didn't change the fact that once the wolf and foil entered the tower, no one left alive.

Tonight wasn't the time to argue. Izzy could see the tension in his shoulders, the low burning fury in his eyes. She was reminded as she watched Rhett glare at the wall that he didn't share everything. If he knew what had caused the curse to accelerate, there was no reason Izzy should expect that he would share it with them.

Rhett sagged into his chair, glancing at them wearily.

"Get some rest," he said. "You'll have tomorrow off...but I expect you to remain within the city walls."

The sharp edge to his words made Izzy stand a little straighter. Had he learned about their foray into the forest on their last liberty? He obviously didn't approve.

"Yes, sir," Collin replied. Izzy let it be answer for both of them.

Rhett nodded, looking back to the moon map pinned to the wall, its white parchment stark against the dark wood.

He murmured, "I'll need you with full strength in the nights ahead."

Collin

Collin raised his chin as bearers carried the iron-bound coffin into the crypt. It was a grim sight, though it was one of the few such funerals he'd watched where only one coffin was entombed. The foil stood among the mourners.

They were all dressed in a pale moon gray, a stark contrast to the bearers clad in the blackest cloth the city had: the living and the dead. The mourners laid rowen and rosemary on the coffin as it passed them. Collin could smell the pungent herb as Izzy crushed her own sprig between her white knuckled hands. He hated that smell. His hands itched to hold her, to *feel* her warmth as reassurance that she still lived. As if the woman at his side was some strange deception. He clenched his hands into fists behind his back and kept his eyes on the funeral.

The crypt where the cursed were laid was half a mile north of Kedar, dug out of a rocky bank set apart from the rest of the tombs. Izzy's sister Mariel was entombed within, right beside their neighbor Rhone. Every time he looked at it he pictured Rhone's long-suffering smile as Collin followed him around, emulating everything he did.

He tried to avoid that last memory. There had been so much blood on the street that night he'd hardly recognized any of them.

The curse had taken Rhone and Mariel before anyone had recognized the patterns, before they knew the signs to look for. And because they weren't isolated when the moon rose as the Marked were now, Rhone had killed Izzy's entire family before the Red

Cloaks struck him down. Izzy would've died with them if he hadn't convinced her to explore the fringes of Kedar with him. He knew Izzy warred with grief over that fact, but Collin couldn't resist being grateful that she, at least, escaped. Even then he couldn't stand the thought of losing her.

He and Izzy stood just outside the gate to silently bear witness. It was a position they'd taken after every wolf moon since donning the cloak, though they always kept their distance. They knew the mourning family wouldn't take kindly to Red Cloaks anywhere near them, no matter how genuine their sympathies.

In the eyes of the people, their order was responsible for most of the corpses laid to rest in that tomb. After all, Red Cloaks conducted the searches for the marked. Red Cloaks locked wolf and foil in the tower along the northern edge of the city to fight and die beneath the impartial full moon. Red Cloaks killed the boy now sealed beneath cold stone.

But Collin knew all of those were the actions of desperate men and women who had little more idea what caused the curse than anyone else, let alone how to end it. None of it was the answer Collin wanted...but he and Izzy had never blamed the Red Cloaks like so many others had. They saved their anger for the one who'd set the curse in the first place.

Collin's resolve broke. He turned his head toward Izzy, taking in the tears that streamed down her face. It took every scrap of self-control he possessed not to brush them away.

"I love you." The grief held in her voice as she whispered to him, telling him the words he'd longed to hear for years, was nearly more than he could bear. He'd wanted more than anything to kiss her then and there, to declare everything in his heart. But that wasn't what she'd needed.

He would've kept her back today if he could. This morning, more than any other, he knew she was reliving her own losses. But he knew nothing he could say would convince her to walk away. He also knew better than to think he could carry her away.

Forcing his eyes back to the funeral in the distance, Collin watched as the black-clad bearers resealed the crypt doors with every protection against sorcery that Kedar knew. The purpose was two-fold: to ensure none of the wolves returned, and to guard their resting place from the desecration of the horde.

They turned back to the city as soon as the mourners began their return journey. They knew the suspicious looks they'd receive from those tearstained faces if they were to keep their place. They'd given up trying to offer comfort to the families years ago.

But they always went. It was a reminder they both needed. Those funerals were the reason they joined the Red Cloaks in the first place: to prevent more families from experiencing the grief they had. Rhett was wrong: containing the curse would never be enough. It needed to *end*. And Collin suspected that wouldn't happen until they found the sorcerer who'd set it in the first place.

He didn't know whether to hope or dread that it was the same sorcerer who supported the horde. It was too much of a coincidence to believe they were unrelated, but to accept that one being stood behind it all? It seemed too simple. It made him fear the hatred that would fuel the rage and destruction that he'd witnessed.

Izzy was quiet as they walked toward home. Collin didn't try to tease her out of her mood. Instead, he focused on the people around them, doing enough smiling and nodding to keep everyone at bay. He swore he could feel Izzy's tension drain away once they passed beneath the arch's blessing.

"I'm going to bathe," Izzy murmured, glancing up at him as she backed away.

"Alright."

She slipped away without another word. As soon as he was sure she wouldn't glance back, he let his smile slip. He knew what she really wanted was to be alone for a while, to hide from prying eyes and concerned friends. Perhaps even to hide from him. Forcing her to stay in the open wouldn't take away her sorrow.

Collin turned away from the doorway Izzy disappeared through, intending to seek out the kitchen in case there were any scraps or chores to distract him. They'd worked in the kitchen often in the months before they were ready to take their vows, and the habit had stuck with him.

"Collin!"

He paused, tensing at the voice behind him.

"Yes, Mercer?" Collin asked with careful evenness as he turned.

The snide smile twisting Mercer's lips didn't bode well. Nor did the way he looked Collin over like he'd caught him stealing Rhett's undergarments and was planning just how he wanted to rat him out. What did Mercer know, or believe he knew, to make him so smug?

"Commander Rhett wants to speak to you."

It was obvious that Mercer believed Collin was in for a reprimand. Which he supposed was possible, even likely. But having *Mercer* of all people give the summons set fire to his blood. He answered a heartbeat later than normal, determined not to show his annoyance. He knew from childhood bullies that *not* reacting was the surest way to get under his skin.

"Then I'll go to him immediately."

Mercer's smirk didn't fade, and Collin walked past him before he could say anything else. Eldon stepped out of Rhett's office as he approached, head hanging. He made an effort to smile when he saw Collin, but it didn't hide the weariness of his bearing.

"How's Izzy?" he asked.

"As well as can be expected."

"Did you watch the funeral?"

"We did," Collin said slowly.

Eldon slowly shook his head but said nothing. He'd already wasted plenty of words trying to convince them to stay back, Izzy especially.

"You better head in," Eldon said.

Dread writhed in his gut. The weariness in Eldon's gaze...for a moment Collin wondered if it was sorrow. There was certainly a warning to his words that Collin knew better than to dismiss. Collin nodded stiffly.

Eldon patted Collin's shoulder as he reached for the door, but that was all the comfort he had as Collin stepped inside. Rhett was waiting for him, though neither of them said a word as Collin stopped before his desk and bowed.

"You're treading a thin line."

Rhett's dark gaze pierced right through Collin, making his carefully held composure feel like no more than a thin veil. Still, he kept his shoulders back and his tone dispassionate. And here laid the cause of their strained relationship.

"What do you mean?"

Collin already knew, of course. But he couldn't risk giving away anything Rhett wasn't already aware of.

"I've warned you about drawing too close to Izzy."

"You have," Collin acknowledged.

"And yet you were found together in a *closet* of all places. Do you care to explain how that was appropriate?"

Collin flexed his hand behind his back. He'd like to pummel Isley. Did he think tattling like a child would earn him a higher place in the Red Cloaks? There was nothing he could say...taking Izzy somewhere they could be so easily found *wasn't* appropriate. He hadn't been thinking of vows or professionalism last night. He needed to get Izzy somewhere she wouldn't feel the need to bury everything behind that cold mask of hers. Some things *couldn't* be buried, not without destroying the person who tried.

"High rank does not mean you are above the rules," Rhett continued. "Our agreement hasn't changed."

Collin clenched his jaw, fighting to swallow back the fury roaring like a dragon in his head. He should stay silent. Nothing he said would change Rhett's mind. But words split his lips against his better judgment, striking the air like falling steel.

"With what you know of Izzy's history, do you really think I wouldn't comfort her? Call it what you want. I won't apologize for being what she needed last night."

"Is that truly all you were doing?" Rhett asked, eyes flashing.

"Yes."

"You're a fool for isolating yourselves. You made it appear to everyone else that you were hiding."

Collin bit back the insistence that they *were* hiding. Hiding was the only way Izzy felt safe enough to relax, and part of that was Rhett's doing.

Rhett stared hard at Collin, waiting for him to respond. When Collin kept his jaw clenched shut, Rhett leaned back in his chair.

"If you break our terms, the consequences will be dire for *both* of you."

"Understood."

Rhett was examining him now, searching for weaknesses. Collin met his gaze with a challenge of his own. He wouldn't admit to anything Rhett didn't accuse him of. It came down to this: would Rhett make that accusation? Or would he continue in purposeful ignorance to keep Collin and Izzy in his ranks? He hand-chose them, raising them to be what Kedar needed to stay standing. He paraded them before the city as the heart of Kedar's defense and the hope of the Order's future. Would he throw that all away because Collin and Izzy were breaking the *one* part of a Red Cloak's vows that Rhett himself never took?

A moon cycle could have passed in the following silence, and Collin wouldn't have been able to tell. Rhett said nothing. Collin didn't buckle.

"You're dismissed," Rhett said, still staring at Collin with narrowed eyes.

Collin bowed stiffly and walked away.

Outside, air washed over his skin with a chill the bright sun couldn't touch. It shook him back to reality, but did little to calm the raging fire in his chest. Viron was dueling with Declan nearby, while

Anson watched with a critical eye. Collin approached them at a march.

"Care for a fourth?" he asked.

Declan looked him over warily. He must not be masking his anger as well as he thought. Commander Rhett had a way of getting through his shields, throwing off the careful balance Collin had worked hard to cultivate. Especially when it came to Izzy.

It didn't matter. They could wonder at his fury all they wanted, he didn't intend to answer any questions. He just needed a way to move.

"Step up," Viron said.

Collin strode forward, taking the practice sword Declan held out to him. He shifted into position and waited for Viron.

He moved like lightning. Collin should've expected it, but he still winced as blunted steel glanced off his shoulder. He gritted his teeth as his bruised muscle throbbed, and Viron stepped back.

"Where's your head?" he asked.

"Doesn't matter. It's a fair hit."

Viron glanced back at Anson. Both looked troubled.

"I'll take over," Andred announced, striding up to Viron.

He gave her the sword without argument, joining Anson and Declan at the bench. Andred attacked without warning, and Collin managed to deflect that first attack. But the second caught him across the ribs.

Andred stepped back, looking Collin over with a critical eye.

"You sure this is a good time for sparring?" she asked.

"I have energy I need to expel," Collin bit out.

Andred didn't look convinced, but she didn't ask again. It wasn't until after a few more rounds, each of which ended with more bruises Collin knew he'd regret later, that Andred lowered her sword.

"That's enough beating for one morning," she said.

And yet the fire within him had only billowed higher. A glance around had Collin giving up his sword, though. He was showing too much. If it was anyone else standing before him, if this was any other time, they'd let him have it for being so distracted. But Collin knew that Andred was holding back. If she wasn't, he'd have a few cracked ribs for his efforts.

He turned his back on the group before he could see whatever concerned looks they were sharing. He needed to get his head on straight, *before* Izzy found him. If sparring wouldn't do it, he'd find something else.

Izzy

Izzy slowly unbraided her hair, staring at empty air as thoughts relentlessly ran through her head. The fate of her family, Mariel and Rhone, every funeral she'd witnessed beneath an uncaring sky in the years since. So much had changed...so much had stayed the same.

The first wolf moon after Rhett took Collin and Izzy into the Red Cloaks, Izzy had been arrogant enough to watch the funeral and say "never again." She'd truly thought that she and Collin would be enough to end the curse, to save more families from the grief she still fought against in the darker hours of the night. And in that she had failed. Last night perhaps more than ever.

She didn't believe joining the Red Cloaks was useless. She and Collin had saved lives. Fighting on the wall, searching for a way to *end* the endless battles...if that was their role then she would do it well. But she hadn't saved them from grief. She hadn't found a way to stop the curse that drove her to this life in the first place. Which meant she wasn't finished yet.

Izzy closed her eyes, wrestling with her own mind. Reliving the past over and over was pointless. Besides, she'd already spent a sleepless night tormenting herself. It was time to turn her mind away from where she'd failed and decide what to do next. She wasn't finished yet...so what was her next step?

Berke's sliver of news from the night before was all she could bring herself to consider. The purpose of the obsidian, the language of the runes...none of it was information she and Collin couldn't have guessed. She regretted not taking time to study the markings on the shards more carefully before handing it over to Rhett. She doubted he or the scribes would tell her anything more than they told Berke. But she could look for answers herself.

Her fingers slowed as she considered that scant information. With quick, twisting fingers she redid her braid. She ought to go to the scribes' library *now,* before her memory faded further. Time alone could wait. Her hair tamed once more, Izzy grabbed her cloak and headed for the door.

She didn't see Collin in the courtyard. The thought crossed her mind to search for him and drag him into the city with her, but she strode beneath the old arch alone. She had hope that he was with their friends, that time with them would wash away some of the heaviness of the past few hours. And if that was the case, her errand wasn't worth disturbing him.

In the city, Izzy tried not to watch the people she passed. But she couldn't help but notice some details: the children sweeping golden leaves from the streets, farmers from the eastern quarter selling sacks of grain, swollen gourds, and the last produce from the gardens they cultivated within the walls. Did they have less to sell than Izzy remembered from the previous year, or were her own worries overshadowing her memories?

She was glad when she reached the sprawling building the scribes called home, marked by the astronomical tower that thrust toward the sky. It was the highest point in Kedar, taller even than the Tower of the Cursed looming over the northern quarter.

The library was older than most of the buildings in Kedar, built of light gray stone that seemed to glow when the moonlight hit it. Beneath the sunlight, it looked as grungy and worn as everything else.

Izzy entered through the wide doors, trying not to pause and gawk. She couldn't help but look around as she walked across the tiled front room, though. On the wall beside the entrance hung maps of the current moon cycle, as well information on sunrise and patterns of stars. A few citizens were inside, engaged in conversation with the scribes over whatever question of lineage or law they'd come with. She walked past them, nodding to the gray-headed scribe who watched her. She'd worn her cloak to avoid as much conversation as possible, and it worked. He returned her nod and allowed her to stride into the library proper without hinderance.

The crimson cloaks that marked their order were expensive to create, and that alone made them unique in Kedar. But there were also punishments for wearing a garment too similar outside of the Order, or even attempting to sell them. That meant that within these walls her cloak was identification enough to gain her entry wherever she went.

The main part of the building was arranged a bit like a maze, twisting corridors connecting dim rooms full of shelves stretching far above her head. Thankfully Izzy knew where to go: it was the only room she'd spent time in.

Rhett had sent them here when they were still training, asking the scribes to teach them about the creatures who fought with the horde and anything they might need to fight dark magic. All Red Cloaks received training on the subject, but few had an education so detailed. At the time, Izzy and Collin accused Rhett of using the scribes to get rid of them. But she now knew that most of the order saw Izzy and Collin's extensive time among the scribes as a sign of Rhett's dedication to them, a sign he'd chosen them as his apprentices. Perhaps they were right. Regardless, she was glad for those long, tiring days.

The scribes weren't the most welcoming group of people, and a few made Rhett seem like a lenient master in comparison. But Izzy would always be grateful for the knowledge they imparted. Thanks to them, she and Collin had a better understanding of their world and the powers operating within it by the age of fifteen than ordinary citizens ever had.

Once Izzy reached the room she was looking for, the easy part of her search was over. It had been years since she read anything there, and all she remembered was that she and Collin had poured over at least one codex that contained definitions for old runes. There were others that would be useful, but finding them...

Izzy stopped at the podium set against the end of one shelf, where the catalogue was set. It was made of thin sheets of wood, each document's information inked onto the surface. They were attached to thin strips of metal, allowing the scribes to add titles within the existing organization. Though Izzy doubted they added to this room very often.

Izzy flipped through the short entries quickly, skimming the information for anything that might prove useful. She began a pile of promising works on one of the nearby tables, slipping flat rods of wood to hold the place on the towering shelves. She didn't dare alter their organization. The scribes might not be trained in combat as she was, but she still wouldn't risk angering any of them. They guarded their halls and records with the fierceness of a mother bear. She only took half a dozen from their places before lowering herself into one of the creaky chairs to begin her work.

The first she examined was a scroll. She skimmed the columns, her movements cautious as she unwound each new section. But she only found one small excerpt related to what she sought: historically, obsidian was favored by moon folk using sorcery. It didn't explain why beyond a claim that the spells used to twist the moon's power out of place adhered better to volcanic glass than the metal and crystals favored by human sorcerers. While the possibility of one of the ancient moon folk seeking their destruction was troubling, she wasn't sure it would assist her search. Izzy began rolling the scroll back to the beginning with a sigh. The familiar motion called back to simpler days, but it didn't dim the weariness already creeping into her mind. She'd known this wouldn't be simple. Izzy hoped the other books she'd chosen would contain more.

They didn't. Izzy wished she could find whatever long-dead scribe wrote the descriptions in the catalogue and throttle them. Even the dictionary Izzy remembered wasn't the boon of information she'd hoped. The only runes Izzy was *sure* she remembered seeing on the shards were generic, related to secrecy and containment. And without a better grasp of what the markings were, she had little to go on.

Her head ached as she picked up her final book, and she wondered if she should put them all away and give up for the day. It was a general text about the moon folk, written long before her grandmother was born, and Izzy knew without looking that reading it would make her eyes ache. But she opened the cover anyway. She was here *now*. She needed to take advantage of what time she had.

Flipping through the leaves as quickly as she dared, Izzy gritted her teeth. Impatience bashed against her skull with every line she skimmed. *This was the wrong day to try this.* She should've chosen a day when she'd slept, when she wasn't fighting against her own grief.

Izzy paused, hand hovering over the edge of the page as blood rushed to her ears. There below her eyes, in a precise ink drawing, was the wolf mark.

Ripping her gaze away, Izzy searched for the beginning of the entry and lowered a shaking hand to the table. The book said nothing about a curse. It called the mark the seal of werewolves who made their home on Mount Talith, swearing to protect *all* the inhabitants of their lands. The author claimed they'd even defended Kedar, though he didn't say against what. It was the first text she'd read that referred to werewolves more than in passing.

At the bottom, in small script, was a reference to another section of the book. Izzy flipped forward in search of it even as she warred with whether she ought to read it. It wasn't wise. She'd likely regret knowing whatever she found. But when she found the entry on werewolves, she read it anyway.

The author said nothing about the origin of werewolves, whether they existed from the beginning of the world or if it was a potential that was discovered later. But that hardly mattered to Izzy. What the author *did* say was enough to light a fire in her chest, burning away any trace of lethargy.

> "As werewolves are connected inescapably to the moon, it follows that they must come from the lineage of the moon folk. Unlike many of the powers the moon folk possess, however, transformation into a werewolf remains possible when the blood is diluted with human heritage. In fact, some argue there *must* be a mixing of bloods for a werewolf to have true control over his transformation. Those of pure moon folk heritage are said to be bound to the cycle of the moon in their entirety, unable to choose which form they take.
>
> "Whether that is true or not, it is known that those with stronger human blood require special rites to transform into a werewolf. And as the blood of the moon folk is diluted, the transformation becomes more difficult. Attempts made by those with too little heritage from the moon folk result in madness or even death."

Izzy leaned back, lifting her eyes to the book spines that filled her vision. This wasn't information she'd heard before, but...she believed it. It fit with all she knew of the moon folk and the curse so well she was surprised no one had suspected it...or at least hadn't shared their suspicion. It gave them another thread connecting each of the wolves taken by the curse.

But what about the foils? Did her sister have moon folk ancestry, however faint? It was possible, if it came through her birth mother, who'd died when Mariel was a toddler. Izzy's own mother didn't, nor did their shared father. She wouldn't have been accepted into the Red Cloaks if they had.

Izzy knew that Rhett and Eldon came here when considering

new recruits, examining their bloodlines in the fragmented records the scribes kept hidden from all but the most privileged. The Red Cloaks were formed as an order to defend Kedar against the city's enemies...enemies who weren't human. And she'd heard that the order had always been very careful with who they allowed into their ranks.

She supposed it explained why no one among the Red Cloaks had ever fallen victim to the curse...and why Izzy was the only one who'd been so closely connected to any of the victims.

Closing the book, Izzy stood and slipped her documents back into their places with calm movements that bore little similarity to the storm raging in her mind. This was not the place to reveal her emotions.

Izzy left with no more than a nod to the scribes she passed, blind to her surroundings and speaking to no one as she returned home. What she'd learned...Izzy wasn't sure what to make of it yet, particularly how it applied to her.

She and Collin were protected from the curse...she should feel guilt over how relieved she was to know that. But she wasn't sure she did. They both faced so many risks, wasn't it just that there was one she didn't have to fear? But that was a pattern of thought she tried to avoid. Her position didn't entitle her to anything.

Slipping into the complex, Izzy went straight to her narrow bunk. She had more to think about before facing her comrades, more to decipher before she spoke to Collin. She would tell him everything. But she wasn't sure yet how to begin.

Collin

Collin knew when Izzy arrived, her freshly washed hair hanging wet around her shoulders. He kept at his work, swinging the heavy ax to split the thick rounds of oak stacked behind the kitchen. He'd already amassed a pile large enough to keep the kitchen going for a week. Baldwin and Keita weren't the type to warn him not to expel his strength. If he wanted to exhaust himself attacking the woodpile, they'd leave him to it.

Splitting wood didn't offer his mind any relief, but at least it gave him a safe way to work out some of his anger.

Collin leaned the ax on a log, tossing the pieces of wood onto the pile.

"What happened to get you so worked up?" Izzy asked.

Collin shrugged, shifting another round of wood twice his girth into place. He took up his ax again before answering.

"Doesn't matter."

"Collin."

Collin paused at the warning in Izzy's voice, looking up. She still looked fragile, even with the glare in her gaze. He forced a smile to his lips.

"Rhett and his rules."

"The funeral?"

Collin didn't answer, swinging the ax down with enough force to crack the wood in two. He hoped she took that as a yes. If she ever found out just how much Rhett knew about the two of them, she'd never let her guard down again. He couldn't stand the thought of watching her close off entirely.

"I went to the scribes' library."

Collin paused with the ax raised, letting the handle rest on his shoulder as he turned to face Izzy. Her expression matched the hesitant note to her voice. Whatever she found, she wasn't sure what to make of it. Or not sure what *he* would make of it.

"Learn anything new?" he asked, leaning the ax against the log he was splitting on.

"Obsidian is favored by moon folk who've turned to sorcery."

"And?"

It was good information, but Izzy wouldn't be watching him like that if it was all she'd learned. She was staring at him like she was looking for a way to tell him she'd stained the rest of his clothes dandelion yellow.

"Only people with moon folk blood can become werewolves."

For a long moment, Collin stared at Izzy in silence. All the implications and questions of that statement were a thick fog in his mind, threatening to smother him as they all crashed in at once. He'd need a clearer head before he'd be able to consider it all. But a few conclusions came easily enough, and he released his breath in a huff.

"That explains a few things."

It was a milder reaction than he actually felt, and Izzy gave him the side eye as she walked closer.

"Am I awful for being relieved?"

Her question came out in a whisper, and she glanced over her shoulder as if afraid someone else would hear. Collin reached for her hand before remembering where they were. He dropped his arm to his side with a silent growl toward Rhett.

"No," Collin said, in a normal tone. "Of course you're relieved, Izzy."

She wasn't convinced, but Collin didn't know how much more he dared say. To tell her that any living being would be relieved, that it didn't make her unfeeling toward the victims...she already knew that. Just as she no doubt knew from his bearing that *he* was relieved. Though with all they knew of the powers the Almighty bestowed on the moon folk, he should've known that was the case. Whether or not werewolves were a creature that was ever supposed to exist was in debate, but there was no doubt that their shift came from the moon.

Izzy didn't say anything as grabbed a second ax from the woodshed and began splitting wood a short distance from him. Collin took that as his sign to let the discussion drop for now. Just as well. Though some of the cracking fire in his chest eased with Izzy's presence, he still wasn't in a place to calmly discuss anything.

For a while they worked in companionable silence. As Collin's shoulders burned, his mind drifted from thoughts of the curse and he couldn't help the rebellious pleasure that snaked through his core. Here they were, just the two of them. But not even Rhett could fault them right now. He supposed he should accept what he could get.

They were stacking the wood they'd split when Alair walked around the corner.

"Enough with the dead trees," he said. "We're going into the city. There's some tavern Dal found that he *swears* has the best pot pie he's tasted."

"I'm not in the mood for revelry," Izzy said, setting her armload of wood into place with more force than necessary.

Alair snorted. "That means you need it more than ever."

"Alair," Collin said in warning. "Now isn't the time."

"You obviously need a distraction." Alair gestured to the pile of thick logs behind them. "That woodpile isn't going to last forever. Save some for the next time you decide to work yourselves to death."

Collin looked to Izzy. He could feel her reluctance, but he also had to admit that Alair might be right. A different distraction might be wise.

"We'll come," Collin said slowly.

"You sound like I'm dragging you off to clean sheep pens."

They both ignored Alair's complaint.

"I'm changing first," Izzy said, as they walked toward the rest of the building.

"Fine," Alair said. "But if you take too long, I'll send Andred in to drag you out."

Izzy waved her hand dismissively as she strode toward the women's side of the barracks. Collin headed toward his own barracks without bothering to look at Alair. He knew better than to drag his feet. Alair would come in after him no matter what state of dress Collin was in.

By the time Collin emerged, Izzy was surrounded by Andred, Dal, Alair, and Berk. She met his eyes with a subdued smile, finger combing her hair as Andred and Berke argued over the proper care for silver inlaid steel. Most of their disagreement seemed to center around whether tarnished silver was as effective against moon drunk animals as polished.

"Keep it polished," Collin interjected, taking his place at Izzy's side. "It's more impressive, at the very least."

"Thank you!" Alair called out with a laugh. "I said that right off, and they insisted I was being vain."

"You *were* being vain," Andred said drily.

"And Collin isn't?"

"Most likely."

Collin feigned offence, turning to Izzy.

"Am I vain?"

He could see the heavy way she held her head and wondered if she'd answer. But her lips parted.

"Only about your hair."

Berke snorted. Collin saw their friends note the small smile that tilted Izzy's lips. It only lasted a heartbeat, but it returned a few times as Andred and Alair continued to argue about the dangers of vanity. Alair glanced back at Izzy to gauge her reaction often enough that Collin knew they were trying to set her at ease. It was enough to calm the part of his heart that hadn't settled since talking to Rhett. He wasn't the only one watching Izzy's back.

Not everyone knew the entirety of Izzy's story prior to joining their order. But those who did, their friends in particular, understood that the tragedies of the curse affected her more personally than others. And perhaps they had a better solution than he did, for tonight at least. By the time they reached Dal's tavern, he could almost ignore the sight of the full moon hanging above them all...and what it would bring as soon as night fell.

CHAPTER FIVE

Izzy

Izzy stared up at the tall gate lit by the moon high above them. The wood shook with the many clubs and fists that pounded against it from the other side, making the wood groan. She missed the old stone-oak gates that stood through most of her childhood. They'd withstood battering rams better than the stone surrounding them. But a few years ago an ogre with a unfortunately strong hold over magic splintered the last of the ancient gates. Now they were left with normal oak that too often broke apart beneath the constant attack.

This gate was the fourth hung this year alone, and already it was a patchwork of reinforcements. The horde had broken through it the night the wolf attacked. Soon they would break through it again.

Glancing up at the sky, Izzy's eyes caught on the moon. It was already tilting back toward the horizon, but still it hung like great eye watching them all. The missing sliver wasn't discernible to the naked eye, but Izzy could feel the difference. There was a charge to the air during the true full moon, a taste like lightning was about to strike where she stood. That sensation was lessened tonight.

Cries from the wall made her tense, her hand gripping her drawn sword too tightly. Her bones ached as the pounding on the gate continued like a battle drum. The archers above them had to retreat an hour before to avoid the magic-fueled fire being cast from an ogre on the other side.

She wasn't sure where this ogre had come from, or what convinced him to join the attack against Kedar. She only knew that they hadn't fought him until tonight. Where their enemies replenished their numbers was one of the secrets they hadn't yet found an answer to. And at this moment, in the midst of battle, it didn't matter why he was there. All that mattered was keeping him from his goal.

The ogre's sorcery apparently wasn't strong enough to set fire to the gate, but it was strong enough that Izzy could *feel* the dread of anticipation among the warriors gathered before her.

Two dozen warriors, watchmen and Red Cloaks mingled. She itched to be among them. As dreadful as the waiting was, the thought of standing back and watching it all happen before her was even worse. She wanted to *fight*, to defend the lives of those around her, not merely watch.

But Rhett's orders were different tonight. They were to watch... and to follow.

She and Collin wouldn't be the first to follow the Horde's retreat in hopes of discovering where they hid. But she prayed they would be the first to return alive.

Rhett was growing desperate if he was willing to try it again. Eldon had argued against his decision, particularly the fact that Collin and Izzy would go out alone, but Rhett hadn't bent. Izzy had seen the truth in his eyes: something needed to change if they wanted to survive the winter. And if he had to risk their lives for a chance to finally gain ground in this war, he would do it.

Izzy hadn't argued, nor had Collin. They knew their peril as well as Rhett and Eldon. What was the point of holding their own lives as precious when they'd be killed with everyone else if the city fell?

Splintering wood joined the pounding clubs, and Izzy raised her sword. She could sense more sorcery on the other side.

Faint laughter echoed across her mind, that death-sweet taste of magic bringing a heavy familiarity that fought to drag Izzy under. *Whose laughter is that?*

The sound of breaking wood knocked her out of her strange reverie, as one side of the gate was torn off its hinges and shoved inward. Men scattered, and dark-clad goblins poured through the gap.

Izzy watched with her sword raised, itching to leap into the fray. She needed to be *moving*. But instead she was standing still, watching the battle before her like a cursed specter. She adjusted her grip on her sword as spearmen surrounded the troll responsible for the broken gate, scrambling to avoid his stone-hard fists. A few Red Cloaks surrounded the ogre responsible for the magic fire. Silver flames coated his skin, lighting his wide grin as he swiped at the Red Cloaks.

Every line of her body was taut, demanding that she step forward. She knew Collin felt it too. If any of the warriors at this gate died tonight while she and Collin held back, saving their strength wouldn't be worth it.

But the gate was well defended. Even as Izzy fought an internal war between orders and conviction, she watched the warriors before her eyes push back the flood of enemies. Once the magic-wielding ogre fell dead to the cobblestones, they forced the fighting back into the narrow gap where fewer enemies could push through to the streets.

Izzy watched closely, tapping her fingers on her belt. If they weakened, if another ogre with his hands dipped in sorcery pressed through the breech, she would spring into action. Rhett could scold her if they survived. She wasn't going to watch unmoving while one of her comrades died.

The moon was hidden behind the city when ogres called an order down the wall. Kedar didn't contain the resources to learn the ogres' language, but these were words they'd long known the meaning of. It wasn't a retreat yet...but it was coming.

Izzy drew a dagger in her other hand, glancing once at Collin at her side. The torches cast grim shadows over his face as he nodded. She turned and plunged into the fight.

They skirted the fiercest fighting, working their way toward the gate itself. Izzy caught a glimpse of Dietrich's familiar form spearing a moonstruck boar who attacked as many goblins as watchmen. A goblin blocked her view before she could decide whether they needed to step in. She dodged his spiked club, sinking her sword through his side. She ripped it free and continued forward.

A human voice shouted, and Collin dragged her down just in time to avoid the chunk of wood coming for her head. The ogre responsible roared a battle cry as he pushed through the broken gate. A swipe of his muscled arm caught a watchman, throwing him against the wall. Izzy and Collin leaped forward as one to put themselves between the prone watchman and the ogre already reaching for his body.

The ogre drew back from Collin's dagger, sneering down at them. Izzy longed to glance behind her, to see if the man still lived, but she knew that would be a deadly mistake. The ogre reached for her.

Izzy stepped aside. She and Collin stabbed their blades into the space she just occupied, both swords piercing the ogre's tough skin as his fist closed on open air. He jerked back with a wild cry of pain that shook the stone around them and made Izzy's ears ring. They stepped back together and raised bloodied blades toward the ogre as he held his bleeding arm to his chest and glared at them with a hatred that made Izzy's skin sting. She held her ground, heart pounding. An injury like that wouldn't weaken him enough to count.

Another familiar order was repeated down the wall: the retreat. The ogre before them hesitated, glancing over his shoulder. He'd turned his gaze downward again before they could take advantage of his distraction, glaring at them with a molten malice that promised retribution.

But there was another shout just outside the gate, a harsh order that made the ogre grimace. He stepped back, offering them one last glare before turning his back on them. He ripped another piece of wood from the gate and let it crash to the stone.

Izzy stepped backwards, pulled by Collin, to avoid the falling wood. But then they leaped over it, casting their cloaks onto the corner of the archway as they passed. They'd be less visible without them.

Once outside the walls, though, Collin and Izzy hung back as the horde ran for the trees. The army wasn't vulnerable in retreat. They employed far more tricks of sorcery to guard their backs than they used against the city. And they kept a rear guard of goblins to sound the alarm if anyone attempted to attack them from behind. Kedar's forces had paid dearly for that knowledge.

Their nightly retreat was why most in the city agreed that conquering Kedar wasn't their main goal: torment was. Even without the moon shining, the horde could've besieged Kedar in truth and starved them out. Instead, they'd drawn out the fight full moon after full moon, year after year. They wanted Kedar to suffer for as long as possible before taking their victory.

They were nearly silent as they ran across the open space, weaving between the fallen bodies the horde trampled underfoot. The last goblins melted into the shadows long before Collin and Izzy reached the shelter of the trees.

There was no cry of alarm as they wove through the trees, following the racket of the horde. As they jogged, Izzy wondered what the forest would be like without their enemies gathered before them. Would it be peaceful here if night wasn't a promise of more bloodshed? She wondered if she'd ever have a chance to find out.

Izzy could see the darker shadows of the wild woods when the trees before them moved. Goblins split away from their shelter to block Collin and Izzy's path, and several oaths passed through Izzy's mind as they slowed before this new resistance. They hadn't counted on being noticed this early.

There were only five goblins. They attacked at once, in an intimidating show of strength. But fighting as one, Collin and Izzy dispatched them quickly. When the last goblin was bleeding out into the soil, they ran on.

Traveling through the deep forest was slower, though. The thick trees and underbrush that created her treasured sense of privacy during the day turned the land into a maze in the darkness. They were forced to follow the tracks of their larger enemies to find breaks in the growth.

Straining to hear the horde ahead of them, Izzy didn't notice their new attackers until a goblin leaped for Collin's back.

"Collin," she gasped, stepping in to intercept the tall creature. Her sword met flesh while he was in the air, forcing the goblin off course and dragging Izzy with him. By the time she'd regained her balance, they were surrounded by goblins. Swallowing blood from her bitten cheek, Izzy put her back to Collin and lifted her weapons.

Whether it was because of greater numbers or more difficult terrain, this fight took longer. Izzy thought she caught two goblins melting back into the shadows when it was clear their comrades would fall, but she didn't have time to worry what they would do. She and Collin had to run to regain ground, and Izzy prayed for sure feet over the rough terrain as they fought to catch up to the horde. If one of them sprained an ankle, there was little chance they'd return to Kedar alive.

The horde was skirting around the south edge of Mount Talith. It was an area they'd searched before, though Izzy only recognized the larger landmarks. For a while she feared they were approaching the arena where Tay was injured, but just when Izzy was convinced they'd cross the road, the trail turned west. They were headed up the mountain itself, now.

Izzy's lungs burned as they climbed the mountain, going as quickly as they dared. Rocks slid out from Izzy's feet, sending her face first into the dirt. She caught herself on her elbows, saving her blades from damage, and scrambled back to her feet with Collin's help. She spit grit out of her mouth as they continued climbing.

There was something different ahead, a light or absence of one. Izzy strained to see it, only for Collin to grab her arm and jerk her to a stop. She followed his gaze and found a massive silhouette rising from the ground on their left. A glance around proved that they were surrounded, and she put her back to Collin's as that silhouette stepped closer.

She glanced back at the tall foe, now bathed in moonlight. It was the ogre they encountered at the gate, his arm a torn and bloodied mess at his side.

Almighty, shield us, she prayed, her heart dropping at the sight of the ogre's hateful glee. She was a fool for not offering that prayer earlier.

This wasn't the worst odds she and Collin had faced, but she didn't like the look in this ogre's eyes. He might be low ranked, a fact she gathered from their confrontation at the gate, but that didn't mean he was weak. At most, it meant he had no talent for sorcery. That wouldn't stop his fists from crushing their bones.

A figure leapt from the circle, a deer driven on by goblins. Others followed. Izzy's focus was ripped from the ogre as she was forced to fight goblin and animal alike, scrambling to meet every blade, club, or antler intent on piercing her skin. Jaws latched onto her leg, and a cry ripped from her throat as she stabbed the badger responsible. Even dead, its teeth were lodged in the leather armor protecting her legs. Dragging its weight slowed her dangerously, but she didn't have a safe moment to free herself from the carcass.

It wrenched away when Izzy had to jerk right to avoid a club coming for her side, her calf throbbing where the badger's incisors had pierced the leather. She gritted her teeth and kept fighting.

"You may as well die quickly, Red Cloaks. This is as far as you go."

The voice was rough and heavily accented, but in their own

language. It made Izzy shudder as she deflected a dagger aimed at her throat.

"Arm still smarts, does it?" Collin asked breezily, as if they weren't engaged in a battle for their lives.

Izzy was caught between exasperation and pride. Did he have to anger the ogre even further?

Izzy slashed a goblin across the stomach. He threw himself backward with a screech, and when Izzy looked for the next enemy to attack there were none. Hope lit in her chest.

Something smashed into Izzy's side, sending her flying through the air and crashing to the rough ground with Collin pinned beneath her. Her first attempt to crawl off him only sent searing pain tearing through her bones.

Her shoulder was on fire, the ache spreading through her entire body and making her head swim. She raised blurry eyes to the ogre and saw him grinning.

Biting her lip until she tasted blood, she grabbed her sword from where she dropped it and forced herself to her feet. She didn't try to use her left arm. She was afraid she wouldn't be able to move it.

She raised her sword against the ogre. Her hand shook. Behind her, Collin was still on his knees. Fear pierced through the fog of agony, and she lunged forward to meet the ogre's attacks before he could reach them. If Collin couldn't fight, if he was more injured than her...this ogre wouldn't touch him. She'd die first.

Perhaps she *would* die first. The ogre was armed only with a rough hewn club and his fists, but he stood nearly twice her height. Speed was her one advantage, and that would soon fail her. Each movement sent a new wave of agony across her shoulder.

Collin stepped up to her left side. The wild tearing in her heart settled back into place to see him upright, even if the brief glance she could afford showed the pained way he stood.

The ogre paused, spinning his large club in his hand. Assessing them? She couldn't tell with his face shadowed.

"I'm glad to have the honor of killing the Blood Children," he said. "You've been a thorn in the side of my leaders for too many years, *infants*."

Blood Children. That's what the horde called them? She waited for Collin to quip back something clever and biting, but he stayed silent. Collin was *never* silent.

She couldn't let the ogre go unanswered. They weren't dead yet.

"For us," she gasped. "Killing you will be just another night."

The ogre's face contorted in a snarl, and he lunged forward.

Miscalculation, she realized as she stumbled backward. This was why she let Collin do the talking.

Collin pulled her further away, behind a thick tree. Her left shoulder knocked against the wood, sending white hot pain that darkened her vision. She blinked and realized Collin had blood dripping down his forehead. She didn't like the desperation in his eyes.

"Time to run?" he asked.

Izzy nodded.

"You think you can run?" the ogre asked.

Izzy saw the meaty hand he was reaching around the tree just in time to sink her dagger into it. While he roared and jerked back, taking her dagger with him, Collin pulled her away from the tree.

They fled, darting between the thick trees in hope it would slow him down. Their gasping breath was the loudest sound in Izzy's ears, a rhythm to which she set her frenzied prayers.

Almighty, be merciful. She wouldn't claim that she'd done a good job following Him over her lifetime. She knew she didn't deserve mercy, that someday this *was* how their lives would end. *But not tonight. Please not tonight.*

"Where's your courage?" the ogre snarled. Breaking branches punctuated his words as he forced his way toward them. "Afraid of a *real* fight?"

Collin didn't reply, and this time Izzy followed his lead. She needed what was left of her strength to keep herself conscious as agony radiated out from her shoulder with every step she took.

"You're not as dangerous as I was told. Gorth will be disappointed when I return with your corpses over my shoulder."

Rough laughter accompanied those words.

"Izzy," Collin gasped, forcing her to the ground. She landed hard on her left side, and a scream ripped free of her throat.

She couldn't think. She couldn't *see.* Agony painted stars across her vision, and her ears rang with the scream building again in her throat. Collin was struggling to sit up beside her, but she couldn't bring herself to move.

Not yet, she told herself. *Almighty, lend us strength.*

Gritting her teeth, Izzy forced herself up, blinking clear her vision. The forest around them was lit with a delicate silver light, leaving no room for shadows. She blinked again. Was shock setting in? Collin tugged on her right side, trying to get her to stand. She followed his prompting only to stumble.

The ogre was taking his time approaching them. The strange light illuminated the gloating smile twisting his lips. Izzy's gaze flicked beyond him, to where the moon hung impossibly large in the sky.

The ogre stopped. Izzy braced for more gloating, for more pain, even for humiliation. She was already searching for any hope of escape they might take while he toyed with them. She found nothing. But as the ogre's mouth dropped open, Izzy dragged her attention back to their foe. He didn't speak. Instead, his eyes widened in fear. A strangled cry left his mouth, and he took one stumbling step backward.

His body crumbled to silver ash.

Izzy clung to Collin's arm, staring at where the ogre had stood with numb horror. The light hadn't faded, revealing the pile of ash already scattering on the wind. Glancing down, she realized the light now surrounded *them.*

She twisted to face Collin, clinging to him with her good arm and bracing for the pain. But it didn't come. As she and Collin stood there, clinging to each other, light danced around them. Dust caught in the moonbeams and glinted like tiny stars. Her ears were ringing again. She *must* be in shock.

But the tension leaked out of her body in spite of herself. She couldn't resist. Wherever the light touched her skin was a soft caress, like her mother tucking her into bed. It settled inside her like the warmth of a winter fire, the comfort of bread baking and the smell of leather oil. It tasted like *home*.

"Izzy," Collin murmured. She glanced up, silver light glinting in his eyes as he stared at a point behind her. Her heart faltered as she twisted in his arms. They weren't alone.

CHAPTER SIX

Izzy

Izzy flexed her empty hand as she took in the group of people standing before her. They were...luminous. The silver light cradled them, settling into their skin so that they each seemed to be made of moonlight. They were also tall, eerily so, with eyes that glinted like stars in the low light. *Moon folk*. They watched Collin and Izzy with a quiet intensity that set her on edge.

"Thank you," Collin said.

The strain in his voice only sharpened her fear. They were miles from Kedar...would they make it back? If they were attacked again, she wasn't sure they'd be able to defend themselves.

But as those worries filled her mind, she never took her eyes off the silent moon folk. The grim death of the ogre still haunted her thoughts. They wouldn't have any chance to return unless these beings allowed it.

The man standing closest to them, with dark hair braided down his back and skin a strange shade of silver gray, was the first to break the silence. His voice was far deeper than Izzy expected given his ethereal appearance.

"You were foolish to take on so many adversaries alone, no matter how brightly the moon shines tonight."

Izzy felt her brows furrow, as confusion flooded her. Did he not understand that for them the full moon was a danger, not an aid? She didn't dare question it. That said, she wouldn't have any of them thinking she and Collin were arrogant enough to attempt fighting an army on their own.

"Our goal was to follow, not attack," she said. She sounded even worse than Collin.

She saw the moon folk behind the leader exchanging glances. The leader, however, kept his eyes fixed on them. Izzy quickly lost patience with the silent standoff, turning to face Collin. Even that slow movement reminded her of the agony throbbing in her shoulder, and she swallowed back a whimper. She fixed her eyes on the hand Collin pressed to his side. Could she see blood seeping between his fingers?

"How bad is it?"

"I've had worse," he replied, his eyes still on the moon folk. "Your shoulder?"

Izzy cast her voice low, hoping it would disguise the tremble. "Dislocated."

"Eris, Silaine. Aid them."

Two figures split away from the group, and Izzy took a half step backwards. Could they trust these beings? Feeling Collin sway, she wasn't sure they had a choice. She looked at him. And seeing fear still lingering in his eyes, she held her peace.

The two figures paused beside their leader. While they looked to him for instruction, he stared at Collin and Izzy as if trying to read something.

"What are your names?"

"Collin, and this is Izzy," Collin answered before Izzy could decide if there was danger in answering. She glanced up at him in exasperation, and he lifted an eyebrow, silently asking what other option they have.

None. That didn't mean Izzy liked it.

"I didn't think moon folk still lived on this side of the mountains," Collin said cautiously.

Izzy thought about pinching him. The time for questions was *before* giving the moon folk their names so freely. Still, she listened closely to the answer.

"We don't dwell in this area permanently. We came to investigate signs of a great disturbance."

A surge of heat flooded Izzy's face, and she was speaking before she was aware of it.

"If Kedar's doom is such a disturbance, I wonder why you didn't come years ago."

Collin's elbow struck her ribs, and Izzy snapped her mouth shut. She didn't need to look at Collin to know that her words were unwise.

In truth, it's not as if she would expect anything different. If the king who claimed Kedar had long abandoned them, why would anyone else care about their fate? They'd been on their own for a long time.

"I...apologize," Izzy said slowly, praying that they wouldn't take too much offense.

"You're overwrought," a musical voice said near her side. "No one here will hold your words against you."

Izzy followed the voice to find herself staring at a woman with skin as dark as the midnight sky. Somehow she glowed as brightly as the others. Izzy listened to her own heart for three, four beats before she'd accepted that the woman's compassionate smile was genuine. Even then, when the woman wrapped her hand around Izzy's uninjured arm to pull her away, she stood her ground.

"We won't separate you," the woman murmured. *Silaine.* If they knew her name, she was determined to remember theirs.

Collin's hand disappeared from her back, and she looked over her shoulder to see a man with similar features lowering Collin to the ground. He caught her looking and smiled painfully, even as the man pried his blood-stained hand from his side.

Izzy's eyes fixed on the wound and blood rushed in her ears. She didn't need to examine it any closer. She knew wounds like that often ended in death. She turned away quickly, trying not to hyperventilate. He would fight. He would heal.

Prodding fingers on her injured shoulder distracted her from her panic. Izzy pulled in a hissing breath. The woman's lips were pursed as she continued to examine Izzy's shoulder, and Izzy bit her already sore lip to keep in the cry working its way up her throat. Her touch felt like a hot brand.

"Neoma," Silaine said.

Another woman stepped forward, stopping at Izzy's other side. Silaine met Izzy's eyes.

"Neoma will brace you while I reset the shoulder."

Izzy nodded, breathing through her teeth. Neoma gripped Izzy around her back and arm, and Izzy leaned into her. Silaine shifted Izzy's arm so rapidly Izzy didn't have time to brace herself. Pain consumed her. She slumped into Neoma's arms as her vision darkened. But even as that agony washed through her, a gentle touch cooled the fire at its source. Silaine pulled Izzy's sleeve away from her shoulder, running her fingertips across the joint.

Neoma eased Izzy to the ground. She concentrated on breathing as Silaine's touch numbed her shoulder better than ice. Izzy didn't question it. Anything that lessened the pain was to her benefit.

When she could breathe without fighting a scream, she twisted her head and found Collin leaning towards her, worry lining his face more than pain. He seemed to have forgotten the man dressing the wound to his side. Izzy nodded to him, and Collin sank back down the ground. Izzy tried not to look at the blood staining the pale hands of the man tending him.

Silaine turned her attention to the wound sluggishly bleeding down Izzy's calf. She stiffened as the woman eased the leather gaiter off Izzy's leg.

"If you're here to investigate a disturbance," Collin said, turning to look up at the leader. "Do you know a way we could defeat our enemies once and for all?"

"Why are these beings your enemies?" the leader asked sharply. "Why do so many hold enmity against Kedar?"

Izzy noticed the woman standing behind Collin when she began cleaning blood away from his forehead. Collin winced as he answered.

"We don't know."

It was obvious the leader didn't believe them. Fire ignited in Izzy's chest. She wouldn't have them mistaken for liars.

"We know Kedar and the occupants of the Pitch Mountains have always struggled to live peaceably, but it's been centuries since we were *besieged.*"

The leader nodded, confirming her word. *Has he lived that long?* The question threatened to set everything spinning, and Izzy brushed it away to finish.

"This army has attacked Kedar every full moon since we were children. We don't know what began it or who leads them, let alone why they seek Kedar's destruction. We only know that we can't withstand it forever."

The moon folk gathered behind their leader exchanged more shadowed looks heavy with meaning Izzy couldn't grasp. Did they believe she was lying? Izzy twisted her head to find Collin, worried she misspoke. But he smiled weakly at her.

Silaine's hand stilled halfway down Izzy's ragged braid. Izzy stiffened, looking up to find Silaine's gaze fixed on her leader. Izzy flexed her hand, wishing again that she had a weapon. Even if using it would be futile. They wouldn't aid her and Collin just to kill them, though...would they?

Silaine noticed Izzy staring, glancing back at her leader once before focusing on Izzy.

"You bear the mark of a sorcerer."

"That's impossible," Izzy said.

"This one bears it as well," the woman tending Collin said.

Izzy turned stricken eyes on Collin, her own shock mirrored in his gaze.

"We've dedicated our lives to fighting against sorcery," Collin said, turning to face the leader. "We have no dealings with magic."

"Hold your peace," the leader said. "No one is accusing you of practicing dark magic. It is clear enough that you are no sorcerer's ally."

Silaine nodded. Noticing Izzy's stare, she explained.

"It is a stain upon your mind, not a poison within your heart. Someone has bespelled you."

Izzy fixed her eyes on Collin. He looked as stricken as she felt. Though when the man kneeling beside him rested his hand on Collin's head, his face twisted in weary exasperation.

"The mark is...familiar," Eris said.

He twisted to face his leader and spoke rapidly in a different language. Whatever he said caused many of the moon folk to fix fearful and pitying gazes on her and Collin. She felt herself tense, and Silaine returned to gently massaging her shoulder. Izzy ignored her.

"Can you get it off?" Collin asked.

Eris shook his head, regret twisting his face. "It would take more time and supplies than we have. You must return to your city soon, lest you're caught by your adversaries once more."

"Even we cannot take on the numbers we've witnessed here," the leader added.

So they were supposed to live with the knowledge that they bore a sorcerer's mark?

"Will it overtake us?" Collin asked.

Most people in Kedar would likely wonder why Collin wasn't concerned with whether it would kill them. Not anyone who'd trained with the Red Cloaks. After all they'd studied, Izzy knew that death was the far better ending for those bespelled.

“Not in its current state,” Eris said. “It is weak, as these spells go.”

That wasn’t comforting. The idea that there was a shadow of sorcery infecting her, weak or not, was a new thorn beneath her skin. If she could dig it out with a knife, she would.

“Flex your hand,” Silaine said.

Izzy obeyed. Her muscles were stiff, and an echo of pain radiated from her shoulder. But each movement she tried came as fluidly as she was used to. Relief made her dizzy, tainted as it was by this new knowledge.

“You are not fully healed,” Silaine said sternly, drawing Izzy’s gaze. “I have sped the process, and you should have the strength to return to your city. But you will need to go gently for a while.”

“The same applies to you,” Eris said. “You each need *rest*.”

“We’ll try,” Collin replied, glancing at Izzy with amusement. Izzy smiled back and realized it was genuine.

Silaine and Neoma helped Izzy stand. As soon as they released her, she stumbled toward Collin. He wrapped his arm around her waist and held her tight.

Panic lodged in her throat as she glanced around them. If they saw, if they told...

Who would they tell? She doubted moon folk had much knowledge or reverence for a Red Cloak’s vows.

“I assume you won’t return to Kedar with us,” Collin said.

“No,” the leader said emphatically. “We have no intention of going near your city.”

Collin smiled regretfully. “That’s a shame. I imagine our commander would appreciate a chance to speak with you.”

“Recent history would suggest otherwise.”

The leader’s words, given with a similar smile, were a milder reaction than the rest of his group. There was suspicion in the way they looked at Collin and Izzy, perhaps even anger. Had they heard lies about Kedar? Or was there a part of Kedar’s history that she didn’t know?

"I hope our paths cross again under better circumstances," the leader said, bowing his head. "We will pray for your safe return."

"Thank you," Collin said, and Izzy echoed him in a quiet murmur.

Eris, Neoma, and the other woman returned to their group, but Silaine lingered.

"As soon as you reach safety, you need to *rest.* Your bodies need time to heal fully."

"We will," Izzy promised, as Collin's arm tightened around her waist.

Silaine accepted that with a nod and turned away. She and the rest of the moon folk melted into the shadowed forest sooner than should've been possible, the light fading with them. Unreasonable sorrow struck Izzy's heart to have it disappear.

She twisted, throwing both arms around Collin. Her shoulder screamed, and she bit her tongue in her effort to keep silent. But it didn't matter. She could ignore that pain, especially as Collin tightened his arms around her waist. She pressed closer, relaxing when she realized that strength had returned to his embrace.

He kissed her head. That simple pressure awoke a wild and desperate voice that insisted it wasn't enough. She'd spent years risking her life, but tonight was the first time she truly thought she would die. If she was killed, if Collin was stolen from her, she didn't want her last thought to be regret that she spent her entire life holding back.

Her heart pounded, flooding her face with heat. All she had to do was tilt her face up, to press her lips to his. After that there would be no going back. Why was it that she was *excited* by the thought of that?

Collin pulled back. Her eyes still cast downward, Izzy crushed the disappointment. She shouldn't trust her thoughts tonight.

"We should start moving."

"I know," Izzy said, a little more sharply than intended.

She walked away before he could ask what was wrong, searching for her discarded weapons. Her sword wasn't difficult to find, nor was Collin's. But a few minutes of searching didn't reveal any sign of the dagger she'd stabbed through the ogre's hand. Perhaps it turned to ash with him.

As they turned back toward Kedar, Izzy snatched up Collin's hand. Her throat thickened when he squeezed her fingers, but she kept her face resolutely forward. The forest was quiet as they picked their way down the mountain. She wasn't sure if she had the coming sunrise to thank for that or the secretive moon folk. Regardless, she was ready to leave that place.

Izzy nearly melted with relief as they approached the gate of Kedar, even if it meant her hand was empty.

Dawn was nearing, the eastern sky aglow with a light that scarcely reached the ground where they walked. In the distance, high on the wall, Izzy could see watchmen silhouetted against the gray sky. But she doubted they could see them. Mist rose from the ground, swirling in silver and shadow, but enough light found its way through to glint on the frost covering the ground. She stayed tense, trying to ward off shivering in the cold morning air. Her shoulder ached fiercely.

As she and Collin slowly approached Kedar, the mist swirling away from their feet, she thought she saw crimson at the base of the gate. Not long after she spotted it, those cloaked figures ran toward them.

Izzy looked over at Collin, sharing one last look of relief before turning back to their greeting party. Alair and Dal were the first, but it was Eldon who walked up to them, resting his hands on their shoulders as he looked at them. The relief lighting his face was painful to witness, again striking dread in her heart over how close they'd come to never seeing him again.

"Your injuries?" Eldon asked, his gaze landing on Collin's torn and bloodied armor.

"Izzy's left shoulder was dislocated, and she has a bite on her leg. I have flesh wounds on my side and head."

"Flesh wounds?" Izzy said sharply.

He shrugged. "That's all they are now."

Izzy's response was interrupted by Eldon embracing her. His hold was gentle, but her shoulder still ached with the contact. She allowed her head to rest on his shoulder, allowed herself one moment to be a young woman needing comfort rather than a fearless warrior, before she pulled away. She took a deep breath as Eldon released her and switched his attention to Collin.

Thank you, merciful Almighty, for bringing us home.

"Did you really stay up waiting for us?" Collin asked incredulously.

"That's a fine way to thank us for our concern," Dal said, slapping Collin's back with a quiet relief that stood in contradiction to his jovial voice.

"Berke would be here too," Alair added, "But he had a few scratches to patch up, and the nurses insisted he stay through the morning."

"You'll see him when you go to the infirmary yourselves," Eldon said, with a stern look Izzy recognized. It never failed to make her curl in on herself like a child.

"I don't think we need it," Collin said slowly, glancing at Izzy.

"No argument. That's an order."

Izzy shrugged, then winced. *Bad idea.* Whatever numbing Silaine had offered her had worn off as morning approached. It felt like she'd caught her shoulder in a bear's jaws.

"We'll go," Collin said, brow furrowing at the sight of her pain. "But we should report first."

Something in Collin's tone must've tipped Eldon off that they had more than the usual to report. His voice quieted.

"What did you find?"

"We didn't follow them to the end," Izzy said, failure bitter on her tongue.

"We were deterred," Collin added. "There are two-dozen goblins and an ogre we won't have to contend with tonight."

Alair whistled, glancing over Collin and Izzy with a respect that soothed the sting a bit.

"But you did find something," Dal said. He glanced at Eldon, as if expecting him to tell them to save talking for their report. But Eldon only watched in silence.

Izzy glanced up at Collin, wondering what he'd say. There was a smile twitching at his lips as he answered.

"We met a group of moon folk passing through the area."

She glanced Dal's direction in time to see his face twist. "Be serious."

"I am."

"What do you say about it?" Alair asked Izzy. "Our Iron girl won't jest."

"They were moon folk," Izzy said. "And it's thanks to them that we're alive."

Eldon's frown deepened with that, but she didn't regret saying it. Dal swallowed his objections. But the smile also dropped from Alair's face, and there was a heavier look to his eyes that made her uncomfortable. Izzy looked away quickly.

"You'll have to shift your worldview a bit, now," Collin said in a light tone. "We have proof that moon folk are just as impressive as the stories."

Dal grumbled beneath his breath, making Alair laugh again.

"You sure it isn't blood loss coloring your memory?" Alair asked. "The stories tend toward more myth than legend."

"It was like they had part of the moon within them," Izzy murmured, her eyes fixed ahead.

"Not so mythical, then. Dal, you owe me that drink."

"Not happening," Dal replied.

"It better not," Eldon added sternly, though when Izzy glanced his way there was a twinkle in his eyes. Izzy fought a smile as the men behind her quieted quickly, remembering who they were with.

Alair handed Izzy her cloak as they neared the gate, which Izzy hadn't even noticed he was holding. She drew it around her shoulders, a sigh slipping from between her lips as it locked out the chill air. Izzy wrapped it tight around herself, letting the warmth embrace her as they stepped into the city.

More than that, she was glad to cover up the signs of their battle with the familiar crimson fabric. The people they would pass didn't need to know how fierce their fight was. She threw her hood up to block most of the faces surrounding her, hiding from their stares. Her eyes forward, her attention on Collin's conversation behind her. Nothing else mattered.

Collin and Alair continued to tease Dal as they walked the streets of Kedar, though they left out any details. They didn't want to spread rumors among the citizens, not when there was already unrest. Eldon walked close to Izzy's side. His steady presence was a comfort, as was his silence.

Few were up and about when they entered the Red Cloaks' estate, but those who were all offered Collin and Izzy a solemn salute as they entered. She nodded to each of them and pulled her cloak tighter around herself. She knew most of them believed she and Collin left on a suicide mission last night. She would never admit to most of them how close it came.

Of course, she wouldn't need to. In a few days rumors of their fight would've reached legendary proportions. Encouraged by Alair, no doubt. She was glad she'd have little opportunity to hear what reached the ordinary people.

Eldon held the door to Rhett's office for them, and Izzy stepped in with Collin close behind her. Rhett looked up at their entrance. Deep wrinkles lined his mouth and eyes, lessening as he met her gaze.

"You've returned," he said. "Good."

Though his words were few, Izzy thought she heard a warmth in them that she seldom witnessed these days. The dark circles beneath his eyes made her suspect that he was more worried for them than he would ever admit.

She gingerly sat on one of the chairs, watching as Collin took the other. Eldon had already settled into his chair against the wall, hands draped over his knees as he leaned forward in rapt attention.

"Our presence was discovered by the horde before we reached the deep forest," Collin said. "At first the resistance was slight, a few goblins left behind to attack us. But the deeper we pressed the more that resistance grew. We were following them up the eastern slope of Mount Talith when we were attacked by a low-ranked ogre and two-dozen smaller adversaries. We weren't able to follow further."

"Do you believe they were set to guard something?" Rhett asked.

Collin turned his head toward her, and Izzy stared back at him as she considered the question.

"They might have been," she admitted, meeting Rhett's gaze. "There was a different feel to the area where we were attacked. But I don't believe we were near the horde's final destination."

Rhett nodded slowly, and the disappointed set to his mouth only increased the weary weight pressing on Izzy's shoulders.

"Regardless, I am glad you've returned. It would've been a heavy loss to our ranks if you hadn't. Defeating an ogre is no small feat."

"We didn't kill the ogre," Collin said flatly. "He was moments away from killing *us* when a group of moon folk intervened. They killed the ogre and tended our injuries afterward."

Rhett sharpened as soon as "moon folk" left Collin's lips, turning to face Eldon. Izzy watched the exchange closely, taking in the troubled set to Rhett's face, the way Eldon tilted his head and shrugged back at him. But she knew she was missing too much to understand what passed between them. It was clear to her that Rhett wasn't pleased by news of Moon Folk.

The leader was right. Rhett *didn't* want to interact with them. But what had happened to make Rhett so wary of them, and to make the moon folk they met so determined to stay away?

"What did they tell you?" Rhett asked sternly, turning around to pierce them with a steely gaze.

"Very little," Izzy said dryly. "The leader called us fools for standing against the ogre alone and asked after our errand, but he wouldn't share much regarding his own purpose on Mount Talith. All he'd say was that they were looking into a 'disturbance'."

"The leader was courteous, and more trusting than I would've thought wise," Collin added. "The same couldn't be said of all who followed him, though. I suspect some disapproved of the aid he rendered us."

Collin left it there, and Izzy resisted looking his way. She was grateful he said nothing of being "marked," but she didn't want Rhett to realize they were withholding something. She didn't want to know what Rhett would do if he knew, regardless of whether it was a punishment or an attempted cure.

Rhett leaned back in his seat, once more glancing toward Eldon. Perhaps he already knew they weren't sharing everything. There seemed to be suspicion shared in that glance, though neither leader asked for the rest.

"I'm glad to have Moon Folk in our territory, for your sakes if nothing else," Eldon said, staring at Izzy with a fatherly look that settled inside her and made her ache and squirm all at once.

His words shook Rhett out of his thoughts. Some of the commander persona dropped away, making Rhett look a little softer and a lot older as he met their eyes.

"I apologize for sending you alone. I knew the results would be the same...I shouldn't have risked your lives on a foolish chase."

Some of the tension drained from Izzy's shoulders with those words, a small but genuine smile lining her lips as she nodded. An apology from Commander Rhett was rarely given.

"We have to keep trying *something*," she said.

Collin added, "And it wasn't entirely wasted."

"It wasn't," Rhett said, that small amount of vulnerability melting away. "We know now that moon folk are in the area. Do not let down your guard because of one night of kindness. The moon folk have their own agendas, and we cannot trust that it aligns with our own purpose."

"Understood," Collin said.

Rhett looked them over a moment, and Izzy nodded her own acquiescence. He didn't press them further.

Eldon cleared his throat. "I'm going to take these two to the infirmary before they can slip my grasp."

Collin flashed her a regretful look, causing a smile to tilt the corner of Rhett's mouth.

"You're dismissed, then. I better not see you until supper."

"Yes, sir," Collin said as he stood.

Izzy followed him, allowing Eldon to prod them out the door and toward the infirmary. Once he walked ahead of them, though, Izzy glanced at Collin. He was already staring at her, her own thoughts mirrored in his eyes. Rhett and Eldon weren't sharing everything. She had no doubt that as soon as she and Collin were being checked over by the nurses, Eldon would return to Rhett to discuss whatever matters they didn't want to share in front of Collin and Izzy.

There wasn't much they could do about that, though. Rhett and Eldon were entitled to their secrets, and there was no true reason they should expect their commander to share *everything* with them. Except she used to believe Rhett told them the full truth.

"Off to be scolded to death?" Alair asked, sauntering back up to them.

Izzy and Collin broke away from their shared look, Collin replying to Alair lightly. Izzy didn't catch what he said, only that Alair laughed. Exhaustion dragged at her limbs. That and the growing ache in her shoulder distracted her from any deeper thoughts. Secrets would wait.

CHAPTER SEVEN

Collin

Collin leaned against the infirmary wall, arms crossed over his chest, and watched Tay and Farren. He and Izzy had finished their own check in with the physician, which had involved a lot of confused looks and mutterings about the mysterious moon folk.

His eyes landed again on Farren, sitting beside the bed and holding her sister's hand. Tay was awake, and aware enough to ask Izzy for news around the compound, but Collin could see her fade in and out. Fever clouded her eyes, and her empty hand picked at the blanket absently. Farren looked like a ghost.

Izzy told the sisters about Dal's dyeing project and the lasting repercussions, both his official punishment and the unofficial consequences his victims were inflicting on him. He'd found nettles in his boots twice, and various men had switched their clothes out with his until he didn't have a single shirt that wasn't stained pink. Tay smiled at some parts, but Farren's attention never strayed from her sister.

Collin took in Farren's haggard face with a chill that sunk into his bones. He knew that Tay's survival wasn't assured as long as infection still raged. Even if she did survive, her return to their ranks was doubtful. Either way, their lives would never be the same.

He'd lost family before, but all when he was a kid. He didn't remember his parents beyond a few scattered memories of laughter and steady warmth. His grandmother had passed when he was fourteen, but even with the ache of losing her he'd been grateful she was out of pain.

But the idea of losing Izzy... He stopped that thought short, casting it to the deep recesses of his mind where it wouldn't torment him. *Almighty, I beg You...protect her.* He never wanted to consider what his life would be without her.

Izzy stood from the bed, quietly bidding farewell to Farren as Tay drifted into troubled sleep. Farren hardly reacted as Collin and Izzy left.

As soon as they were out of sight, Izzy drooped. Sorrow overtook her expression, and Collin ached to take her in his arms. He settled for squeezing her right shoulder instead. She glanced up at him with a wan smile.

They turned toward the mess hall, and Collin hoped there was someone in there who could drag them back out of the mire visiting Tay and Farren sank them into.

He flexed as they walked, assessing the burn in his side. Two days had passed, and the wound already appeared weeks old...a fact that had made the physician peer at him with pursed lips. A few days more and Collin wondered if it would be anything more than a scar. Izzy's recovery was slower going, meaning they were still banned from their morning practice, but she was healed enough to return to light duty at least. And yet Rhett and Eldon continued to leave them on relief, ordering them to keep within the city walls.

He had little hope of returning to their work for another week at least, and the inactivity might drive them insane. This would be the first time either of them had more than three days off duty for four years. He didn't understand why others lamented their long hours.

But neither of them challenged Rhett's orders. Collin knew that they *needed* to heal, and to heal completely, before the moon fully waned. He was sure Rhett and Eldon were planning what to try next, and that Collin and Izzy would be the ones they sent. They knew the forest best, these days.

He dreaded the next full moon. They'd be on duty for three nights at least. Would another young man be claimed by the wolf curse? The thought made him sick.

Berke and Andred were seated across from each other when Collin and Izzy entered. They took places beside their friends after grabbing their meal. They were debating again, this time over leather care. Berke, who'd apprenticed at a tannery before being recruited to the Red Cloaks, was set in his opinions. Catching the smile sneaking across Andred's drooping mouth, he suspected their disagreement had more to do with Andred poking the bear than an actual difference of mind.

"What about bloodstains?" Collin asked, wanting to prod a little further. "Should they be cleaned off, or left to set?"

"Left to set, surely," Andred said. "Skin takes no harm from contact with blood."

"Hide and leather are hardly the same," Berke said.

Collin glanced at Izzy and was pleased to see the amusement lightening her eyes. But Mercer's loud voice dimmed that smile again. Conversations all around them dropped to listen in, though Collin didn't turn around to look. He raised his cup to his lips as Mercer bragged loudly enough to carry around the room.

"It's set for the Waning Crescent. The Watch Commander is already having the training grounds rearranged to hold it."

Collin turned his eyes to Berke.

"Tournament between us and the watch," he explained. "Rhett announced it while you were in the infirmary."

A frown tugged at Collin's lips as he turned to Izzy. *Why now?*

They'd wanted a tournament, but that was before the unexpected wolf set everyone on edge. And an informal tourney among Red Cloaks was far different from an event like Mercer was talking about. It would involve the entire city. He even claimed citizens were allowed to join, as long as they passed the Watch trials first.

"Ten of the highest will be brought among us for training," Andred added, as Mercer and his friends boasted of all the events they intended to enter.

"*Ten*?" Izzy asked.

Andred and Berke nodded.

"Seems Rhett wants to get ahead of the losses," Andred said, far more quietly.

Collin's mind returned to Tay, tossing with fever, and Farren's vacant gaze. He wished he disagreed. Izzy was staring at her plate, and the set of her jaw made Collin wary. But it seemed she didn't intend to reveal her ire here. She likely wanted to face Rhett directly. Collin doubted that conversation would change anything, but he'd go with her. He was tired of no explanations. If they couldn't drag out answers regarding Rhett's distrust of moon folk, at least they could get his reasoning for dedicating a day for mere sport only halfway through the waning cycle.

They finished their meal quickly, going straight for Rhett's office. Waiting outside for Viron to finish speaking with the commander, he and Izzy leaned against the wall and said little. It wasn't a restful silence, and Izzy shifted her hands every few seconds. Her nervous energy made him smile, despite the cause. She wanted a knife grip in her hand.

Viron stepped out, and Izzy lost no time in slipping in through the open door.

"Izzy," Rhett greeted, "Collin. Sit."

They obeyed, though Izzy's nervous energy had her picking at the wood grain of the worn chair.

"How is your healing progressing?" he asked.

"I'm cleared for training, as long as I keep it light," Collin reported. "Izzy has a few more days at least."

Rhett nodded, his eyes landing on Izzy. Collin thought he already knew why they'd come. But he didn't broach the subject, instead letting the silence drag on. When Izzy said nothing, Collin stifled a sigh and broke it himself.

"Why set a tournament now?" he asked.

Collin found no surprise in Rhett's expression, only resignation.

"You take issue with the timing?" he asked, leaning back in his chair.

"The wolf's death has set everyone on edge," Izzy said, her voice tight with pent up emotion. "The attacks are still fierce each night...it doesn't seem like a good day for mere *competition*. The citizens might think we're taking time to play in the midst of their peril."

Rhett was silent once Izzy finished, but Collin knew it wasn't in consideration. His gaze made the air of the room heavy, though neither of them broke beneath their commander's stare.

"Do you doubt that I considered this?" he asked.

Izzy's hand gripped the chair tight. Collin braced himself for a scolding.

"This tournament is meant to remind the people of Kedar why they place their lives in our hands. They don't see what occurs on the walls each night. A tournament will demonstrate our competency, while revealing who is ready to come into our ranks."

"Are you sure they'll see it as a reminder?" Izzy asked.

Her voice was quieter, but hard as steel. Collin stifled a smile at the way she stared back at Rhett, unbreaking before his stern glare. Iron Girl, indeed.

"I intend to encourage it," Rhett said finally. "Anything else to say?"

Rhett glanced at Collin with that. He shrugged, meeting Rhett's eyes steadily. He didn't agree with the timing of this tournament any more than Izzy, but he could see that arguing was useless.

"No," Izzy said, displeasure coloring her voice.

"Good. I'm glad to hear of your quick healing. You will be off duty for the rest of the days leading up to the tournament, to facilitate your recovery."

They were expected to participate, then. Collin clenched his jaw, biting back unwise words as he held the door for Izzy. Collin could feel Rhett's eyes on his back as they left.

They put some distance between themselves and their commander before speaking a word, seeking out a quiet corner in the armory. Izzy sighed, crossing her arms over her chest as she leaned against a windowsill. She didn't quite manage to hide her wince when she leaned on her left shoulder first.

"I still don't like it," she whispered. "I don't see how parading our strength in front of everyone will encourage trust."

"Rhett is taking a risk," Collin agreed, standing as close as he dared. Mercer's bragging resurfaced in his mind, drawing a frown to his lips. "I'm not looking forward to new faces, either. No matter how necessary."

Izzy huffed again, pushing away from the wall.

"I'm going to get the oil," she said. "Some of these spears need desperate attention."

Glancing around, Collin saw what she meant. Dust was heavy on the seldom-used weapons. They couldn't afford to let any of their arsenal fall into disrepair. There was always a chance they'd need it.

"I'll join you later," Collin said, stepping toward the door. "I have something to check on."

Izzy cast a sly look over her shoulder. Collin smiled brightly. He had explanations ready if she asked, each more outlandish than the last. But she didn't question him. Collin watched her walk away, her thick braid hanging down her back with the tail twisted in one big curl. She wrapped her fingers in it when she was deep in thought. He understood why...even now memory tormented him of his fingers threaded through those smooth strands, brushing them away from her face.

He kicked himself. He couldn't afford to let his thoughts stray, not now at any rate. Glancing around, he forced himself to walk away before anyone caught him staring at Izzy's back. Hopefully a walk to the south quarter would dispel some of the nervous energy making him twitch.

Yesterday he'd spotted something while wandering with Izzy, and he wanted a closer look without her hovering over his shoulder. More than a tournament came with the waning crescent this cycle.

Izzy

Izzy hummed absently as she ran an oiled cloth over the blade of a scimitar, frowning at the spots of rust. Few, if any, currently in the Red Cloaks trained with the curved swords. But she still hated to see any weapon showing signs of disuse.

When she and Collin were younger, they kept each of these weapons looking newly forged. Those were the days before Rhett declared them ready to fight beside the rest of the Red Cloaks. She supposed most would've been plagued with boredom polishing weapons for hours at a time, or helping the cooks peel potatoes, or sweeping the long corridors. But she looked back on those days fondly. She was with Collin, and that was all that had really mattered to her.

Rhett and Eldon struggled to keep her and Collin occupied in that first year. They were the last recruits accepted into the order under the age of eighteen. Some days Izzy wondered why Rhett raised the age after them. Other days she wished Rhett had forced them to wait. If she'd had time to grow up a little, to know her own heart better, she never would've taken those vows.

Now, though, she had no idea who she was outside of the Red Cloaks. What would she have done if she hadn't been offered a home in these walls? Would she and Collin be married by now? Or would their fear of separation have come to fruition?

Izzy reached for a wooden crate of silver-tipped arrowheads, careful not to touch the razor-sharp edges as she wiped away the dust. Footsteps broke the silence, and Izzy dropped her humming. It wasn't Collin.

"Mind if I join you?"

Izzy twisted to find Eldon smiling down at her. An answering grin lit her face as he took the seat beside her.

"Why aren't you home with Abby and Maizy?" Izzy asked, as Eldon dripped oil on one of the clean cloths Izzy had piled beside her.

"They're helping with the harvest feast at the orphanage," he explained.

Izzy nodded and turned her eyes back to the arrowheads. She'd only seen two harvest feast in that place, and they weren't memories she enjoyed. It was beautiful, of course: one of the few occasions when the orphanage was truly decorated for the season. But the feast also served as a farewell to those aging out of the orphanage's care, one final night of safety before they were thrust out into the world whether they were prepared or not. She'd deeply feared that fate before Eldon took her home with him.

She remembered Kedar's orphanage as a place of overflowing halls and narrow beds, itchy clothes and keepers that didn't always love the children they were supposed to care for. Survivors of the curse were held in suspicion in those days. Perhaps they still were. In any case, Izzy found herself nearly friendless in that worn manor.

Nearly, but not quite. Some of the keepers had hearts warm enough to make up for the rest. Eldon's wife was the warmest of them all.

Would Eldon and Abby have kept her if Izzy had decided *not* to enter the Red Cloaks?

"There are troubled thoughts behind those eyes," Eldon said.

Izzy shrugged, setting aside one arrowhead and claiming another in silence.

"Little Star," Eldon said gently. "Share your thoughts with me."

The seldom used nickname broke down the last of her resistance, though she kept her eyes averted as she spoke.

"I wonder what my life would've been if I hadn't come here, I suppose."

"Are you regretting it?"

There was no judgment in Eldon's voice, but still Izzy shied away from the accusation.

"No," she said, trying not to consider if it was a lie. "I just...have no idea what would've happened to me."

"You wouldn't have gone back to that place."

Izzy looked up at the subtle fire in Eldon's voice. His gentle gaze locked her in place.

"You drew our attention with your skill in...evasion. But we would not have cast you back if you hadn't accepted our offer. Collin, either."

Izzy nodded slowly. She knew that her secret meetings with Collin were what drew Rhett and Eldon's attention. She'd met Collin often enough that the headmaster had threatened to cast her out several times. He'd tried locking her up...it had never worked.

She could see that Eldon was thinking of those days as well. A chuckle rumbled in his throat, and he glanced at her with amusement in his eyes.

"Not many children can evade adults so regularly, especially with a Red Cloak in their midst."

"I was determined," Izzy said, her voice breaking.

Izzy looked away as her eyes burned. She swallowed thickly as Eldon covered her hand with his.

"Feeling isn't a flaw, Star," he said. "It's what separates the living from the dead."

"Not a heartbeat or warm breath?" she countered, glancing up in time to see Eldon shake his head.

Eldon reached beside him, and Izzy noticed the bundle of worn cloth for the first time. He passed it to her.

"An early birthday present, since you're sharing the day with the tournament. Maizy insisted I chose this one."

Izzy pulled the wrapping away to reveal a dagger. The leather sheath was tooled with swirls, the hilt set with a single opal the size of her pinky nail. She drew the blade from the sheath and her eyes widened at the silver inlaid along the length of the blade.

"I noticed you're a blade short," Eldon said.

It was similar length and weight to the dagger she lost to the ogre, but *far* more decorated. In all honesty, it was fancier than she needed. But she couldn't deny its value. The silver inlay alone must have cost a fortune.

"It's beautiful," was all she could make herself say.

Eldon wrapped his arm around her shoulder.

"It's past time you have a weapon to fit your station. Don't tell Collin, but Maizy has one picked out for him as well."

A watery laugh broke free of Izzy's throat, and she rested her head against Eldon's shoulder.

"Thank you."

Eldon didn't reply. But he held her for a moment longer. Izzy gripped her new dagger and closed her eyes, enjoying her moment of simple, unrestricted affection.

CHAPTER EIGHT

Izzy

Izzy breathed in the twilight air that was already growing cold for the night. People crushed in around her, easily filling the large space in the center of the Watch's Garrison. There was plenty of time to examine her surroundings as she and Collin edged slowly up the line toward the signups for tournament events.

She didn't come here often. She seldom assisted Collin's pranks, and the last tournament to involve the entire city was held outside the walls. She'd been so young then, though she hadn't felt like it. She'd matured far more than three years would suggest.

The Watch had far more equipment than the Red Cloaks. Izzy felt a twinge of jealousy as she took in the large facilities, but it wasn't true regret. The Watch was too large for her. They weren't individuals here, weren't fully family. Izzy preferred being recognized for her own strengths, rather than be one face in a crowd.

Someone knocked into Collin's back, forcing him forward. He reached out to Izzy to steady himself, and the brief contact made sparks dance along her arms. He sighed.

"They all have to see at once," he muttered.

Izzy smiled sympathetically, tensing when an unknown shoulder brushed against her back. She stepped a little closer, wrapping her hand around the hilt of her new dagger to keep from reaching for Collin's hand.

"Rhett owes us," Collin said.

"Yes," Izzy agreed.

They'd tried volunteering for wall duty after the tournament so they wouldn't have to participate. Rhett had insisted that their participation *was* their duty. Most of Kedar knew their names and story. Rhett had made sure of it. Now he wanted them to serve as an example of what the Red Cloaks were capable of, demonstrating to all of Kedar how Collin and Izzy had grown into their place within the order.

The look of pride in his eyes as he said it made Izzy feel guilty for dreading the entire affair. She fought to protect and defend, not for sport. She didn't like performing.

She already felt like she was on display. It didn't escape her notice how many of the watchmen focused their attention on Collin and Izzy, whispering among themselves. Most met her gaze boldly enough. A few ducked when she caught them staring.

Izzy tried to forget about them when they finally reached the board. Collin took up the ragged quill and scratched their names onto the list for two-on-two weaponed fights. Izzy looked over the rest of the events. Archery, knife throwing, strength contests...

Archery was forbidden until her shoulder fully healed, and she had little chance of winning any contest of raw strength even against other women. She'd seen several women of the watch who were twice her size in nearly every direction.

Her eyes focused on the one-on-one weaponed fights. Several familiar names were already written in.

"We should sign up individually," she said, quiet to avoid eavesdropping from the crush of people behind her.

"We'll never hear the end of it if we do," Collin said, eyeing her.

She locked eyes with him, recklessness heating in her chest.

"Rhett wants us to show them our strengths. So we should."

Izzy watched that same challenge light in his eyes, and he turned to write his name beneath Hendrick's. Izzy took the quill to write her own name on the women's list. Seeing Andred and Edina already listed, she knew she didn't have a chance of winning. But that was the idea. Strength didn't mean much until it was set beside weakness.

Collin turned to slip out of the way, and Izzy followed so close her knees brushed the back of his cloak.

"Collin, Izzy," Dal called somewhere to their right. Collin turned into the crowd, and they slipped between watchmen and Red Cloaks until they reached their friends. Anson and Berke were there as well, taking in the people surrounding them.

"What did you sign up for?" Dal asked.

"Two-on-two, and one-on-one," Collin replied.

Berke looked at them, confusion deepening the lines between his brows. "One on one?"

Collin shrugged. "Figured we'd give it a try."

Berke and Dal didn't look like they believed him. Neither did Anson, for that matter, though his attention was mostly on the strangers around them.

"I thought I saw Isley when we came in," Collin said.

Berke sighed, but it was Dal who answered.

"He tried to talk him out of it, but Isley was determined."

"Are you hoping he's eliminated early?" Izzy asked.

"Don't know," Berke said. "He's good when he keeps his focus, but some days he has the attention span of a sparrow."

Berke's brows were low over his eyes, and he shook his head again. She knew he felt responsible for Isley. Partly because they were cousins, partly because Isley's mother had begged Berke to keep him safe. But they all knew that Berke couldn't shield Isley forever. He'd taken the vows of a Red Cloak, and that brought danger.

"See that kid?" Anson asked, pointing at a teenager several years younger than Izzy.

"Yeah," Dal said. "Who is he?"

"Distant cousin of mine. His name is Cole."

"Poor kid," Dal said, shaking his head in exaggerated sorrow. "He doesn't stand a chance."

Izzy looked the kid over before saying, "Don't judge him so quickly. You said the same about Collin and me."

Berke laughed, and Dal grimaced at her.

"You two are a rare breed. You had the arrogance beaten out of you *long* before those matches."

"And you're sure he hasn't?"

"He hasn't," Anson said. "Trust me. He could use some humbling."

"We shouldn't speak so loudly in Watch territory," Berke rumbled, glaring at a knot of watchmen obviously listening in.

"They're doing it," Dal said, flicking his hand at the small groups all taking in the competition.

Izzy knew he was right. She continued to catch men and woman alike staring at her and Collin, whispering what she assumed were predictions about how well they'd do. How many knew her name, she wondered? How many were hoping for a chance to defeat the Commander's apprentices?

Blood children. At least there was little chance of *that* nickname spreading through the city. It was bad enough to be called such by their enemies.

She recognized Brenner as he turned away from the lists, and she nodded to him as their eyes met. He barely had time to return the gesture before being swept up in conversation with fellow watchmen.

"Did you visit Tay today?" Berke asked.

"No," Collin said, glancing at Izzy.

"The fever broke. They said she'll pull through, and now it's a matter of how much strength she can regain."

Not enough to rejoin them at the wall, Izzy already knew that much. Would Rhett keep her in the Red Cloaks? Or would he push her into retirement? If Tay went, Farren would go with her. The sisters never did anything separately.

"Is Farren sleeping better?" Dal asked.

"Tay convinced her to take the sleeping powder the nurses have been trying to force on her, so at the moment she's probably sleeping like the dead."

"Good," Izzy said.

She knew the dangers of going long periods without sleep. Farren could end up worse off than Tay if she didn't begin resting.

"Alright, I've been stared at enough," Dal said. "Anyone ready to get back?"

Berke's answer was to start cutting a path toward the large gate that led into the city. Izzy let Dal and Anson pass before following in their wake.

Izzy breathed a sigh when they left the crowds behind. The streets were blessedly quiet, and the few people still out mostly ignored the Red Cloaks walking past them. Izzy reveled in how cool the air was now that they were free from the crush of bodies, ready to be back in their *own* territory. The Watch and Red Cloaks were allies, but they were also rivals. Izzy didn't enjoy spending time beneath the weight of their stares.

They were halfway home when Collin grabbed Izzy's wrist, tugging her off the main road. Izzy went without argument, though she glanced up in question as they plunged into shadow. Collin only flashed her a bright smile.

They shouldn't be doing this. Rhett had been watching them closely these past few days, and he'd know if they delayed their return.

Or would he? There were other Red Cloaks still at the Watch Garrison. Who was to say they didn't stay longer? When Collin led them to a new road and Izzy realized where he was taking her, the last of her reluctance vanished.

Through alleys and narrow streets, all the way to a long, twisted building. The upper floor was long abandoned, the floor weakened by years of rain falling through the broken roof. The lower floors were kept as storage, mostly. The more habitable dwellings were occupied by poorer families.

They didn't go in through one of the worn doors. Instead, they slipped around to the back corner, scaling the exposed bricks until they reached a wide windowsill jutting out from the wall. It was far larger than the windows in any house Izzy had lived in, fit for the manor this building once was. Even in its disrepair it served a purpose: Izzy slipped through easily, searching out the stone lip on the other side. Collin copied her.

This was perhaps the most secluded place within Kedar. This room wasn't safely accessibly from within, and once inside they were hidden from nearly every angle below and around them. She wasn't sure if anyone other than Eldon and Rhett knew about it. This is where she and Collin first met the two leaders after they'd followed Izzy from the orphanage.

She used to know the path to this place better than anything. She'd sneak here at least one night a week to meet with Collin, in the days when it seemed every adult in their lives was determined to break them apart forever.

"Alright," Izzy said, turning to face Collin. "What do you have?"

The stars were coming out now, the light of the setting moon revealing only half of his face. He was smiling.

"What makes you think I have anything?"

Izzy jabbed a finger into his arm. "You're terrible at keeping secrets from me."

"True enough."

He reached into his pocket, pulling out something on a long leather cord. Holding it in the moonlight, he slowly unfurled his fingers to reveal a milky white stone carved into a waning crescent moon. Izzy's breath caught, and she held out her hand. Blue flashed in the depths of the stone as he tipped it into her hand.

"Strange to choose a moon of all things," she said, holding the charm closer to her face. "When every threat to our lives has been beneath its light."

"You don't have to pretend to hate the moon like the rest do. Our best moments have happened beneath its light, as well," Collin said.

Izzy couldn't disagree. She finally ripped her eyes away from the charm to meet Collin's gaze, wishing she could see him better.

"I love it," she breathed.

The half of his face Izzy could see was smug.

"I knew you would."

"Don't get cocky," Izzy scolded.

"I thought that was one of my charms."

He took the necklace from her, carefully easing the leather cord over her head. His hands lingered near her neck, slowly drawing her braid through and running his fingers down the length of it. Izzy's skin electrified wherever he touched. She brushed her fingers over the charm where it laid against her breastbone, tilting her head up. Collin's gaze burned. He drew his hand across her jaw, his thumb resting against her chin.

Izzy leaned toward him, wanting as little distance between them as possible. He knew her so well...but could he guess the thoughts rushing through her mind? Did he know she was wondering how his lips would feel against hers? His gaze dipped to her mouth, and she knew he was thinking the same.

Collin leaned forward, and a smile tugged at her mouth as he did. She'd gladly throw caution to the wind for one night.

But he turned his head at the last moment, so their cheeks brushed. She felt his breath on her temple, heard the ragged edge to it. His fingers wrapped around the fabric at her waist, as if desperate to hold her close. Izzy realized her own hands rested on his shoulders.

"We should go," he whispered.

A hollow ache settled in her core, a harsh counterweight to her soaring thoughts. She nodded. But when he tried to pull away, she held him close.

"What about my other birthday present?"

He hesitated, and fear struck that this would be the year he would refuse. That he would say it was too little, that it was too much. But rather than say anything, he shifted his head to press a chaste kiss against her forehead. Never mind that he lingered a little long, or that Izzy's eyes fluttered closed as she wished she could pause the moon's setting to extend this moment. What had begun as a strange and childish tradition had become so much more.

But time didn't pause for mortal beings, and Izzy wasn't selfish enough to ask the Almighty to stop it for her. When Collin pulled back, she let him. Even though the absence of his warmth was dart straight through her heart.

Even in the shadows, she saw the war Collin now fought to lock up every desire, every scrap of tenderness that could prove their undoing. Izzy was doing the same. And by the time they returned to the darkened street, they were the two dedicated Red Cloaks Kedar knew.

Izzy already had years of practice hiding her regret with everything else.

Izzy breathed deep and slow, ignoring the burning demand in her lungs, as she stretched out her legs. She and Collin had abbreviated their usual sparring, taking just enough time to warm up and clear their heads.

They'd been reluctantly cleared by the physicians yesterday, giving them little time to prepare for the tournament already getting started across Kedar. But as Izzy carefully rolled her shoulder she didn't feel any of the burning or tearing that she had the first few days.

She shouldn't be healed. A dislocated shoulder took several *months* to recover from, and here she was nearly whole less than two weeks later. She'd know better than to think the legends exaggerated from now on.

Collin stepped aside, letting Izzy enter the mess hall first. She didn't think much of it...until a riot of voices hit her all at once, nicknames and well-wishes and teasing remarks about her old age. She blinked, frozen where she stood until she heard Collin's chuckle behind her.

Eldon and Rhett were absent, likely already observing the Tournament. But every other person she considered a friend—and a few others she suspected simply enjoyed celebrating things—stood before her. The cooks, Baldwin and his wife Kieta, stood in the center with a large plate of sweet bread. The scent of cinnamon and yeast made her mouth water from there.

Izzy stepped forward, smiling as she approached Baldwin and Keita. It had sugared flowers scattered on top. They must've saved them for months.

"Thank you," she said thickly, taking the platter from their hands.

"Thought we'd forget you with the excitement, didn't you?" Baldwin said with a wink.

Keitra only grasped Izzy's arm and squeezed.

Collin steered her to the nearest table, decorated with chrysanthemums, pumpkins, and bright leaves scattered across the wood. Everyone else crowded around for a piece of the rare treat. She spotted a few other platters scattered around the room, but didn't say anything. She wasn't opposed to having everyone press in on her, wanting a piece from her plate. Celebrations were meant to be shared.

"You have to take more than that," Dal said, snatching the plate from Izzy's hand. "You'll make us look like pigs."

He shoved a different one into her face mounded with nuts and dough all saturated with cinnamon, a pale sugared violet on top.

"Trying to slow me down?" she replied, gingerly picking the violet out of a glob of melted sugar.

"Never! I'm not naïve enough to think that would work."

"I never get moon bread for *my* birthday," Alair quipped, sitting with a plate mounded higher than Izzy's.

Collin snorted as he took a seat beside her. "You haven't spent hours scrubbing pans, either."

Conversation waned after that, everyone devouring their breakfast with silent glee. Izzy made sure to take two of the hard-boiled eggs also on the tables, scarfing them down quickly so she could savor the moon bread. She should feel guilty for how many resources Baldwin and Kieta had used for a single meal, but instead she only felt warm. Private gestures were all she'd expected, not a celebration. She glanced sideways at Collin, already nearly finished with his food, but he shook his head and shrugged. Perhaps Baldwin and Kieta arranged it all.

They finished and walked to the Watch Garrison together. Izzy had dreaded this day since she'd heard about it, but their companions' excitement was catching. Surrounded by family with cinnamon still warm on her tongue, her blood was racing by the time they entered the crowded Garrison. Izzy tried not to gawk at how many people had come.

Makeshift stands had been erected around the larger events, allowing more of the crowd a decent view of the soldiers below. Large stones and gate beams were laid out for contests of strength. They paused while Berke checked his place on the list, continuing as a group to the weaponed matches.

They passed knife throwing, and Izzy had a moment of regret watching the participants practice. She'd almost signed up. But she had enough to focus on already.

A narrow path to the sword arenas was roped off, allowing them to reach the list of who would face who. Izzy searched for her name, finding it placed beside one she didn't recognize: Vera. From the Watch, then.

Collin groaned, and Izzy turned to find him hanging his head while Berke grinned through his bushy beard. A glance at the men's list showed their names side by side.

Alair slapped Collin's shoulder. "You can always claim you're still healing up, save face a little."

"If I have one left once Berke is finished," Collin replied.

Berke laughed. "Not to worry. I'll save most of my energy for the watch."

Collin shook his head, but he made little effort to disguise his smile as they searched for a place to observe until their names were called.

There were two arenas for the one-on-one fights, separated by men and women. Only three matches passed before Collin and Berke were called into the roped off arena. Izzy threaded her fingers together beneath her cloak, watching with more worry than was warranted. She fought to keep her expression composed. She trusted Berke not to take advantage of Collin's recent injuries, but accidents happened.

She needn't have worried. Berke defeated Collin within seconds, his large sword resting where neck met shoulder. If it was a real blow it would've taken Collin's head off. She narrowed her eyes as Collin left the arena. He'd moved too slowly. If it was her, he would've avoided that attack...not with ease, but with efficiency.

"Are you sure the moon bread didn't slow *you* down?" she asked as he left the arena.

He only winked.

Izzy heard her name called moments later. She entered the arena to stand across from a steely woman half a dozen years older than her. Izzy wondered if they were matching public perceptions. Vera certainly looked like she was forged of iron.

Izzy didn't move when the announcer called, letting Vera attack first. She regretted it as Vera whipped forward like a snake, forcing Izzy into a two-handed grip. She was stronger than Izzy guessed; her shoulder burned from deflecting her attacks. Izzy moved quickly, testing for weaknesses in between Vera's sweeping attacks. Izzy saw when Vera's defense faltered. She didn't waste time, pressing her advantage until her guard folded entirely and Izzy slipped her sword tip to press just below Vera's breastbone. Vera froze, breath heaving, as a few scattered cheers and Dal's voice calling "iron girl" surrounded them.

Izzy lowered her sword, nodding to the woman. She nodded back, but brushed past Izzy to march out of the arena and into the masses.

"You don't seem excited," Collin teased as she left the arena.

"Should I jump up and down?" Izzy replied, though she tried to soften her expression.

Alair's name was called, and they shuffled their way toward the other arena. They were peering around trying to glimpse Alair's fight when Collin leaned down, whispering just beside her ear.

"Now they'll think you're the better fighter of the two of us."

"They wouldn't if you hadn't thrown your own match," Izzy whispered back.

He chuckled. "It would've been a different battle if they'd matched me against Mercer."

Izzy shook her head but said nothing more. For a while they simply watched the matches, analyzing skill levels and predicting who Rhett and Eldon would want to recruit. The sun flooded the Garrison when her name was called again.

This time the woman she stood against was nearly a head shorter than her. Izzy examined her carefully, taking in the lithe way she stood. This woman would be quick.

She *was* quick. This time Izzy's guard was the one pressed too far, and in less than a minute they both stood frozen and gasping, the watchwoman's sword pressed to Izzy's side. The woman pulled back her blade, and Izzy nodded to her in what she hoped was a gracious manner before she left the arena.

While Dal and Alair gave their sympathies, Collin only smiled cunningly.

"Now the fun begins," he whispered when she was close.

They watched Berke go against a watchman who was half his size but also half as quick before making their way to the larger arena where they'd fight next. Their names were written in near the bottom of the first round, giving them some time to watch. Andred and Claret were in the arena right then, going against two women from the watch. Claret was disarmed and eliminated, but Andred defeated both women on her own.

Izzy watched these battles more closely. The one-on-one matches were fairly mixed between the Watch and the Red Cloaks. Collin wasn't the only one matched against someone from his own order. But here there seemed to be a clear divide between Watch and Red Cloaks, pitting the two groups against each other in each match.

Of course, some were Watch against Watch to make up for the disparity of numbers. There were far more watchmen available to sign up, even with those on duty around the city. The divide would grow muddier in further rounds, of course, but it provided an interesting contrast to observe.

When the Watch fought on the walls, they stayed in greater numbers, usually six or eight. Many of them struggled to keep up a good defense against even numbers, especially against the Red Cloaks. There were exceptions, of course. Izzy thought she could pick out the ones the Watch Commander had trained personally: they always looked to him first when their match was over. He apparently had his favorites for recruitment.

Mercer and one of his closest friends fought two watchmen they were obviously familiar with. They made it to the next round by a clean fight, much to Collin's disappointment. Soon enough their own names were called to the waiting area near the entrance to the ring, and they wove their way toward the ropes. She rolled her shoulder as she unclasped her cloak. The ache was manageable.

They laid their cloaks over their opponents', Tallis and Kyne, but were left to wait. Izzy couldn't help but look around at the observers as the four watchmen in the arena fought. These rounds were longer than the individuals, giving her more time to pick out faces and guess at their thoughts.

She'd seen some earlier in the day who wore expression of suspicion, even anger. But most seemed to have left already. Those who remained carried the fire of excitement, or the desire to be entertained. She wasn't sure Rhett's message would get across.

Izzy didn't realize she was hunching her shoulders until Collin poked her. She turned and found him watching her with a far more tender look than was safe in such a crowd.

"Ignore them," he said. "We'll show them where our true strength lies."

She nodded, letting out a slow breath and willing the tension to leave with it. Cheers and groans of disappointment marked the end of the battle.

The watchmen filed out, the angles of their heads clearly distinguishing the victors. Tallis and Kyne entered the arena as soon as they were out of the way, and she and Collin followed. Theirs was the first match she'd seen with Red Cloaks set against each other, and she couldn't help but wonder why. Did Rhett mean to imply that the watchmen weren't challenge enough for them?

The announcer told them to take their places, and Izzy let those questions flow out. Cold focus washed over her mind as she drew her blunt sword and dagger. They were weapons she knew as well as her own hands after hundreds of mornings sparring with Collin. Settling her feet into a familiar stance at Collin's side, she glanced up at their opponents and her focus fractured.

They looked nervous. She knew they'd seen Collin and Izzy fight, at the gates and in training. Were they worried she didn't know how to hold back, how to *not* go for the killing blow?

This was why she hated fighting for sport. With the cacophony around them and the steel in her hands, there was hardly a difference between the fight before her and the battle she faced nearly every day. Even knowing she wouldn't be taking the lives before her, that they all would come out of this arena alive and well, it was too real.

But when the announcer told them to begin, Tallis and Kyne didn't hesitate. They charged Collin and Izzy, angled to drive a wedge between them. Izzy gritted her teeth as Tallis forced her a step away from Collin, and then two. He didn't seem concerned that he was isolating himself as well as her.

Izzy raised her sword and dagger before her face, locking his sword between them. In one movement she twisted the blade from his hand and raised her dagger to his throat. Tallis lifted empty hands, eyes wide, and she backed away. By the time she turned to help Collin, Kyne was on his back with Collin's sword resting on his chest.

The audience cheered as Collin helped Kyne to his feet, slapping his back as they left the arena. Izzy slipped out just behind Tallis, quickly redonning her cloak as if it could shield her from the crowd. Fingers tapping her shoulder made her spin, and she allowed her grin to break through as she stared up at Collin. He grinned back, ducking his head.

"Smile for everyone else, too. This isn't a trial, you know."

Izzy kicked his shin. But as he stumbled backwards, she fought to keep her smile and glance around at the crowd. Most of them already had their focus on the next match. There was one man staring at her and Collin, though: an older man with snow white hair that struck Izzy as...familiar. But a taller man stepped between them, and as soon as her sight of the man was cut off the sensation of familiarity vanished with it.

"My condolences on the slaughter," Alair said too loudly, drawing Izzy's attention back to her immediate surroundings.

"Someone had to fight them," Tallis said, rubbing his throat where Izzy had held her dagger.

Guilt rose in Izzy's throat, until Tallis glanced at her and she realized he was smiling.

Alair patted his shoulder consolingly. “I’m sure they’ll disarm their next opponents just as quickly.”

“Don’t be so sure,” Andred said, appearing behind Alair with eerie suddenness. “The Watch Commander is setting us against his best.”

Izzy agreed. Not all of the Red Cloaks won their matches.

“Our commanders are playing games,” Collin said.

Andred shrugged. “Of course they are. It’s a competition for them as much as us, only they’re setting the board.”

“Are they competing for highest honors, do you think?” Alair asked, his eyes trained on the match nearby. “Proof that one order is more skilled than the other?”

“Or that one protects the city more than the other,” Izzy said quietly, wary of others hearing.

Tallis and Kyne looked at her sharply, but she didn’t flinch. She wasn’t going to pretend that, as much as they fought together, there was always an edge of rivalry between the Watch and the Red Cloaks over who was truly the city’s protectors. Numbers versus training.

Andred nodded as if she agreed, but Alair didn’t look convinced. Or perhaps he was frowning at the women of the watch disarming Declan.

“Who’s winning at the singles?” Collin asked.

“Dal and Andred are still in it,” Alair said. “But there’s a couple watch boys who might beat us out. And one citizen, oddly enough.”

“That ‘citizen’ is Hendrick’s nephew,” Andred said. “It’s not that strange.”

“I thought he was only seventeen,” Collin said.

“Turns eighteen in a few weeks. “

“It’s a good opportunity to prove his value,” Collin said.

Izzy left the discussion to them, satisfied merely listening as their conversation turned to comments on the fights playing out before them. Most of the matches only took one or two minutes, hardly the drawn out performances the Red Cloaks occasionally put on during festivals. It felt like hardly any time had passed before she was being called back into the arena with Collin.

This time they were set against two watchmen, both built like oak trees. She'd seen their first match, though, and knew that they possessed a speed that belayed their size. She kept her guard high as she took her place beside Collin, wary of their greater strength. But she was also prepared to exploit their weakness: during their first match it was clear that they fought as individuals, not as a unit.

When the two men barreled toward them, Izzy and Collin sidestepped as one and focused on the blond-haired man on the right first. Collin engaged his sword, and Izzy darted in to thrust her sword at his gut. He reluctantly backed out of the fight with a scowl that Izzy hardly saw. She and Collin had already turned to face the second man.

He held them off better, using his longsword to keep them at a distance. But he was used to fighting goblins, not Red Cloaks. This time it was Izzy who distracted him, though even deflecting his blows made her shoulder ache fiercely. Collin slipped to the watchman's unguarded side while Izzy feigned a thrust toward his gut. The man froze a moment before his sword came down on Izzy's arm, Collin's sword resting along his neck.

Izzy backed away from the blunt blade, examining the watchman carefully.

"Well fought," Collin said, a little out of breath.

The watchman nodded stiffly, grinding his teeth. Both he and his comrade avoided their commander's gaze as they left the arena, walking through the path that cleared before them in the crowd. Izzy forced her gaze away from them as Alair slapped her back with enough force to ring through her bones.

"Well done," he said.

She hoped her smile in reply didn't look like a grimace.

Berke's shadow overtook her. "What did I miss?"

"They fought off the two bears you were tossing rocks with earlier," Alair said.

"And left victorious?" Berke asked, one bushy eyebrow raised.

"Obviously," Collin said with a grin, throwing his arm over Izzy's shoulders.

Izzy stiffened, her mind screaming "forbidden" as her pulse quickened. But their friends didn't act like Collin's gesture was unusual, continuing their discussion as usual. Izzy still didn't relax. If she did, she'd lean into him. And *that* would draw dangerous attention. She couldn't give any outward sign that the weight of Collin's arm across her shoulders, the taste of his closeness, made the tight knot in her chest ease.

"The Watch Commander thought his bears had you," Andred said, and Alair grunted his agreement.

"He neglected to teach them to fight *together*," Izzy said.

"They fight like trolls," Alair said. "Odd strategy in my mind."

"Effective on the wall, though," Collin said. "The berserker trolls prove that."

Alair grimaced and conceded Collin's point with a nod. Izzy stifled a shudder. When battle madness took trolls, they crushed *everything* in their path. Sometimes they killed their own allies, but too often it was Watchmen and Red Cloaks in their path.

The fighting rush had hardly faded from Izzy's limbs when they were called into the ring again. A glance at the list showed over a dozen pairs still remaining as she and Collin entered the arena.

They were set against fellow Red Cloaks again: Liam and Raith. They were more experienced than Tallis and Kyne, and Izzy took her stance warily. She'd seen them sparring and knew they'd be a challenge.

They also focused on separating Izzy from Collin, but their method was far more effective. Izzy was forced backward, her guard strained as Raith bore down on her. He brought a dagger to her throat, chest heaving as he stood over her. But he flicked his eyes downward, feeling the pressure of the dagger she'd brought to his ribs at the last moment. They were both eliminated. Rather than expressing the frustration she expected, he grinned down at her as he pulled his dagger away from her skin.

Izzy nodded before turning toward Collin, backing toward the rope as she anxiously watched his own fight. A sword hit the dirt, and the frenzy of motion stopped. It took a pounding heartbeat for Izzy's mind to comprehend the sight before her, even as the cheers drowned out all else. Liam stood with his dagger nearly to Collin's ribs, but Collin's own blade already rested against the base of Liam's neck.

Both men broke into grins as they sheathed their knives. Izzy stepped forward and lifted the sword from the ground, handing it to Liam as he and Collin walked toward them.

"Thank you," Liam said, taking the blade. "And well fought."

"Same to you."

"Getting a little slow there, Izzy?" Alair said as Izzy wrapped her cloak around her shoulders.

Izzy stared at him, lifting one eyebrow. But Alair knew her too well. His smile didn't falter as he slapped Raith across the back.

"That's the first impasse I've seen," Alair said. "Seems you two are well matched."

"Not the first, surely," Raith replied, gesturing to Izzy and Collin. "You've seen them practice in the mornings."

"Those don't count," Collin said.

"Why? Are you going to claim you *let* Izzy get that close?" Alair shook his head.

Izzy dared to meet Collin's gaze, letting a wry smile overtake her lips before schooling her expression once more. Sometimes he *did* intentionally let her get close, and she did the same. Not that she could explain that.

Dal entered the group, head hanging.

"Who'd you lose to?" Collin asked.

Dal grimaced. "Hendrick's protégé, Sabriel."

"Good for him," Collin said, earning a withering glare from Dal.

"Is Mercer still in?" Andred asked.

"Barely. I thought Isley had him for a second, but no luck."

"Maybe Sabriel will humble him next."

Izzy kept her silence, edging closer to their group as another round of applause made the air around her heavy. The sun was finally high enough to warm the air, but Izzy missed the chill. She was growing tired of the frenzy around her. As other events finished, more and more people came to surround the arena she stood beside. More and more eyes to watch her every move. She stifled a sigh when her name was called again.

In this match, she found herself settling into the same disconnect she sought out on the wall. Fight, breathe, and never stop moving. She and Collin won the match and left the arena. Izzy left her cloak off, knowing their time would come again quickly. This time they fought Andred and Claret. Izzy suspected they would've lost, except Andred had pulled a muscle in her leg in the last match and was moving slower than usual. She offered Collin and Izzy a rare smile as they left the arena together.

And then it was time for the final match. Collin and Izzy were set to go against a team of watchmen, Caston and Giles. She'd watched their previous matches and knew that they'd made it this far because of skill, not luck. They'd likely earn a place among the Red Cloaks whether they defeated Collin and Izzy or not. Weary as she was of this day, she still had something to prove. She and Collin were recognized as two of the best warriors in Kedar, but they were only the best when they were *together*. She wanted the entire city to acknowledge that they belonged by each other's side.

Izzy kept her gaze down as she entered the arena, the midday sun a blinding reflection against her sword. Archery was the only tournament event still taking place, and it seemed every eye in the garrison was focused on them. She took a slow breath, not truly noticing the murmuring around her, and raised her eyes.

She started at the sight before her. Caston carried a mace. It was a training mace, smooth wood rather than the steel spikes used in battle. But still fully capable of breaking bones if wielded correctly. And based on the way Caston held it, he would wield it well.

Izzy turned, searching out Rhett in the crowd and lifting an eyebrow. Maces were for fighting against plate armor, or in the Watch's case trolls' rocky hide. Not the light leather she and Collin wore. And Caston hadn't wielded it in any of the previous matches.

Rhett was scowling, and Izzy wondered if the Watch Commander was playing his contest a little harsher than Rhett agreed to. The rules said nothing about changing weapons, but it had been an unspoken agreement that all would stick to swords and knives.

She glanced at Collin. He was examining the watchmen warily, but when he turned to her there was a fire of revolt in his eyes. Izzy felt it ignite within her, too.

The Watch Commander wasn't a fool. He wouldn't honestly *want* his men to incapacitate two of the Red Cloaks who kept his soldiers alive during the full moon. Which made Izzy wonder if he expected them to protest. The Red Cloaks prided themselves on facing any fight that came before them...did he want them to contradict that oath before the city?

Izzy despised being manipulated. She was no tool to be molded to suit the purpose of another. The Watch thought she and Collin couldn't handle unfair odds? They would learn better.

The pain in her shoulder sharpened, the memory of the troll's unseen blow sending ice through her veins. She clenched her jaw and forced those memories away. A mace wielded by an ally in contest wasn't the same as an ogre's club. And she wouldn't let the actions of a dead foe influence her now.

Turning her gaze back to Caston and Giles, she lifted her chin and met their gazes with a challenge. Collin turned to let the announcer know that they would continue with the fight. Both watchmen wore helmets, making it difficult to make out their expressions. She didn't know if either of them were unnerved by

Collin and Izzy's refusal to back down from their challenge. All she knew was that neither hesitated when the order to begin rang out.

She and Collin were more cautious this time, edging around the arena to stay out of range of the swinging mace. And Caston seemed content to approach slowly, sure of his eventual victory. Giles stayed behind, shielded by Caston. For a while Collin and Izzy slowly circled with them, each searching for an opening in the other's defense that wasn't there.

Izzy turned, glancing at Collin for less than a heartbeat. He had turned too, and in that brief meeting Izzy knew they had come to the same conclusion. If they wanted a chance of winning this match, they would have to take a risk.

Izzy took a slow breath, sinking lower as she counted to four in her head. On that fourth beat, they both lunged forward. Collin ducked the mace, lifting his sword to tangle in its chain. Izzy stayed low and slid all the way to Giles feet. She knocked the flat of her sword against his wrist, breaking his grip, and twisted her blade to press the tip to his stomach. Seeing a flash of teeth, Izzy pressed a little harder, forcing Giles to take a step backwards. Her spine tingled in her vulnerable position, but she held fast.

Behind her, the crowd gasped as screeching metal tore through the air. She didn't move until startled cheers broke across the crowd.

Turning, she found Collin holding Caston's sword to his throat, Collin's own sword tangled with the mace on the ground. Only then did Izzy lower her blade, stepping back to give Giles some space. Her shoulder bumped against Collin's, and she let out a heavy breath. Warmth spread through her limbs as she and Collin faced their defeated opponents. For a moment, no one moved. But then Izzy and Collin bowed as one, offering a sign of respect to the men who'd thought to humiliate them. Caston and Giles stiffly returned the gesture before leaving the arena. Caston held his hand to his shoulder like it pained him.

Izzy tried to leave with them, but Collin held her back. And before she could look to see why, their friends were surging into the arena and surrounding them. She barely had enough time to sheath her sword before hands grasped her arms and waist, lifting her onto Liam and Dal's shoulders. Izzy fought to steady herself, glancing over to see Collin being carried on Berke and Alair's shoulders. He was laughing, and the sight broke through her reservations like they were never there. She grinned, holding onto Dal's head for balance. Laughter broke free of her lips when he yelped that she was pulling his hair.

Their friends carried them all the way to the victor's platform across the garrison, where the rest of the victors were already waiting. Someone handed Izzy her cloak when they set her down, and she threw it around her shoulders as she and Collin took their places near the center. Her head spun as she took in all that surrounded her. Collin's shoulder pressed against hers, Rhett and the Watch Commander announcing the winners one by one, her friends' grinning faces just below her...the mingled expressions filling her vision beyond.

Izzy straightened as the two commanders approached, lifting her gaze to meet Rhett's eyes. His face was composed, but the pride glinting in his eyes filled her chest with warmth.

"Collin Fastolf and Izzy Pryor, Guardians of Kedar."

The title startled Izzy out of her foggy elation. Her cloak weighed heavier across her back as she looked out once more at those watching. All she found was the excitement that filled the garrison like a contagion. Still, she had the cold sense of an enemy among that sea of faces. And that the title Rhett bestowed on them so proudly was one more target written across her back.

CHAPTER NINE

Collin

Collin walked blindly, his eyes focused on Izzy beside him. He should be paying attention to their path, searching for signs of goblins who'd harried a group of hunters the day before. But they were still far from where he expected to find them, and he struggled to take his eyes off her. Her braid was looser this morning, allowing strands to slip free and frame her face. She was laughing, shaking her head as she gave him that scolding look he loved so much.

"I'm just saying, the black eye at least gives him a reason to be in a bad mood," Collin said.

She laughed again. The sound was quiet, like raindrops on leaves, but he wasn't sure there was a sound he loved better.

She was fingering the cord around her neck. She hadn't taken off her necklace since he gave it to her. She'd only take out the charm when she thought no one was looking, but the quiet awe in her eyes as she twisted it back and forth in the light made him glad he bought it. Forget the cost. It wasn't as if he had many expenses to use his wages on.

Izzy glanced at him, and her lips curled up in a hint of a smile. "What are you staring at?"

Half a dozen sentimental answers passed through his mind, all discarded. He could only push it so far.

"You look relaxed," he said instead. "Glad to be away from the recruits?"

She rolled her eyes. "A bit."

Collin didn't answer, and after a moment of patience Izzy continued.

"As *honoring* as it is for Rhett to have us help train them, it's not my favorite task."

Collin smiled at the twist to that word. He knew as well as she did that Rhett only ordered them to help train the recruits to keep them busy.

"Perhaps it's payback for all the years Rhett and Eldon trained *us*."

Izzy nodded. Collin grabbed her hand on impulse, his smile renewed when she held tight to his fingers. Then he forced his eyes to the forest around them. No matter how much he longed for some time just for the two of them, they were out here for a purpose.

"Were we so awed by everyone when we joined?" Izzy asked.

"Probably," Collin said, narrowing his eyes as he looked around them. Something was off. But what?

"We grew up holding the Red Cloaks in reverence like everyone else," he continued, as they climbed upward.

"That's my least favorite part of working with them," Izzy said. "They shouldn't *want* to stare at us, no matter what they saw at the tournament."

"I don't think it's our skill alone that amazes them. I think it's the fact that we're still so *young*. Some of the watchmen have kids our age."

"And they equate age with experience," Izzy said.

"Exactly. They forget that we have nearly as many years in the Red Cloaks as Andred and Alair."

"You can't disagree that the people we're training should know better," Izzy said, flashing him a stubborn look. "Especially Sabriel."

"Sabriel is..." Collin trailed off, considering the seventeen-year-old who, despite being younger than the recruitment age, was already training with the rest. "I haven't figured him out yet."

"Nor have I."

Thoughts of Sabriel's piercing stare dropped from Collin's mind as he looked around again. A deep foreboding was rising in his gut, and that demanded more attention than the strangers in their ranks. He took a closer look at the trees, the leaves fading from into shades of gold, brown, and scarlet. A week more and the maple groves would be the same shade as their cloaks. Some of the leaves were frostbitten, and he knew they were only half a moon cycle from hard freezes. Time was running out. Or at least it felt like it was. But that didn't explain the insistent sense that they'd come here recently, despite a lack of any memories to corroborate that. He still saw little sign that the goblins they hunted were nearby.

Collin took another look at the trees and adjusted his path, falling silent as he followed that faint sense at the back of his mind. He knew it would disappear if he tried to analyze it. Izzy quieted, following his lead without question.

She trusts me too much. His mind went back to the tournament, even as he searched the trees for foes. Caston nearly broke her skull open, and she never even turned around. All because she trusted him to have her back. The truth of it was that Collin shouldn't have been able to wrench the mace from Caston's hand like that. He also hadn't had the right angle to draw his opponent's sword to use against him. All he knew was that when he saw Caston turn to attack Izzy, he saw red.

They made their point: Izzy with her unwavering trust, and Collin with his determination not to fail her. But the memory of it still chilled him. She shouldn't place her life in his hands so completely. There might come a night when he was too far away, when he *couldn't* move the stars to see her safe. What then?

He shook those thoughts from his head. He was already on edge, and questions of "what if?" would accomplish nothing. Flexing his hand, he realized he'd drawn his sword a few inches out of his scabbard. And looking over, he could see Izzy with her gifted dagger bared. Dread coiled tight within him, making it hard to swallow. He didn't have the faintest idea what was causing it...but he didn't need to. It was a sign that those they searched for were nearby and that was enough.

He forced his eyes forward again, slowly creeping forward. It wasn't long before he caught glimpses of a stone wall in among the trees. Collin stopped, reaching for Izzy. She grabbed his hand and squeezed it tight. Why did he feel like he remembered this place?

No matter the reason, they had to investigate further even if it wasn't what they were searching for. He stepped forward, Izzy moving with him. She dropped his hand, and Collin tried to ignore his regret as they approached the stone cottage taking shape before them. They moved forward as one, prepared to face whatever they might find.

The sight that greeted them wasn't what Collin expected. But the subversion of his expectations wasn't comforting. If anything, it made him more wary.

An old man was working in a small garden alongside the house. He straightened slowly, wincing and holding his back. But Collin didn't drop his guard. Anyone who lived in this kind of isolation, anyone who survived in a forest as full of danger as this one, wasn't harmless.

He was taller than most men Collin knew, with skin so pale Collin could see blue arteries in his neck even from where he stood. Collin wasn't sure why the moon folk came to mind. He bore little similarity to the moon folk they'd met...until he looked up. Collin froze, and Izzy inhaled sharply. He couldn't say what it was about the old man's gaze, whether it was the peculiar paleness of his eyes or the set to his face as he examined him. But it set every nerve on fire as he stood there.

"Greetings," the old man said, his smile at odds with his gaze. "It isn't often I have visitors this far out in the forest. What brings you here?"

Collin looked him over silently, analyzing the feeling of abject vulnerability coursing through him despite the sword in his hand. He'd never felt its like before. Or had he? The old man stared at them a moment, unbothered by their silence. He flapped his hand at their sword and dagger before shuffling toward the open door.

"There's no need for that. Come in, and I'll give you some tea to warm your bones. The air has a bite to it today."

Collin lifted his arm to stop Izzy from approaching, though she hadn't shifted from her place at his side. The old man looked back from the doorway with expectation.

"We've met you before," Collin said slowly, wondering if those words would be what broke the fragile ice surrounding them.

The old man beamed. "Yes, several times. I wondered when you'd break through that memory charm. I was a bit disappointed my cousins didn't break it for you."

"You're the obsidian sorcerer," Izzy said evenly.

"I am." He dipped his head graciously. "Artyom, pleased to finally meet you properly."

"You won't make us forget again?" Collin asked, bitterness creeping in despite his caution.

Artyom shrugged. "It would be more effort than it's worth now. I'm growing tired of working from the shadows, anyway."

There was no sign of fear or regret in Artyom's bearing, and his ease chilled Collin to the bone. How many times had they met this man? How many times could he have killed them with ease and chosen not to? Collin couldn't begin to guess why the sorcerer responsible for so much death would choose to leave them alive, and that worried him most of all. He didn't know where they stood here...

but he knew they were in more danger standing before this old man than fighting any ogre or troll.

"If that's the case, then would you answer questions?" Izzy asked.

Collin resisted the temptation to turn to Izzy. What possessed her to ask that? But the sorcerer folded his hands in front of himself and smiled benevolently. The expression made Collin's skin crawl.

"I will," he said. "Of course, if you ask how best to kill me I will lie. But ask anything else, and I will give you the truth."

Collin narrowed his eyes. The ease with which he stood before them, completely ignoring the weapons in their hands, made him wary. Where was his pet wyvern?

The thought came from nowhere, startling him. Wyvern? Foggy memories of threatening hisses and baleful eyes struck him, and he resisted the resurfaced knowledge with desperation. There were more of those memories struggling to break through, more encounters they'd been made to forget. He couldn't afford to let them distract him now.

Artyom was confident he had them outmatched. There was no other reason he would be so genuinely at ease.

"Are you going to kill us after you answer us?" Collin asked.

Artyom chuckled, the scraping sound awaking more memories Collin shoved aside.

"I haven't decided yet." Artyom said. "Probably not. I haven't killed you any other time you came upon me, have I?"

"Why not?" Izzy asked.

The sorcerer's lips twisted in a secretive smile, his eyes darkening. "That's a question I won't answer today. Try again."

When they were slow to speak, the sorcerer leaned against the doorframe and clucked his tongue.

"Come now, speak to grandfather. I'm enjoying a chance to talk to you. Watching you rise through the years has made me...fond of you, in a way. Congratulations on your victory at the tournament.

You're the most worthy of any of them to bear the title of 'guardian.' Not that it means what it used to."

Collin edged closer to Izzy as the sorcerer rambled, wishing he could grab her and flee. Izzy tensed when Artyom mentioned the tournament. Collin held tight to his sword and didn't break eye contact with the man. He wished he could afford to attack him and get it over with, but the more this man said, the more Collin was sure that they stood before a foe far more deadly than any ogre. Their best chance to survive might be to humor him.

"Are you behind the attacks on Kedar?" Collin asked, forcing his voice to stay easy and light.

"I wouldn't go so far as to say I'm *responsible*. Those you call the 'horde' genuinely hate you. I merely...supply them."

Collin didn't ask the natural question following that. He already knew what the sorcerer meant. And he had no intention of satisfying that gloating glint in the man's eyes.

"Did you set the werewolf curse?"

Collin sighed inwardly as Izzy asked the one question he was hoping she'd leave alone.

Artyom sharpened, standing taller as the shadows curled around him.

"In a manner of speaking."

Collin glanced sideways, meeting Izzy's gaze for the briefest moment. *Almighty, deliver us,* Collin prayed. They were in far over their heads.

"But if you're looking for someone to blame," Artyom said. "Look no further than your mighty commander."

Izzy straightened. Collin seized her wrist, squeezing tight in warning, but she spoke anyway.

"The blame belongs to whoever inflicted dark magic against innocent people."

Collin watched with a sinking stomach as Artyom snapped. That smug civility vanished, his face contorting in wild and untamed hatred. Spit flew from his lips as he spoke.

"*Rhett* is the cause of the curse. Bloodshed began with him, and it will not end until he *atones for what he did*."

Collin stepped backward, taking Izzy with him. But Artyom followed them, his shadow reaching out to touch them as he continued.

"If I must take his precious children to finally break him, so be it."

The air around them was thick and heavy, tinged with the sweet scent of rot. He recognized the taste of sorcery. Digging in his pocket, Collin grasped the carved stone inlaid with silver, purchased alongside Izzy's necklace. It was one of the few charms against magic that actually had a chance of diffusing whatever spell Artyom was crafting, as long as it was still captured within the air.

Artyom raised his arms, mouth opening to finish whatever spell he was forming. Collin's heart pounded as he waited for the right moment. He had one chance. He had to make it count. Izzy tugged on his arm, holding her silver-inlaid dagger before them both to ward off what it could. Artyom let out a breath heavy with twisting, malicious words. And Collin leaped into action.

Rather than toss it to the ground, as intended, Collin threw the stone at Artyom's face. He caught it with unnerving ease. But his face twisted from hatred to agony, and he flung the stone from himself like it was a hot coal. Collin was already dragging Izzy backwards when Artyom lifted his eyes, piercing Collin through with his gaze.

"If you betray me to your Red Cloaks," the sorcerer spat, "I will *drive* you so far from each other you will never again witness the same moon. Your lives will end in blood and betrayal!"

That was the last Collin heard as he and Izzy fled down the mountain. He let Izzy chart their path, keeping his own attention at the trees where he expected the wyvern to fall on their heads. But other than the sorcerer's hatred splitting the air, the forest was quiet as they ran.

They didn't stop until they were at the base of the mountain, near their tree. Izzy turned toward him, and Collin crushed her to his chest. Their chests heaved, limbs trembling from exertion, but they stood wrapped in each other's arms until their hearts calmed. All the while, the sorcerer's threat echoed again and again in Collin's mind. *Blood and betrayal.*

"We should go," Izzy said. "We have to tell Rhett."

"No."

Izzy pulled back and stared up at him in disbelief. Collin gripped her a little tighter.

"We don't know what curse he'll use to make good on his threat. I will not let you be taken from me."

Izzy's lips parted, then closed as her jaw set in that stubborn look he knew so well.

"He can't separate us if he's dead."

"But what if he isn't defeated? If something goes wrong, if he targets us, what do you propose we do?"

Izzy shook her head fiercely. "We *can't* keep this to ourselves."

Collin bit back his *why not,* heaving a frustrated breath. When Izzy spoke again, her voice had quieted.

"We can't defeat him on our own, Collin. And he *needs* to be defeated."

Fire and ice raced through Collin's veins, tasting too much like fear. He forced his hands to loosen around her arms before he bruised her, though desperation demanded he hold on tight enough no one could ever take her away from him. He *couldn't* lose her.

And yet he knew she was right. They couldn't take on a sorcerer of this caliber on their own. It was a mercy from the Almighty that they escaped alive today. Artyom had been toying with them for months, perhaps even years, and they'd had no idea.

"We can't trust that he'll leave us alone, no matter what we say," Izzy pressed. "The only way we're safe is if he's dead."

A heavy sigh was dragged from Collin's lips as he stared down at Izzy. He didn't have to say anything: she knew he'd given in.

Izzy threw her arms around Collin's neck, half strangling him with her grip. Collin didn't care. He wrapped his arms around her back, pulling her tighter against himself and burying his face against her neck.

"I won't let *anything*, magic or mundane, take you from me," Izzy whispered.

Collin didn't reply. He couldn't bring himself to point out that there were some things they couldn't guarantee, even fighting together. *That's never stopped us before.* Resignation slowly filled him, deadening the fear with a numbness he despised even more than the weakness of terror. But there was no way to escape it.

"We should go quickly," he said, when Izzy released him. She nodded resolutely.

They ran through most of the forest, pausing only to don their cloaks once more. Neither of them spoke a word, especially when they reached the city gates and were forced to slow. Collin didn't meet the stares of those watching them pass, didn't smile and try to win them over. His mind was fixed on the woman at his side as he fought to convince himself that they weren't dooming themselves with this choice.

Rhett stood in the courtyard, giving orders to the recruits all holding blunt swords aloft. Collin walked up to him, ignoring everyone else in that courtyard.

"We need to speak to you privately," he said.

It only took one glance over the two of them before Rhett was walking toward his office.

"Short break, don't waste it," he announced over his shoulder.

Collin marched two steps behind Rhett, glancing over once when Eldon joined them. None of them said a word until they were in Rhett's study with the door shut behind them. Rhett stepped behind his desk and turned to face them.

"Explain."

"We spoke to the sorcerer supporting the horde," Collin announced. He added bitterly, "Apparently we've spoken to him several times now."

Rhett sat, looking grave. "Tell me everything."

Collin took a breath, dread making his tongue heavy. But once he forced his voice into action, the encounter was dragged from his lips a detail at a time. Including the sorcerer's accusation that Rhett was to blame for the wolf curse.

Rhett changed when Collin repeated the sorcerer's claim, grief aging him two decades as he looked at Eldon. The sight chilled Collin to the bone. *Did* Rhett carry responsibility for the curse?

"You already suspected it was him," Eldon said.

"I was hoping to be proved wrong."

"You know this Artyom," Izzy said, the first words she'd spoken since they'd entered.

Rhett's gaze flicked to her, and he closed off again. "I've interacted with him before, years before you joined us."

"Why would he...

"We'll prepare for an attack immediately," Rhett said, standing. "You will need to mark out exactly where the sorcerer dwells. You are *not* to leave the city until I give the order."

"Why?"

Rhett turned back to face him. "From what you tell me, Artyom knows of your activities. If you return to the forest, you are inviting trouble."

"Will you let us lead the attack against him?" Izzy asked.

Rhett looked them over, his face stern.

"No."

"You think you can protect us from his retribution?" The words slipped from Collin's lips without thought, a fire to his voice that he *knew* was unwise. He didn't even try to hold it in check. "After every threat you've had us face, you'll hold us back *now?*"

"If you believe you have a chance of defeating this foe, you've learned nothing of what I've taught you," Rhett said fiercely. "My decision is made. There *will* be consequences if you disobey me."

He turned on his heel and marched out. Collin and Izzy mutely watched as Eldon glanced back at them with a rueful smile and followed Rhett.

Izzy stepped forward, and Collin followed her out the door numbly. Eldon was taking over the training exercise, his normal good humor strained as he gathered them back together. Collin could see Rhett's back disappearing down a hallway.

Collin didn't move until Izzy grabbed a fistful of his sleeve, tugging him out of view.

"What is he hiding from us?" she hissed as they walked down an abandoned hall.

"I don't know," Collin said. "Dal and Berke might."

"But will they tell us?"

That Collin didn't know. There were a few topics that neither of them would willingly discuss, and Collin didn't doubt that this was one of them. Would Rhett send them to attack the sorcerer and leave Collin and Izzy trapped here, waiting for news?

"I'll see what they'll tell me," he said, though it was a sour thought. Answers were only a small part of what they needed, now. But how far could they push before Rhett stopped turning a blind eye?

Hours later, Collin and Izzy were reclining in the courtyard, soaking up the last warmth in the stone as the air grew chilled, when Liam stumbled in. His cloak was torn, doing little to conceal the deep burn covering his upper arm. Alair and Dal were the first to make it to his side.

"What happened?" Dal asked, throwing Liam's unwounded arm over his shoulder.

"Wyvern attacked us," Liam gasped. "Tallis...he didn't make it."

Collin froze. *Tallis*. He followed Liam's progress toward the infirmary, but inside his mind was reeling. Another loss...another brother fallen. Had Artyom sent his wyvern after Liam and Tallis before their confrontation, or because of it? Collin turned his head, meeting

Izzy's grief-stricken eyes. He didn't look away until movement drew his attention.

Rhett was walking toward the infirmary, his face a grim mask. He paused when he saw Collin and Izzy staring at him, but didn't so much as nod before turning away and disappearing.

Izzy was right. None of them were safe until Artyom was dead. Steely resolve filled his veins as he stared down at Izzy.

"We're joining that attack."

"Agreed."

CHAPTER TEN

Izzy

Izzy walked cautiously, making no noise as she and Collin approached the Red Cloaks Rhett had sent after the sorcerer. They'd sneaked out of Kedar just after muster, making an appearance so Rhett would believe they were following his orders. He'd know better once they failed to arrive to train the recruits, but they were already too deep in the forest for him to stop them.

Izzy clenched her teeth, forcing her head not to turn with the flight of a bird on her left. She was on edge. New moon or not, she wasn't sure this was the right day for this. Sorcerers had sources for their power other than the moon.

But she wasn't about to suggest they turn back. Eldon was out here. Alair, Dal, Berke...their friends. Even Hendrick and Viron, though not close, were still their brothers. She couldn't stand to lose any of them.

Tallis's death was already too much. They'd held his memorial beneath the setting sun: one more marker in the crypt for a Red

Cloak who never made it home. No new name would join that lonely list, not if she had even a prayer of preventing it.

Collin turned, beginning to angle toward the group rather than walk parallel. Izzy stuck close to his side. They still wore their cloaks, standing out far more than Izzy was comfortable with, and once they began approaching they moved quickly. They still emerged from the trees to find half a dozen weapons aimed in their direction.

Izzy stopped, leaning back on her heels as she raised an eyebrow at Dal and the crossbow he aimed at her. He lowered it slowly.

Berke cursed. "We might've shot you."

"With your aim?" Collin retorted.

Eldon stepped toward them, interrupting the pleasantries. His eyes were fire.

"You're supposed to be in Kedar."

Collin said easily, "We decided to join you instead."

Izzy knew no one was convinced by his casual words. There was a hardness to his eyes, a set to his shoulders that made it clear they weren't going anywhere. Izzy stood ramrod straight at his side, hand resting lazily on her sword pommel as she silently challenged any of them to try sending them back.

"You were ordered to stay behind for a reason," Eldon said.

"I'm sure we were. But if the reason isn't important enough to *explain* to us, then it isn't important enough to keep us out of this fight."

The accusation bordered on insubordination. Who was she kidding, it *was* insubordination. But she lifted her chin, standing by his words. They wouldn't be kept in the dark. And they wouldn't let their brothers walk into a serpent's den alone.

Izzy glanced around the group, taking in the guarded looks. She ended by settling her gaze on Eldon, who was scowling with his arms crossed over his chest. He met her gaze, as if asking if she really was party to this.

"We know what we're walking into," she said. "We aren't leaving you to handle it alone."

At that, Eldon looked resigned.

"Berke," he said, gesturing to Izzy.

He unhooked a crossbow from his belt, along with the quiver of darts. She stepped forward to receive them, clipping it into place with the ease of long practice.

"I assume you have your own plans," Eldon said testily.

"The sorcerer apparently enjoys toying with us *specifically*," Collin said. "Hang us out as bait, and we might buy you more time to get into a good position."

Eldon's scowl only deepened.

"Of course that's your plan," Dal said. "Always taking the showy task."

"You'd rather be the bait?" Collin asked, keeping his eyes on Eldon.

Eldon took his time thinking it over, but when he sighed Izzy knew he'd agree to Collin's plan. No matter how much he disliked it, he couldn't deny that it might be the key they needed. Artyom's fascination with her and Collin should serve *some* purpose for good.

"The rest of you, same orders as before," Eldon said. "We can't count on taking him by surprise. Ready yourselves for the worst."

Everyone gave their assent, and Izzy eyed them with apprehension as she walked toward the front of the group. Alair winked at her, and a smile flickered on her lips. But she couldn't stop picturing the crypt, lamplight flickering across the wall of the lost.

Once she and Collin were beside Eldon, he started walking again.

"You're on your own explaining your disobedience to Rhett," Eldon said quietly.

"We know," Collin replied.

"What defenses did you bring?"

Izzy touched the silver inlaid dagger Eldon gave her, and Collin gestured to the silver threaded shirts they wore beneath their armor. She'd noticed the same protection glinting in the sleeves and collars of her comrades' shirts. A glance down revealed silver tipped bolts in her quiver, as well.

Silver inlaid crossbow bolts were too rare and expensive to use on the wall, but it seemed Rhett was sparing no expense on this task. She hoped it was enough. Silver didn't fully cancel out magic, it was merely harder to manipulate. It ensured their weapons couldn't be turned against them. She hoped it would also be enough to slip through any defensive spells Artyom might've set around his home.

Izzy swallowed with difficulty, tugging at the leather cord around her neck. The moonstone charm rested against her chest, still cool to the touch. It never warmed. She'd already grown used to the sensation, but now she couldn't decide if it was a comfort or an ill omen.

They split up before coming within sight of the sorcerer's home. Collin and Izzy continued straight through the trees, planning to step into view in front of the door. Everyone else surrounded the house out of sight. The plan was to close in once Collin and Izzy had Artyom distracted, preventing his escape.

Almighty, guard us and guide us, she prayed silently, taking a slow breath as she loaded her crossbow. Collin had already drawn his sword.

Artyom was standing in the open door when she and Collin stepped into sight. The glint of his teeth bared in a grin made her shudder inside. He spread his arms wide before him, and a chill took the air as a spell built around him. Their time was already up.

"Collin, Izzy. Welcome. I see you've brought friends..."

Izzy raised her crossbow and shot at his face while he still spoke. But it stopped a handbreadth from his nose. The magic Izzy felt building in the air remained, suspended as Artyom tipped his head to look around the bolt. He was still smiling. Her stomach dropped.

"So that's how it will be. Very well."

The sorcery withdrew, like the air itself inhaled. Then Artyom cast his arms outward in a dramatic gesture and flung two dark stones to the ground. Darkness spilled out from the stones in a swirling, devouring fog. It stole her sight before Izzy could reload, as the screeching war cry of goblins came from the north.

Izzy hooked the crossbow to her belt, drawing her sword and putting her back to Collin's. Her eyes flicked around, desperately trying to pierce the darkness as the sounds of battle surrounded them. Their friends.

Would they survive in the dark? Would they cut down one of their brothers in the chaos? A lump filled her throat, and she offered a silent, desperate prayer for their lives as Collin took a step toward the hidden door.

Nothing attacked them, their foes occupied with the rest of the Red Cloaks further out. She kept her shoulder blades pressed to Collin's back as he slowly took them toward where the cottage should be.

He took a final step and his presence disappeared from her back. But he grasped her wrist and pulled her forward before she could stumble, drawing her out of the darkness. Sight returned with a startling suddenness, and she squinted in the cloudy light. She exchanged her sword for her crossbow as she and Collin stepped through the open door.

Artyom stood across the room, scooping vials and half-carved stones into a leather bag. He straightened when they entered. Izzy struggled to reload her crossbow as Artyom retrieved another spell stone from his pocket.

"You two have admirable determination," he said, lobbing the stone in their direction.

Izzy and Collin split apart to avoid the crackling magic. It hit the floor and bled tar-like ooze that snapped with lightning. It spread across the floor. Izzy left Collin to smash the stone, raising her crossbow to take aim. The bolt shot out, aimed for his heart. But once more it stopped before reaching his skin.

He flicked away the bolt with an indulgent smile that curdled her insides.

"You do realize such repetition it futile. You might..."

He cut off when Izzy leapt at him with her gifted dagger, having discarded the crossbow for a weapon surer to leave a mark. He fell back before the weapon, lifting his hands in a strange gesture. A hastily spoken word threw Izzy across the room. Her back slammed into the wall, and she fell in a crouch.

Her limbs shook as she stood, feeling like someone had shoved a torch into her ribcage. She glanced and Collin and met his worried gaze.

"You should've listened to me," Artyom said, his voice echoing in the small space. "I admire you, I really do. You have the same unbreakable will as another young man I once knew."

Izzy forced herself to take a step away from the wall, raising her dagger in front of herself as weapon and shield as magic suffocated the air around her.

"But perhaps your lives were also meant to end in tragedy."

She and Collin were creeping toward him. Izzy kept a close eye on the two black stones he was rolling in his hands, waiting for the moment he'd inflict his magic on them once more. Her very bones ached, but she gritted her teeth and prepared herself to lunge.

A ghostly chuckle drew her gaze upward in time to see the smile creeping across Artyom's face.

"Tell Rhett it will all end soon. His child soldiers will join his fate."

Collin and Izzy leapt forward at once. Artyom's hands twisted once more, and another muttered phrase flung Collin across the room. Izzy kept moving, thrusting her dagger toward his unguarded stomach.

It plunged through open air.

Izzy hit the ground on a roll. When she was back on her feet, she twisted...Artyom was gone. Her eyes met Collin's where he knelt on the floor, one hand pressed to his shoulder. Helpless terror washed through her, and her hands shook. They'd failed. *Oh heavens, what evil will he create now?*

Collin stood slowly, his gaze heavy, and somehow Izzy found the strength to follow. Artyom might have disappeared, but he'd left his ambush intact. Only a heartbeat more passed before they both turned toward the door, surging back into the darkness to help their friends.

CHAPTER ELEVEN

Izzy

Izzy's toe brushed against the broken shards of obsidian. She's stumbled upon it through pure mercy. Once the first was broken, the darkness faded to a twilight haze that they were able to fight through. Miraculously, none of their number had died. But that didn't mean they'd come out unscathed. She and Collin were the only ones uninjured, unless she counted the deep ache from being tossed around like rag dolls.

Izzy winced at Alair's pained cries. Collin was helping extract the poisoned quills from his back, while Dal bound the wound on his arm to slow the bleeding. She and Berke were searching for the second stone so they could dispel this unnatural haze while Eldon took a look at what Artyom left behind.

Izzy glanced up, but Collin wouldn't look at her. Her throat swelled as she lowered her eyes back to the ground. She took a shaky inhale. He was right in his reluctance. Alive and free, there was nothing stopping Artyom from making good on his threat. What revenge would he choose?

She'd barely begun to imagine all the ways he could separate them before she crushed each thought to dust. She would not be torn from Collin's side, no matter what dark magic Artyom worked. She glanced up at the sky, though the moon wasn't visible.

Izzy crushed that thought too. Werewolves only came from bloodlines intwined with the moon folk. Her family and Collin's had dwelt in Kedar for generations without count. They were safe from the curse.

That voice whispered again, *your sister wasn't invulnerable.* But her sister was the foil, not the wolf. And half of her sister's lineage Izzy didn't share.

Obsidian glinted below her, catching the light she still couldn't see. She crouched, bringing the hilt of her dagger down on the obsidian with all the strength left in her arm. Darkness rolled back like night fleeing the sunrise. A sigh slipped from her lips as the oppressive taste of sorcery faded from the air.

Glancing up again, she found Collin watching her. Their eyes locked, and Izzy's heart sped until she felt every beat pulse in her head. Her gaze swam with the sudden heat, and she ripped her eyes away. She forced air in and out of her lungs as she stared at the leaf-strewn ground.

She was allowing herself to be emotional. But she couldn't afford to be overwrought, not this far from safety. She didn't have time for fear and regret until they were all back within Kedar's walls.

Eldon left the small house with a sack thrown over his shoulder. He limped from a bite on his thigh, but his expression revealed nothing but resolute authority.

"Time to leave," he said. "Izzy, Hendrick, take rear guard. Collin, lead us out of this place. We need the quickest path back to Kedar."

Izzy mutely took her place, glancing once at Hendrick. His gaze was stormy, and her eyes strayed to the bloodstained cloth tied around his arm before she focused on forest around them. Her hands flexed around her sword and dagger as they began walking.

If they were attacked, they would lose someone. Alair couldn't even walk on his own.

Please protect us, she prayed, searching the trees for enemies. *Please guide our next actions.*

She couldn't know what Artyom would do next, but she had no doubt that his retribution would be brutal. She wasn't prepared to face the consequences of their failure today.

Collin

Collin didn't glance at the carved blessing as they entered the Red Cloaks' estate. Viron and Hendrick took Alair toward the infirmary, others crowding around for any information on what had happened. Most went to Dal and Berke for explanations.

There must've been something in Collin's bearing that gave away his ill mood. He was glad for it. A dull fire still ached in his ribs from Artyom throwing him with his magic, and the pain only fueled the blaze of fury filling his head. He was in no place to answer meaningless questions.

Eldon had already disappeared in Rhett's office to report. He was surprised he hadn't demanded he and Izzy follow him to answer for their disobedience. Collin assumed it meant he'd found something in the sorcerer's belongings that he didn't intend to reveal to Collin and Izzy, which only stoked his fury.

Spotting Dal and Berke separating themselves from the frenzy, Collin marched toward them. They watched him approach warily, not resisting when Collin grabbed their sleeves and tugged them somewhere more private.

"Tell us what you know about that sorcerer," Collin said, releasing them and taking a step backward.

"We don't know much," Dal said. "Most of its old rumor."

"We still have a right to know," Izzy said.

Izzy. Even the sound of her voice drove a fracture through his chest, his heart pounding as though he was sprinting. How was he supposed to protect her when their enemy had escaped into the shadows?

Berke and Dal glanced between Collin and Izzy before Dal sighed.

"There was a man called Iah who joined us, about a year before I took my vows. He wasn't from Kedar. One morning he showed up and demanded to speak to Rhett alone, the next morning he was training alongside the rest of us. Not long after that, Rhett began taking teams out to the forest to eliminate small groups of moon sorcerers who'd settled around Kedar. Iah always went with them."

"You think he knew about them," Collin said.

"The rumor was he was related to one of them," Dal said. "That he came to our side to help protect Kedar against whatever they were planning."

"Artyom escaped Rhett's attacks?" Izzy asked.

Dal shrugged. "I assume so. He's using the same methods as before, as far as I can tell."

"He is," Berke said. "And Iah was definitely mixed in with it before he came to us. They all knew him. It didn't stop him from killing as many as the rest of us, though."

"Why haven't we heard about him?" Izzy asked.

Collin had been about to ask the same thing. Gossip and rumor passed swiftly through the Red Cloaks, and a good story would be told for years after it happened.

"He and Rhett's daughter Tahlia were...close," Dal said. "He was involved in her death, and after that we all knew better than to talk about it."

Collin opened his mouth to ask involved *how*, but Berke spoke over him.

"Only Rhett and Eldon know how she and Iah died, and none of the rumors have enough weight to make them worth anything."

"I know Rhett didn't like Iah getting close with Tahlia," Dal added. "He added to the vows around then, but they refused to take them. I thought for a day or two that Rhett would back off and revert to the old vows, but..."

"They both got killed, and Rhett kept the new vows," Berke finished. "The wolf curse started three moons after that."

Collin leaned back, not daring to look at Izzy.

"I've heard Rhett watched her die," Izzy said quietly. "Is that..."

"As far as I know," Berke said. "It happened in the forest, but he came back carrying her body."

Now Collin looked down, needing to see Izzy's thoughts. Fear was hidden deep within her gaze. What had happened that night, the reason Iah and Tahlia had died...Artyom believed Rhett was responsible. And as little as Collin trusted the sorcerer's word, it seemed Rhett *had* been involved. But what part did he play?

Mercer distracted them all, speaking in a voice that carried across the courtyard.

"I don't know why this was hidden from us."

Collin turned to face Mercer, his shoulder brushing against Izzy's. Rhett hadn't announced the mission against the sorcerer that morning. Collin wondered what rumors had already spread.

"If more of us were involved, perhaps whatever this task was would've been a *success*."

Collin flicked his eyes to Rhett standing a few paces away. He didn't interrupt Mercer, but the scowl and set of his shoulders made it clear that Mercer's outburst wouldn't go unpunished. Collin almost pitied him. Apparently Mercer hadn't yet learned that Rhett's silence was far more dangerous than his scolding.

Mercer flung a hand in Collin and Izzy's direction. "They disobeyed orders. We *all* know it. And yet here they stand, uninjured and unrepentant. How many times will they be allowed to do as they please while the rest of us are held back?"

"I will handle their disobedience," Rhett growled. "Just as I will handle yours if you say another word on the matter."

Mercer glared at Rhett, his hands curling to fists at his side. But he turned his glare to the ground and bowed his head.

"You're dismissed."

Mercer stomped off in silence, not even his friends following his path.

Rhett turned, and dread twisted in the pit of Collin's stomach.

"Follow. Now."

Collin held his head up as he walked across the courtyard, not meeting anyone's eyes though he felt their stares. He knew without looking that Izzy did the same. He also knew that she was nearly overwhelmed. Her defenses wouldn't hold much longer.

If only he could take her away somewhere, to hold her until the confidence in every line of her body was more than a lie. It half killed him to walk into Rhett's office without so much as a glance back at her. He didn't know what punishment Rhett would inflict, but he trusted it would be painful. Their disobedience wasn't so forgivable with Alair half dead and the sorcerer who-knew-where.

Izzy closed the door behind them, and silence overtook the room as Rhett rounded his desk. He met their eyes with an iron stare.

"I expected better."

Out of the corner of his eye, he saw Izzy flinch.

"Do you believe me to be incompetent?"

Rhett's voice was dark and calm, but his eyes were seething. He hadn't seen Rhett this angry for years. Collin held still and didn't answer.

"Do you doubt that I understand the full danger of a sorcerer as powerful as we've witnessed?"

Again, he nor Izzy answered. Now wasn't the time to offer a defense. Rhett leaned across the desk toward them, fingers curled into claws digging at the wood, as his words fell like a hammer on steel.

"Have you lost all trust in my leadership?"

Silence stretched on, heavy as it picked against Collin's mind.

When it was clear Rhett expected an answer, Collin reluctantly spoke.

"After seeing what this sorcerer is capable of, we weren't willing to leave our brothers to fight him alone."

"That wasn't your decision," Rhett snapped.

Izzy's voice broke in, heavy with repressed emotion.

"Since the day we took our vows, you have ordered us into the fire without looking back. And now that it comes to the battle that could determine the fate of everything we're meant to protect, we're supposed to sit quietly and *wait?*"

"Yes," Rhett barked. "Because that is what I ordered. I know this threat far better than either of you, and I trusted you to *obey me*."

It was Collin's turn to break, looking away to the wall behind Rhett's back. Blind obedience had never been his strong suit. But breaking Rhett's trust...that hurt.

"We have a right to fight for our lives, whether you allow it or not," Izzy said.

Collin tensed. What would Rhett take from those words? They hadn't told him of the sorcerer's threat...Collin didn't want him to know *now* of all times. Keeping his eyes forward, rather than turn to look at Izzy, took every scrap of willpower Collin had in him.

Rhett straightened, his tone suddenly low and calm.

"What do you mean by that?"

Izzy was panicking. He could feel it. One glance down revealed her desperately searching for words, and a pleading glance in his direction sealed his decision.

"Did you think we wouldn't notice this sorcerer's obsession with us?" Collin asked, praying he wasn't digging them a deeper hole. "Red Cloaks come back scarred, maimed. Others never come back at all. But we have multiple encounters with this sorcerer and all he does is charm our memories away?"

Collin paused, staring at Rhett and searching for any sign, any hint that he would explain. But Rhett only stared back, as expressive as a stone wall.

"There's something about us that makes the sorcerer treat us differently," Collin continued. "You may not see fit to tell us why, but that won't stop us from using it to our advantage."

"And doom yourselves in the process."

There was a wildness to his gaze that Collin didn't recognize, a fury in his words that took him aback. Thus far Rhett had kept his voice quiet to prevent any eavesdropping from outside, but Collin had no doubt *those* words had carried beyond the thick walls. Collin leaned on his heels and said nothing, wondering just what Rhett knew that made him lose control at the thought of Collin and Izzy risking themselves.

It was Izzy who answered, softly. "But we're doomed already, aren't we?"

Doomed already. Those words were an itch deep in his soul, picking at his sanity. The sorcerer's words rang through his head, that their lives were always meant to end in tragedy. Collin didn't believe in fate. But the thought that their downfall was already inevitable still struck a new terror deep in his soul. And meeting Rhett's gaze, he saw that terror mirrored back at him.

Rhett looked away, gathering himself so quickly that anyone who knew him less would doubt what they'd seen. Collin knew better. Rhett was frightened, and that in itself spelled out doom.

Rhett stared at the moon map, tapping his finger on the edge of his desk. When he turned back to them, his gaze was set as steel.

"You are forbidden from leaving the city until ordered otherwise. If you disobey, the consequences *will* be harsh. I'll have no one question my execution of justice."

"What would you have us do in the meantime?" Collin asked.

"Are you asking us to *stop* seeking a way to save Kedar?" Izzy added.

"You've sought and found nothing," Rhett said coldly. "Now leave my sight."

Collin leaned against the cold wall, staring out at the silhouettes of broken pots and a cart likely twice as old as he was. The Red Cloaks' compound didn't share walls with anything else; Collin assumed whatever Governor oversaw its construction didn't want to brush shoulders with the common people. Along the front the wall faced the road, but back by the kitchens that separation meant there was a narrow corridor between the wall from the next houses. It was one of the hidden corners of Kedar, mostly used to house useless things that were soon forgotten. Collin knew that the house above him was empty.

He rubbed at his chest, frowning at the burn that had yet to fade. How much of Artyom's spell still lingered for it to ache so fiercely? With as much as he'd studied sorcerers, he didn't know if this lingering shadow should worry him or not. All he'd done was throw them across the room. But with sorcery nothing was as it first appeared.

The tree above him rustled, distracting him from his troubled thoughts. Collin smiled to himself as he waited. Soon enough Izzy dropped the stone just before him. The only part of her he could really see was her hair, glinting silver in the scant starlight that made it into this shadowed alley.

She'd barely straightened when he reached out, pulling her to his chest. She pushed back.

"We can't risk..."

"Don't overthink it," Collin hissed, keeping her close.

She stayed tense, but Collin didn't relax his grip. Slowly, reluctantly, she melted against him. He closed his eyes as she wrapped her arms around his back. Warmth rose in his chest, digging talons into his flesh. It demanded that he hold her closer, that he rid the world of any who would try and separate them. Even those who thought they meant well.

Collin grit his teeth, revoking that last thought. He wouldn't confuse enemy and friend, not even if they tried standing between him and Izzy.

They couldn't afford to go to their hideout tonight. Too many people were watching them, and the longer they were gone the greater the chance someone would notice. But Collin *needed* time alone with her. Based on how tightly she held onto him now, Izzy needed it too.

If this was all he got, one moment of holding her, the risk was worth it.

Izzy shifted, and Collin held tighter to keep her from pulling away, but she merely tugged them down until they were sitting against the wall. She twisted to lay her head on his chest with a sigh that sounded like it came from her soul. Collin buried his nose in her hair and breathing deeply as a breeze sent leaves cascading around them. He brushed one from Izzy's shoulder.

There was no moon tonight. As they sat there, clouds devoured what little starlight shone and left them in silken darkness. Collin didn't mind. The rest of his senses were consumed with the woman in his arms, and the darkness only added to the sense that it for this moment it was *just* them. No watchers, no accusers, no gossipers. Just them.

How he longed to claim her outside of the shadows.

"Everything went wrong today," Izzy whispered.

That was all it took for dreads and doubts to come careening back into Collin's mind. He sighed and pressed his lips to Izzy's head for one more moment. Then he leaned his head against the cold stone at their backs.

"It would've gone worse if we'd been on our own," he admitted.

"But you were right," Izzy said, her voice thick with the tears he knew she was fighting not to shed. "What if we can't fight against whatever he does to take his revenge? What if he drives us apart?"

Collin's arm flexed, holding her closer to his side. His voice came out in a low growl.

"He won't."

Izzy was silent for a moment, and far in the distance thunder filled the sky. More leaves fell around them as the wind picked up.

"I wish Rhett would *tell* us what he knows rather than insisting on shielding us."

"You think that's what he's doing?"

"You disagree?"

Collin considered it, remembering the wild look in Rhett's eyes. He didn't disagree. Rhett was trying to get them *out* of the sorcerer's focus.

"There's more to Rhett's story with this sorcerer than anyone is telling us," Collin said. "And somehow we've been dragged into the middle of it."

Izzy twisted to look up at him. "That's obvious."

He could barely see the edges of her smile, but temptation washed over him with new, fervent heat. Temptation to kiss her until all thought of sorcerers and Rhett's secrets melted away, to discover what it felt like to have her face cradled in his hands and his lips against hers.

It was hardly the first time such thoughts had struck. But tonight they were harder to resist. It was Izzy who broke the moment, turning her head to lay on his chest again. Collin tried to banish the disappointment, the frustration, and readjusted his arms around her. This was enough. It *needed* to be enough.

CHAPTER TWELVE

Izzy

Izzy tightened her belt, her sword and dagger a comfortable weight against her hips. Collin was still searching for his preferred knife on the rack, muttering about ignorant recruits as he did. A tired smile stretched her lips as she watched him.

They wouldn't need their weapons. Rhett hadn't assigned them anything beyond training the recruits for three days, and Izzy doubted that would change anytime soon. At this point she wondered if he'd keep them within the city until they went mad simply to make his point. Or perhaps he really did believe he was protecting them. What would he do, she wondered, if he knew Artyom attended their tournament? That he walked Kedar unknown and unmolested?

But what would the point be? To prove to Rhett that Artyom had no fear of them, that he could stand comfortably in the midst of Kedar's protectors and emerge unscathed? She doubted it would change Rhett's mind.

She couldn't forget it, though. Most of her memories of meeting

Artyom were still foggy, but not the tournament. Not the look in his eyes when he realized Izzy saw him. It sent a shudder deep within her. At any moment he could take his revenge.

Izzy bit her tongue and tried to force away those thoughts, to bottle up her fear and hide it away where it wouldn't torment her. It didn't work as well as it usually did. She must be a coward at heart, because deep down she hoped desperately that they wouldn't have to face Artyom's retribution on their own. She *wanted* Rhett's protection. She wanted it to be enough.

And yet, if it took hiding away in these halls to be safe, she would rather run to the battle. She had never lain passive and let others decide the course of her life, not when she had any chance of making her own choice. And she doubted the Almighty would be pleased if she and Collin waited for events to unfold without them simply because the risk was now personal.

A shadow blocked the morning light filtering through the door, and Izzy glanced back to see Mercer walking toward them. He glared, though his lips slowly twisted in a smirk. He ran his shoulder into Collin's as he passed.

Collin turned to watch Mercer's back with a narrowed gaze, but when he looked back at Izzy he only shrugged. She didn't like that Mercer looked pleased with himself, but it wasn't worth starting a confrontation. They left without glancing back.

Most on duty were already gathered in the hall. Collin's searching nearly made them late, and Izzy glanced over with a raised eyebrow. He rolled his eyes as they wove their way toward the bench were Dal already sat. He moved his feet before Izzy could kick him, winking as she took a seat.

"The bruising is improving," Izzy said. "I can see both of your eyes now."

"I live for your compliments, Izzy," Dal replied drily, gently touching the blue bruising around his eye.

Something jostled their bench, and Izzy peered around Collin to see Alair taking a seat beside him. He looked awful, dark circles beneath his eyes only emphasizing the sallow tone to his skin. One arm was still in a sling. But the fact that he was strong enough to come was cause for relief.

"Are you sure you're supposed to be out of bed?" Collin asked.

"Don't kid yourself," Alair said with a sideways look. "I don't intend to lift anything heavier than a dinner knife. But even the nurses agreed that I needed to get out for a bit."

"I know the feeling," Collin muttered.

"Restricted to the city is hardly the same as being strapped to a bed."

"You were not strapped down," Izzy said.

"There were threats. Anyway, it's good to show everyone I'm still kicking. Andred said people were already planning my funeral."

"Not us," Collin said. "You're too stubborn to die in a bed."

"Exactly. Where's the glory there?"

"And of course glory is the main consideration," Izzy said drily.

Dal elbowed her. "Personally, I'd rather die a withered old man in my bed."

Everyone quieted as Rhett and Eldon stood at the front of the room.

"Dietrich, take Lewis and Anson to the road south. We have reports of threats to travelers in Mount Talith's shadow. Dal and Berke, you'll be taking the trainees west for training today."

Dal groaned, and Izzy almost smiled. Except if Dal and Berke had the new pups, what were she and Collin to do? Rhett wouldn't meet their eyes as he continued giving out assignments.

He finished without mentioning Izzy and Collin, and Izzy turned to see what Collin thought of it. Movement caught her eye beyond him as someone stood. It was Mercer.

When Rhett paused, Mercer spoke loudly, "I have oath-breakers to report."

Dread blossomed in her stomach. His smirk, the way his eyes had trailed after them... He couldn't mean them. They'd been careful.

"We'll discuss it in private," Rhett said.

"We'll discuss it *here*," Mercer countered. "I won't let you sweep it under the rug for the sake of protecting your chosen ones."

"Mercer," Rhett barked. "Sit down and be silent."

Mercer ignored him, turning instead to gesture in Izzy and Collin's direction. Adrenaline thrummed in her veins, and her hand gripped her sword hilt as his eyes met hers with a malicious pleasure.

"Collin and Izzy have forsaken their vow of celibacy. They've been engaging in an illicit relationship for months, if not years."

Izzy stiffened, blood draining from her face as she met Mercer's smug satisfaction. Silence yawned in the room until she swore they could hear her pounding heart announcing her guilt. What could she do?

Nothing. She couldn't fight her way out of this. She couldn't run. All she could do is wait for the blade to fall and pray it wouldn't end everything.

"You better have definitive proof for an accusation that serious," Eldon said, his expression stormy. His fury was a hollow comfort. He knew the truth...there was only so much he could say to protect them.

It took every scrap of willpower and practice to keep her face impassive, and she had little self-control left over. Her fingers found Collin's without thought, and he squeezed her hand briefly before pulling away. Her heart broke a little at the absence.

"I've seen them sneak out of the compound at night five times in the past two months," Mercer said. "And sneaking back in thrice."

How? How had he seen them *that* many times without their knowledge? As Mercer laid out his accusation, Izzy glanced at Rhett. The grim set of his face stood at odds with the look he gave her, a moment of regret so brief she doubted she'd seen it. Izzy looked down.

"Who knows what other duties they've neglected to share one another's bed."

Izzy's head snapped up, and Collin stood so abruptly the bench rocked.

"Say one more word about Izzy's virtue, and I'll cut out your tongue," he snarled.

A few of the newer Red Cloaks quailed at the sound of his voice, but Mercer only crossed his arms over his chest and raised an eyebrow.

"Protective of your lover, are you?"

Collin took a step toward him. Dal and Alair stood on either side of him before Izzy realized they'd moved, gripping Collin's shoulders and telling him to sit down.

"This isn't helping your case," Dal said, quietly but fervently.

They were hardly audible as Rhett's voice filled the room.

"We do not deal in speculation and slander. Is this your only evidence?"

Izzy stood too, her shoulder brushing against Dal's. He didn't look at her, and she wasn't sure if he still stood there in a show of loyalty or to stop Collin from attacking Mercer. Either way, she was glad they didn't stand alone. It was a single, phantom comfort, but it was something to hold on to. This wasn't enemy territory, this was their *home*. Surely that would count for something.

Except she knew it wouldn't, not if any part of Mercer's claim could be proven.

Time seemed to trickle on impossibly slow, a dozen dreadful possibilities passing through her mind, before Mercer spoke. Had he really seen them?

"I followed them three nights ago and found them in a position reserved for married couples."

Izzy's faced burned, injustice rising to choke her. It was true, the way Collin held her that night *was* usually reserved for married couples. But she and Collin had *never* gone as far as Mercer was implying.

"All from the mouth of a single witness who's made no secret of his jealousy," Alair said, his voice strong even though he was leaning on Collin for support. "Accusations in *this* order rely on more than one man's word."

That was true. But even if all Mercer had was his own claims, he'd done his damage. She didn't dare look at Rhett.

"I'm not the only one who's witnessed their misconduct."

Collin snorted at the word, crossing his arms over his chest. Izzy wished she could be so dismissive. It was all she could do to keep her panic from showing on her face and condemn them both.

It wasn't one of the men seated around Mercer who stood, but someone near the front. He glanced around the room with wide, nervous eyes and Izzy's heart fell to see it was Isley. Collin faltered beside her. Isley glanced once at Rhett, half facing him, before dropping his gaze and speaking.

"I have come across Collin and Izzy in private moments. Their conduct goes beyond friends or comrades, particularly in their... embraces."

Izzy turned to Rhett. He met her gaze, and the world dropped out from beneath her feet. There was no mercy in his bearing.

"I remember a case a few years ago," Mercer said. "A red cloak got his lover pregnant and received thirty-nine lashes before the city as punishment. I wonder how that compares."

Izzy swallowed with difficulty, clenching her jaw so tight her teeth ached. She remembered that day, too. Remembered the cries, and blood, and standing beneath the hot sun forced to watch his humiliation. A brief glance around revealed that all their friends had averted their eyes. A chill spread through her heart. Would their own order turn on them as Izzy's own neighbors had?

"Will you ignore their disobedience when it's laid out for all to see?" Mercer asked.

Izzy's heart pounded in the silence, though only three beats passed before someone else stood. It was Hendrick. His solemn gaze only heightened her dread, though he focused his gaze solely on Mercer.

"Sit down, and for moon's sake *shut up*," Hendrick said. "I'm tired of listening to your whining."

"You—"

Hendrick spoke over him. "Everyone with eyes in this city knows Collin and Izzy share a bond deeper than most, and that they're two of our best warriors because of it."

At this point, Izzy wasn't sure if Hendrick's words were support or further condemnation.

"They could spit in Commander Rhett's face and still be the pride of this order." Mercer said bitterly.

"No," Hendrick said evenly. "They must abide by our rules like anyone else. They should be punished."

Izzy's heart fell, and she was scarcely aware of Dal steadying her.

"But getting a girl with child and refusing to take responsibility is a far cry from a few embraces after battle," Hendrick continued. "And I, for one, am not willing to lose two of our strongest defenders for the sake of one man's wounded pride."

She supposed that was the best defense she could hope for. Their friends' silence hadn't escaped her. Izzy had thought they'd been so careful, so secretive...but how obvious were they in truth? Had their disobedience merely been *overlooked* by those who knew them best?

Eldon spoke up for the first time. "We have time to investigate your claims more fully..."

Mercer puffed up to say something, but Rhett cut him off.

"Speak another word, and you will face lashes as well."

As well. Izzy's heart slowed, a curious numbness overtaking her as Rhett turned his gaze to her and Collin. She knew it was inevitable now. The only question that remained was how harsh their punishment would be.

"How do you answer this accusation?" he asked, void of all emotion.

For the barest moment, Izzy wondered if they could deny it, if they could explain it all away as Mercer twisting the truth and Isley misunderstanding. She dismissed it before the idea fully formed. She wouldn't lie. She wouldn't deny Collin.

"I don't deny Isley's accusation," Collin said, and pride grew in her heart at how steady his voice was. "Nor do I deny that we seek out time alone outside the compound."

"Nor do I deny it," Izzy said.

Collin added in a growl, "What I *do* deny are Mercer's description of our *actions* while alone. Our virtue remains intact."

Embarrassment colored Izzy's cheeks, and she struggled to keep her head up. The accusation, false as it was, brought shame slithering through her gut.

Izzy waited with held breath for Rhett's response. He could press them. He could demand that they share, in detail, what they *did* do while alone. He could force them to either lie regarding their motive, or to admit before everyone that their love for one another was far different than brother and sister in arms. She trembled at the thought of what would follow that confession.

"Collin Fastoff and Izzy Pryor," Rhett said dispassionately. "For disobedience and for misconduct, you will submit to five lashes."

Izzy blinked, leaning toward Collin. Dal squeezed her shoulder before retreating.

"Dietrich, Viron. Take them outside. This will be settled within our own order. And *anyone* who carries tales or accusations outside these walls will face the same."

Izzy hardly noticed the glare Rhett aimed at Mercer, or the stricken look Eldon wore as he followed Rhett toward the door. Nor did she resist when Viron laid a hand on her shoulder and began leading her toward the door, though separation from Collin felt like she'd leapt from a cliff.

That numb futility lasted until they were outside, to a forgotten corner of the compound with a post driven deep into the ground. It was so seldom used most ignored its presence. The sight of it drove a wedge into her soul. The fullness of what she was about to face washed over her like cold water as Viron began removing her weapons and armor.

She was stripped to the thin-strapped camisole she wore beneath her shirt before being led to the post. Collin's back and chest were bare, and she fought not to look. Not now, not when it was shameful.

"Collin first," Rhett said dispassionately.

"No," Izzy said.

Her voice shook, but still she raised her head to stare at Rhett. A fire flickered in her chest, unquenched by the dread and shame washing over her, and it crackled hotter as she glared at her commander.

"If we're being punished for time spent together, we will face that punishment *together.*"

Rhett stared back at her until she thought his gaze would burn through her skin, but he nodded. They were both led to the post, their hands bound to a metal ring set above their heads. The vulnerability of the position settled fear close to her bones. There would be no resisting. But she could see Collin, and she stared into his eyes as her only lifeline.

He stood tall and tense, fury in every line of his body. But unshed tears glinted in his eyes with a silent, heart wrenching apology.

It's alright, she wanted to tell him. *Pain is nothing. Not as long as we're together.*

But she knew if she opened her mouth, her composure would shatter. So she clenched her jaw and spoke only with her eyes.

Eldon walked behind Collin, uncoiling the rope in his hands. Which meant Rhett stood behind her. She only met his gaze briefly before looking away, not willing to accept the apology in his eyes while he held that dreaded whip. He might hate this. But he would still follow Rhett's orders.

Izzy fisted her hands, tense as a bowstring as she waited for it to begin. But Collin shifted, grasping at her fingers, and she took hold of his hands with all the strength of desperation. What those watching might think of the gesture was only a fluttering leaf at the back of her mind, soon disappearing entirely. Let this further condemn them. She didn't care.

"Obedience," Rhett said.

The first lash fell like fire across her back. She bit back a cry, shoulders flexing as tears burned in her eyes. She didn't look away from Collin, though witnessing the agony twisting his face was worse than her own pain.

"Integrity."

The second lash fell before she was ready. Her fingers spasmed in Collin's grasp, and his hold tightened. Her knees trembled, terror running along her veins as she waited for the third. Yet, when it fell she held her silence. And with the fourth. She would not give Mercer or anyone else the pleasure of listening to her pain. She would not break before them, not for this. Even as she felt the whip tear across her ribs and shoulder-blades, ripping through her skin as vengefully as any blade, she kept her lips *shut*. Her legs threatened to buckle after the fifth lash, but Collin held on and she found the will to keep standing.

The silence was deafening. Izzy didn't move, didn't speak, didn't even breathe. And she never took her eyes away from Collin.

"Return to the hall," Rhett ordered with that wretched dispassion. "Collin and Izzy will be released at midday. Their punishment is complete and sealed. No one will speak of it."

Shuffling footsteps marked the order's obedience. She knew a few hesitated before turning away, knew that Eldon was one of them. But she didn't try to look at any of them. It was only when they were alone, finally alone, that she let her head fall against the post.

"I love you, Starlight," Collin whispered, his words hardly more than a pained breath as he held her hand. "I love you."

CHAPTER THIRTEEN

Collin

Collin looked around, silently greeting those on the street who met his gaze. Fewer looked at him than he was used to. Hardly anyone had offered any show of respect as they'd walked through Kedar. He didn't miss the strange show of homage, but the change concerned him. Dal had told him public opinion of the Red Cloaks had plummeted since the last wolf was killed in the street in front of neighbors and loved ones. Apparently, Rhett's tournament hadn't improved anything. Collin couldn't say it hadn't had some effect, though: no one shook their fist at them, no matter how much anger simmered in their averted eyes.

It was easier to watch the strangers surrounding them than Izzy, her face a mask and her back arrow-shaft straight. He walked the same way. The slightest shift of his shoulder blades tugged at the scabs across his back, reawakening the fire he really wished he could forget. But he knew for Izzy it was more than that. It was the weight of the stares behind them, the new recruits who hadn't met their eyes all morning but who certainly watched them when their backs were turned. They'd all witnessed their whipping. And though they'd thus far kept to Rhett's orders not to mention Collin and Izzy's punishment, it was obvious they were thinking about it.

Collin knew vengeance wasn't his to take, but it was still a fortunate thing that he hadn't seen Mercer since his accusation. If they crossed paths alone, Collin wasn't sure if his will would be strong enough to walk silently by.

The three recruits walking behind him spoke in hushed tones, and Collin listened without turning around. He'd tried to break the tension, at first. Now he found he didn't care enough to try.

Neither of them had spoken to Rhett or Eldon since it happened. Not when Eldon untied them from the whipping post and told them to get to the infirmary. Not when Rhett failed to mention their names during assignments the day after, or that morning when he told Collin and Izzy to familiarize a few recruits with every weak point in the city wall. He was happy to keep that silence.

A commotion to his right drew his eyes, and he found a haggard young woman being held up by a few older women. Or held back. Her eyes fixed on Collin and Izzy with a wild intensity.

"Go away," she cried. "Leave us alone. Haven't you done enough?"

Collin heard Izzy's sighed, "oh no" and realized why the woman looked familiar. The foil...the woman who watched her transformed lover die in the streets hardly two weeks ago. One of the recruits tried to sweep forward, but Collin raised his arm to forestall him.

"He's dead. Isn't that enough? He's *dead*!" She bent over double. "Haven't you tormented us *enough*?"

Collin glanced down and found Izzy white as a sheet as she stared at the bereaved woman. Her words had dissolved into sobs, and she clung to the gray-haired woman at her side. Izzy raised her fist to her heart and bowed silently.

Collin turned back to the crowd. "We grieve your loss."

An unfamiliar man stepped forward, red with fury. "You have no right to pretend you share in her grief."

Collin didn't respond right away, looking around to measure the situation. He saw only two emotions in the many people surrounding him: anger and fear. None of it aimed at the Red Cloaked recruits at his back, *just* at Izzy and himself. His chest grew cold and heavy.

"We didn't mean any offense," he said. "We'll move on."

"Why are you here in the first place?" a woman demanded, gaining courage from the rage of her companions.

Collin thought he'd seen her mourning the wolf, as well, though her face was hardly recognizable contorted in rage and grief.

"It isn't enough you look on in our mourning. Now you invade our normal lives as well? We can't even pass a crescent moon without your bloody forms walking our streets, watching all?"

This was quickly getting out of hand. Collin took a step back, brushing a hand against Izzy's shoulder to draw her back with him. But Sabriel stepped forward past Collin's shoulder, his own expression tight with insult.

"Show some respect," he growled. "You have no idea what these two have done to protect you."

Collin wanted to groan. He also wanted to grab Sabriel and drag him back to headquarters by his shirt collar. But the deed was done now, and the first man to speak up took another threatening step forward. Of course, Collin saw plainly that his shaking fists had little to do with his anger. He feared Collin and Izzy's retribution.

"And what do you claim to protect us from as we bury our sons and daughters? Do you believe the wolf will return even from that silver bound tomb? Or do you look on to ensure we follow your *commander's* orders?"

"That's not..."

Izzy fell silent, realizing what Collin had: nothing they said would convince these people of anything. They were searching for someone to blame. Apparently, he and Izzy made convenient targets. At this point, it was a matter of finding the path of retreat that would do the least amount of harm.

"What's the problem here?"

When Collin turned to find half a dozen helmets glinting in the sunlight, he wondered if this day would continue getting worse. A squad of watchmen was hardly what they needed to calm these people down. But he recognized the man leading them: it was Brenner, the watchman who helped them carry Tay through the city. Collin found concern in his steady gaze, not wariness.

None of the people answered, most of them staring intently at their own feet. Apparently they still held the watch with respect, or at least were wary of the possibility of being thrown in the stocks for a day.

"We've unintentionally disturbed these good people's morning," Collin said easily, ignoring the confused and wary looks various people cast his way.

Brenner did *not* ignore them. He nodded to Collin, and it was clear he knew Collin was understating the matter. But he didn't seem inclined to call him on it. His eyes went beyond Collin.

"Wyeth," he said. "Good to see you, my friend. How's training?"

"It's going well thus far," Wyeth said hesitantly.

"Good to hear it." Brenner met Collin's gaze again. "Glad to cross your path again."

"And glad it's under better circumstances," Collin replied.

Brenner glanced around as if he wasn't sure it *was* better circumstances. The crowd was still quiet. This was likely the best retreat they were going to get.

"Get moving," Collin said over his shoulder. "We have three spots left to reach."

After a slight hesitation, they continued their trek toward the northern wall. Collin nodded once more to Brenner before turning to follow. He didn't look at any of the citizens who shuffled out of their way as they passed, but he caught a glimpse of Izzy looking back and knew without asking she was watching the foil.

The rest of their outing was more awkward than before. Collin waited until they were back within their own territory to turn on the three recruits. His anger must've shown in his eyes, for one of them stepped backward. He locked his attention on Sabriel.

"Did you recognize the woman who was upset?"

Sabriel glanced around, first at his fellow and then at Izzy.

"No," he admitted.

"She was the foil on the last full moon. She watched her friend lose himself to the curse and die in the street, *at the hands of Red Cloaks.*"

Sabriel's face fell in understanding.

"She has reason to be distraught," Collin said. "And demanding they show greater respect toward us is not going to correct any misunderstandings the people of Kedar have of our roles or motives."

"I apologize for my rash words," Sabriel said, casting his gaze to the ground.

Izzy spoke up, quietly but with an iron edge to her voice. "It is our greatest task to shield the citizens of Kedar from the danger that assails us. Of course they don't understand. If they did, *we* have failed."

Now all three of them were staring at their boots, looking like scolded puppies. Collin looked around them once more as he said his final piece.

"If any of you came here seeking your own glory, give up that thought *right* now. Glory means nothing here."

"Sabriel," Rhett barked behind them. "Wyeth, Becker. Join the others."

The three young men dispersed, looking warily over Collin's shoulder. Collin was stiff, hands fisted at his sides, as he fought the instinct to snarl at the sound of Rhett's voice. The instinct to brandish his sword at the man who'd hurt Izzy and called it justice. But he fought back the wild temptation and turned to face Rhett's approach.

"What happened?" Rhett asked.

"We ran across the foil," Collin explained dispassionately. "Our presence in the city caused...unrest. The citizens in that quarter believed we were there to keep them in line."

Rhett sighed. "More of the same."

Collin disagreed, but said nothing. He had his gaze fixed on the wall over Rhett's left shoulder. Rhett stared at them for a long, heavy moment and said nothing.

"You'll observe their training after midday," he said. "You're dismissed until then."

Collin offered a shallow bow in unison with Izzy. Rhett said nothing more as he turned to walk away, stiff as a board. Izzy sagged beside him when he finally left their sight. Glancing down, he met her regretful smile with a similar look.

Perhaps if they could afford some time to themselves, it would be a true reprieve. As it was they knew better than to try.

"Let's see if Baldwin and Keita have any leftovers they need cleared out," Collin suggested.

Izzy nodded. They walked side by side, as usual, on their way to the kitchen. Collin fisted his hands behind his back, digging his fingernails into his palm to ignore the growing itch beneath his skin that protested every inch of distance separating him from Izzy. To ignore the low-throated snarl demanding he remove every obstacle that stood between them, no matter whose blood he shed in the process.

Izzy

Izzy breathed slowly and steadily through her nose, ignoring the aching in her lungs that demanded she gasp like a fish. Many of the recruits around them didn't hide their lack of breath so well. Her fingers shook as she tugged on the buckle at her side, and even that small movement awakened the simmering fire along her back. The cuts had pulled open...hours ago. She didn't want to know what sweaty, festering mess they were now.

Collin brushed her hand away and unbuckled it for her. She murmured a relieved thanks, but didn't dare look at him. It seemed every time she did *someone* was staring, judging them. They hadn't found a moment of peace together since Rhett had left them tied to the whipping post.

That morning he'd ordered them out of the city—carefully forbidding them from entering the deep woods—to test the new recruits' endurance. They'd wandered the fringes of the woods by every path she and Collin knew for hours. They must've circled Kedar four times, the walls and watchtowers always just out of sight. Even after all that, she wished she was still out there.

Collin had taken the back of the group, pushing on the stragglers, while she led their way. There were a few moments where she'd been able to forget the panting bodies behind her and pretend she was alone, outrunning every fear and doubt that plagued her in the quiet. But even then she hadn't been able to rid herself of Carolin's voice, that wretched, gasping wail.

He's dead. Isn't that enough? He's dead.

Eldon came out to take over, asking the trainees how they did. Izzy didn't look at him. Even hearing his voice brought an ache in her heart that crawled up her throat and made it twice as hard to breath evenly.

She might've had an easier time forgiving him had he sent the whip across *her* back. But seeing him wield that whip, knowing he was directly causing the agony Collin endured before her eyes...it was hard for her to forget. Especially since, broken vows or not, she still didn't believe she and Collin and done anything wrong.

Izzy silently raised her other arm for Collin to unbuckle as well, though usually she'd pull free easily enough. Then she mutely turned her attention to the straps along his sides. His shirt was bloody when he pulled the leather away.

"We should get it over with," Collin said, jerking his chin toward the infirmary.

Izzy grimaced, but followed. No one in that building would be pleased with the state of their wounds, not after the strict warnings the physician gave them when they were first bandaged. But it wasn't like they'd had a choice.

The entryway was quiet...until one of the nurses caught sight of them and the scolding began. Izzy exchanged one last, rueful look with Collin before a second nurse set up a screen around her to shield her privacy. She was thankful when the nurse, Rosalyn, helped her out of her soaked shirt. Even more thankful when she proved far quieter than the nurse tending Collin, who's warnings about infection could likely be heard through the building.

"This will sting," Rosalyn said apologetically.

Izzy knew it would. She held her breath when Rosalyn first pressed the cool cloth to her torn skin. There was no pride here, no reputation to uphold. But she still wouldn't let anyone hear her pain. Especially not Collin.

She bandaged Izzy's wounds with gentle and efficient hands. By the time she was tying the last bit of gauze in place, the salve she'd worked into the torn skin had begun to soothe some of the burning Izzy had endured all afternoon. Some of the tension drained from her shoulders as that heady relief took hold.

Rosalyn walked around to Izzy's front, her hands already clean. Her lips were pursed as she stared at Izzy, but Izzy stared back steadily. What could she say? The physician didn't have a say in their activities, not when it was punishment they were recovering from.

"If you're on duty tomorrow, you both need to have your backs rebandaged beforehand."

"We'll come early," Izzy said quietly.

Rosalyn accepted that with a nod before helping her ease a clean shirt over her head and arms. Izzy wasted no time standing once she was decent again. She heard Alair talking quietly with Collin on the other side of the screen. As little as she wanted to face him—face anyone—she wanted to know how he was doing. She hadn't really seen him since he defended them against Mercer.

Circling the screen, she found Alair sitting on the edge of the bed, grinning at Collin where he stood with his arms crossed lazily. When Alair glanced her way, his smile didn't falter. Izzy blinked. She couldn't bring herself to smile back, though she wanted to. She supposed she expected everyone to see them differently since their punishment.

"Collin was telling me you gave the trainees a lesson in humility today."

"I wouldn't go that far," Collin said.

Alair laughed. "Running them into the ground must've been humbling, at least a little bit. The Watch prides themselves on their stamina."

Izzy edged closer to Collin. "At the very least, we wore them out."

"Alair," a rough female voice called toward the back of the long room. "If you're not back in bed by the time I've gathered your medicine, I swear I'll strap you down."

Alair gave Izzy and Collin a meaningful look as he stood, and Izzy failed to hold back her smile. So he hadn't been exaggerating.

"If they don't let me out of here tomorrow, you better stage a prison break," he muttered.

"Are you truly asking us to risk the wrath of that woman?" Izzy asked.

Alair made a face. "At least bring me a few of whatever Kieta made for dessert."

"That we can do," Collin said, gingerly patting Alair on the shoulder as he passed. He continued through the room with the air of a wounded martyr, though his voice oozed charm as he neared the nurse.

"Idella, darling. I'm touched by your concern, but I can hardly lay around all day."

Izzy could barely make out Idella's suspicious response as she dragged him back toward the bed claimed as his. Izzy and Collin slipped out before her attention could turn to them.

"Collin, Izzy."

Izzy paused as they stepped outside, her smile dropping when she saw Eldon approaching. She met his eyes, but said nothing...even when his smile turned regretful, the lines around his eyes looking deeper in the late afternoon shadows than she was used to.

"You're having dinner at my home tonight, Abby's orders," he said. "She made pumpkin bread for you."

Izzy's resolve fractured. She couldn't disappoint Abby; she had no part in any of this.

"Give us a few minutes to change," Collin said.

Eldon nodded. "I'll be waiting here."

She and Collin turned away, going to their respective barracks in silence. Izzy didn't pay attention to the other women milling around before going to supper, giving her full focus to pulling clean clothes from her trunk. She didn't change her shirt, not wanting to endure the pain it would require. But she changed into a clean pair of pants: old, soft, and free from the dirt and sweat of the day.

The thought of getting away, of having some time free of the watchful eyes that followed her here, was a welcome one. But she feared Eldon's motivations...and she feared the way Abby would look at them. She had no doubt Eldon told his wife what had happened. What would she think of the whole affair?

She'd known Abby longer than Eldon or Rhett, and she was the closest she had to real, *blood* family. Izzy didn't want to disappoint her. But that wasn't quite right...it was more that she didn't want Abby to be one of the many expecting Izzy and Collin to be...sterilized. Nothing more than a cloak and a reputation.

Izzy fingered the cool stone around her neck absently, slipping it out of sight before she reached the courtyard. Collin was already there, but the words he exchanged with Eldon were stilted. The tension didn't improve when she joined them. Eldon didn't try to coax them into speaking as they followed him to his home, and the silence didn't break until he opened his front door.

A scrawny figure barreled toward them, throwing herself at Collin and Izzy with such a joyful greeting that all her unease melted away. Every hard line melted from Collin's form, and Izzy grinned down at Maizy.

"You stayed away too long," she accused.

"Apologies, lady," Collin said, ruffling her hair.

Maizy scrunched her nose, withdrawing only enough to seize their hands and drag them inside.

"I just finished sewing a wool skirt all on my own, though Mama guided the cutting. It's green *just* like the pines, and even Maya said it was beautiful."

Izzy exchanged a smile with Collin as Maizy continued her rushed story, switching topic whenever she took a breath.

"There are a few mums left in the garden, and Thomas threatened to pluck them until I told him that if he touched even *one* I'd clock him! Mama scolded me, but I'm not sorry. Thomas wants to destroy anything beautiful, and I can't *stand* him. Just because he's ugly doesn't mean the rest of the world has to be."

It was that hopeful view of the world that made Izzy most glad Abby and Eldon had adopted Maizy into their home. Such a spirit wouldn't have lasted in the orphanage, not under the authority of the headmaster.

"And what about your studies?" Collin asked. "Still lamenting all the dusty books you have stacked up?"

There was a spark of mischief in his eyes as he spoke, and when he glanced at Izzy it seemed his smile was just for her. Her own turned soft as Maizy expressed her horror at her treasures being called "dusty."

"Did you know in most of the continent they call Moon Folk elves?" she said, guiding them to two worn seats set around the table. "It sounds so *strange*. And they have all sorts of wonderous stories of what their cities look like, and the gifts they offer to humans who befriend them. Not like the fairies. I think they're always beautiful and cruel and *awful*."

"Don't say that where they can hear you," Izzy warned teasingly.

Maizy ignored her, still ranting. "Thomas says they're nothing but tall tales, that all the fairy abductions were just drunk men wanting an excuse to tell their wives. I wish *he'd* get abducted."

"Maizy," Eldon said warningly as he took his own seat.

Maizy looked instantly chastised. "Sorry, Papa. I don't really. I just wish he wouldn't try to sound *older* than me all the time. Twelve isn't much different from eleven."

"Want Izzy and I to visit?" Collin asked. "I'm sure we could make an impression."

Eldon chuckled as Maizy's face brightened with the possibilities.

Izzy lifted her gaze as Abby appeared in the doorway to the kitchen, drying her hands on a towel embroidered with daisies.

"Thank you for having us," Izzy said with a smile that felt more genuine than any expression she'd worn all day.

"Of course," Abby replied. "It sounds like you need a bit of a reprieve."

She glanced at Eldon as she finished, and some of Izzy's happiness dimmed. Her back ached where the wood pressed against the skin, and she shifted uncomfortably. But Izzy found no censure in her words, and she tried not to let the reference bother her. Maizy soon distracted her again.

"What did you think of your birthday gift?" she asked with shining eyes.

"It's perfect," Izzy said. "The most beautiful weapon I've ever seen."

Maizy beamed. But that innocence dimmed, just slightly, with her next question.

"Has it kept you safe?"

Izzy softened. "It has."

Collin poked Maizy's arm, distracting her.

"Is your plan to join the faeries and fly away? You're thin as your precious flower stalks."

She batted his hand away. "Say that again when I'm taller than you."

Collin raised his eyebrows, glancing at Izzy with laughter in his eyes.

"You've told us about the garden and your sewing," Izzy said. "But what about your friends? What mischief have you gotten into?"

Izzy easily settled into Maizy's excited storytelling of all the outrageous occurrences at the orphanage. Though Eldon and Abby had adopted her, she still returned each day Abby worked there. She didn't resent the time she spent in those halls, not like Izzy did. And hearing about life outside of Izzy's own experience gave her a chance to relax like she hadn't in ages. By the time Abby brought out dinner, she found herself laughing with Eldon like nothing was different.

Collin and Eldon exchanged notes on the new recruits, who had the most potential and who might cause trouble. Izzy's face hurt from smiling as Eldon recounted Collin and Izzy's struggles in their own training and Collin accused him of exaggerating. Izzy was content to listen, for the most part. It was enough to be surrounded by family, of a sort, without any expectations.

Abby stood, grabbing empty bowls from the table.

"Maizy, time to clean up."

Maizy stood without protest, though her reluctance was palpable. But when Izzy moved to join them, Abby shook her head with a soft smile.

"Stay. You have things to talk about."

She gave a meaningful look toward Eldon, and the warmth drained from Izzy's chest. She turned slowly and found Eldon watching them with a pained twist to his mouth that soured her stomach. He said nothing until Maizy and Abby were in the kitchen, the clanking of dishes and their conversation spilling from the open doorway.

"I hope you know how much I detested taking part in your punishment," Eldon said.

"We know," Izzy murmured.

"I suppose Rhett's hands were tied once Mercer opened his mouth," Collin said reluctantly.

Eldon nodded, glancing at the window showing a small piece of twilight sky.

"With all the questions and doubts arising...if Rhett loses control over our own, it's over."

"So he made an example of us," Izzy said. She tried swallowing back the bitterness that came with the thought, but it still bled through into her words.

"He proved his impartiality."

"And he's left you to tell us what happens next," Collin guessed.

Izzy suspected the same, and Eldon's pained expression confirmed it. So this wasn't a simple reprieve.

"Forgive me. What I say next I say out of love for both of you."

She reached beneath the table and grabbed Collin's hand. Eldon's gaze flicked downward, noticing the action, but he didn't mention it.

"For the most part, we have turned a blind eye to the time you spend alone. You've done an...admirable job keeping professional when in view of others. But you can't continue as you have. You need to make a choice."

Izzy's breath caught, the panic of drowning filling her lungs, her throat, her mouth. *A choice?* A cruel, fatalistic voice whispered that she always knew this was coming. Every stolen moment, every gentle touch and secret embrace...it was just one more cut of the whip, wasn't it? *Choose.*

How was she supposed to choose between her breath and her heartbeat? She'd made the Red Cloaks her entire life. But Collin...she and Collin weren't a knot someone could pull apart. Their threads were spun together too closely to separate.

In a way, her choice was obvious. She would never leave Collin's side, not if an army stood against them. But to leave the Red Cloaks in disgrace? To abandon their duty at the height of this strange war?

She held Collin's hand in a death grip and stared at Eldon. Whatever stricken expression sat on her face made Eldon's own features fall. But he didn't take it back.

"It isn't a decision I envy you," he said. "If Rhett had demanded I take the new vows, I would've left the order without hesitation. He knew that. But...you both took those vows."

"When we were too young to fully understand what we were giving up," Izzy said.

Eldon conceded that with a nod. "You two are the reason Rhett raised the age to eighteen. We realized long before you did that you'd sworn yourselves to a life you hadn't fully understood."

They'd known. They'd understood. And yet...

"Whatever you choose," Eldon continued. "Rhett will make it as easy as he can. If you remain in the order, he won't separate you unless it becomes necessary. If you choose to leave...he'll give you the chance to leave quietly."

"Quietly?" Collin growled. "After he's held us up to all of Kedar as his chosen ones?"

Izzy flinched, holding tighter to his shaking hand. He was right. There would be no quiet departure for them, not unless they left Kedar completely.

Leave Kedar? A thrill of excitement shot through her veins...or perhaps it was terror. She'd never imagined what life would be like outside of this city, not really. Despite the many evenings she and Collin had spent when they were young dreaming of all the wonders they'd see in far-off places, Kedar was always where she imagined living out her days.

Izzy's lips parted, and she wasn't sure what she planned to say until the words met air.

"Do you believe that it's wrong for us to love each other?"

Eldon didn't answer.

"Do you believe it weakens us? Leaves us vulnerable?"

Eldon glanced back toward the kitchen, where Abby and Maizy's voices offered a bright contrast to this dreadful conversation.

"An oath is an oath."

"We're leaving," Collin said, standing abruptly and pulling Izzy up with him.

Izzy didn't look at Eldon as they went to the kitchen door to offer tense farewells. Maizy threw herself into their arms again, protesting that they hadn't stayed long enough. But Abby only looked on sadly and told them to visit again soon.

"You are always welcome here."

"Thank you," Izzy said, as she and Collin backed away. Neither of them looked at Eldon as they left.

Izzy shivered in the cold night air. The only spot of warmth was her hand in Collin's. Neither of them let go, not even as they wove through the streets back toward headquarters. Neither of them spoke for a time. Collin's silence, Izzy knew, was an attempt to rein in his fury.

Izzy...there was nothing she could say. Their time had run out, just as she'd always known it would. But now that she was faced with the ultimatum she'd always feared, she was numb. Weighing each side, searching for a way out of this corner Rhett had backed them into...she couldn't do it.

When they were a few streets away, Collin pulled her away into a shadowed corner.

"Izzy," he said desperately, brushing his free hand against her hair.

"I can't, Collin," Izzy gasped. "Not tonight. I can't...I'll drown in it."

He stilled. And slowly, painful as drawing an arrow from her flesh, he pulled back and released her. She wanted to throw her arms around him and say she was sorry. She wanted to reassure him that what she'd always said held true: she wouldn't let anything come between them. But her lips might as well have been sealed.

Collin said nothing more, not even when they split apart in the courtyard to go to their separate beds. It hurt knowing his silence was her own fault. But she couldn't find anything to say before he disappeared. Izzy forced herself to turn away to her own barracks. In silence she wove her way between the bunks and fell into her bed fully clothed, squeezing her eyes shut as hot tears slid down her face. It was a long, torturous wait before sleep claimed her.

CHAPTER
FOURTEEN

Izzy

Izzy gripped the edges of the bench tightly, watching Rhett speak to Viron at the front of the room. Collin sat beside her, still and silent, but she hadn't looked at him since they took their seats. Rhett hadn't mentioned either of them during muster.

The numbness that had washed over her last night was still in place, but growing thinner by the hour. Beneath it was a twisting mass of turmoil she was afraid to even acknowledge. Once she did...

Rhett walked toward them, and Izzy stood with Collin. Meeting Rhett's gaze was automatic, but her thoughts as she stared at him were a bit different. In many ways it felt like a lifetime since he took her into this order...a lifetime she'd spent looking up to him as more than a commander. Now she didn't know *what* she saw when she looked at him.

"Take the day to...consider matters," he said.

Collin tensed at those words, and Izzy reached for him instinctively...only to let her hand drop back to her side.

"Are we bound to these walls?" Collin asked, and Rhett scowled at the fury hidden behind those words.

"No. Go where you please. Just don't be foolish."

He turned away and Izzy was glad to follow Collin out of the estate. They left their cloaks hanging in the armory. She should've been glad to escape its weight, but as they walked through the city she felt vulnerable without it. They were recognized even without the telltale marker, and in the eyes that stared back at her she saw far more fear than she'd ever wanted to.

When did that fear begin? When did they become the embodiment of Rhett's authority over the city when all they ever wanted to do is *protect*? They weren't his enforcers. But she had no idea how to begin convincing Kedar of that.

Izzy hardly took a full breath until they reached the shelter of the trees. But even then, she didn't look at Collin. Not until they were in the deep, tangled woods and Collin spun to pull her into his arms.

Her shoulders stayed tight, even as the weight of his arms around her eased some of the howling deep in her chest. She hated the confusion in his gaze when he pulled back.

"Collin," she said, her voice full of the ache and pleading she hadn't allowed herself to feel.

She couldn't finish. All night she'd tormented herself with what to do, and she hated every answer she found. And now, looking into Collin's familiar golden eyes, she found that same turmoil mirrored back at her. But a reckless glint entered his gaze.

"Let's leave."

"What?"

"The order, Kedar, everything. Leave it behind and never look back."

Izzy's mouth dropped open, though nothing came out. Collin's hands flexed, his fingertips digging into her arms, but she hardly felt it. There was a wildness to his face that she didn't recognize, a savage recklessness. It sparked a new fear in her heart.

"We can't leave."

"Why not?"

"The fight isn't over," she sputtered. "Kedar *needs* protectors, and..."

"Why does it have to be us?" Collin asked desperately, bringing his face closer to hers. "We can't shield a city. Why do we have to live as if it's *our* efforts that tip the scale?"

Izzy's lips parted, but she said nothing. Why *did* they have to live like that? She wasn't arrogant enough to believe Kedar would fall without them. But if it *did* fall and they weren't there...would that mean they'd betrayed everyone?

This conversation, this anger...she didn't know where it had come from. It was as if Rhett and Eldon's ultimatum had snapped something deep within him, and Izzy was lost trying to navigate it.

"If we left, and Dal or Alair fell, or Berke or *Eldon*. Moon take us, if they broke through and hurt Maizy...I don't think either of us could live with ourselves."

Izzy watched a war play out before her eyes, a war between whatever wild anger had entered Collin's heart, and the loyalty that she knew defined him.

"It isn't wise to let down your guard."

Izzy twisted toward the voice, her sword half out of its sheath before she faced the speaker. She stilled when her eyes met those of the moon folk gathered before them. But the leader wasn't looking at her. His gaze was fixed on Collin, with tight lips and a set to his eyes that Izzy recognized. She'd seen her comrades wear that same look when the fallen were carried to their tomb. She looked up quickly, but found that that wildness had faded out of Collin's expression.

"Moon's sake," he said with a breathless laugh. "You certainly make an entrance."

"Are we intruding?" the leader asked wryly.

"No," Izzy said. "We were just...discussing something."

"To what honor do we owe the visit?" Collin asked.

Any hint of amusement dropped from his face as the leader said,

"We come bearing a warning. Our search has yielded troubling answers. The sorcerer behind the attack on Kedar..."

"Artyom," Izzy said.

He stared at her in surprise. "You've met him face to face, then?"

Izzy wasn't sure why he'd assume that by a name. She wasn't sure why she'd spoken at all.

"Twice since we last spoke," Collin said. "Suffice to say we won't be inviting him to dinner."

The leader nodded, "Artyom has sent out a call, bringing far more allies to his cause than he has thus made use of. He is gathering strength to assail Kedar for the last time."

More allies? Izzy pictured the shifting mass of shadows they'd faced for years, and her mouth pulled down in a frown.

"What's different this time besides numbers?" Collin asked.

"The final full moon before winter overtakes the world offers greater strength. And do not underestimate numbers. Thus far he has drawn vagabonds and outcasts to his cause. When the full moon rises, your city will be facing the worst beings each of the races has to offer. And our sources say he has promised Kedar to their vengeance in its entirety."

Meaning man, woman, and child. Izzy flinched from the very idea of the carnage that would follow the city's breach.

"Will you do more than watch?" Collin asked.

"The time when our people and the citizens of Kedar fought side by side has long passed."

Thought of yellowed pages and a rough sketch flashed through Izzy's mind, but she pushed it aside as Collin spoke again.

"You can't help us, or won't?"

There was an accusation in Collin's words, but the leader took no offense. He offered a rueful smile and spread his hands before him.

"It is not so easy to distinguish for us. We have those we are beholden to obey, and they have forbidden engaging Artyom directly. As for his allies...fighting them risks upsetting the fragile balance that rules our world."

Izzy bit back the insistence that it was their world too. That *they* were not the ones to upset their own balance. But she couldn't keep the disappointment from showing on her face. It was obvious the leader noticed it, and he stared at them as his lips twisted in grave consideration.

"We will offer you what knowledge we can," the leader said, as if coming to a decision. "Your leaders have not taught you everything you ought to know. Artyom and his allies are not the *only* ones who benefit from the moon's light."

"Aibek," a woman said warningly behind him. "We must go."

"Wait. What do you mean by that?" Collin stepped forward.

"Do you mean *we* can benefit?" Izzy asked.

The leader grimaced. "We will find you another day, when we are more free to explain."

"Just tell us..."

"Farewell," he said over Izzy's protest. "Don't venture near the mountain."

Izzy hadn't made it two steps before the entire group faded, leaving nothing but empty woods where they had stood. She stopped short and stared, searching in vain for any sign of their presence. *How...*

Collin huffed. "Cryptic elves."

Izzy turned to look at him.

"What? That's what Maizy called them."

Izzy continued to stare, waiting for that anger to return, for the wildness to take over his gaze...and instead saw his expression collapse into shame.

"Forgive me," he said, grasping her arms again. "I don't know why...I can't lose you. I can't."

"You won't," she said fiercely, stepping closer. She reached up and rested her hands against the sides of his face. "You will *never* lose me."

One of his hands gripped her wrist, holding her hand against his cheek, but he didn't look convinced.

"I'm..." Izzy's voice broke, but she fought to form the words. "I'm not retreating. I just... I *can't* afford to fall apart, Collin."

"Maybe it would be better if you did," he murmured.

She shook her head. And before he could argue she stepped closer, pressing her forehead against his and closing her eyes.

"I will *not* give you up."

Her voice trembled, but her words were fierce. And she meant them with her whole heart.

"Alright," Collin said softly.

"That's all you have to say?"

"What's left for me to declare? You know my heart is yours."

A wet laugh escaped her, and Izzy threw her arms around Collin's shoulders. She buried her face against his neck, her throat thick with tears as he held onto her with the desperation of a drowning man. She still didn't know what to do. But she was *not* letting go.

Collin

Collin stared at the carved blessing above his head as they passed through the arch. *Please, Almighty, give me a clear mind and a steady heart.*

He wasn't sure what came over him in the woods, what momentary madness or long suppressed desperation, but he couldn't afford to give into it again.

They couldn't abandon their people, especially not now. If someone had suggested it to him, he would've dismissed them with disgust. So why, in that moment, had the fate of Kedar felt meaningless? Izzy was justified in her confused concern, no matter how much seeing her look at him that way hurt. It wasn't the first time in the past few days that all reason had abandoned him, and it was starting to worry him.

He wouldn't give Izzy up. If Rhett cast them out of the Red Cloaks and they had no choice but to fight alone and uncloaked when the full moon came, he would do it. But walking away?

Deep down, Collin supposed he did wish they could leave everything behind. But he also knew it was a coward's way out.

The few people in the courtyard stared as he and Izzy passed. Isley, in particular. When Collin met his gaze, he lowered his head with an air of shame. Collin couldn't fully banish the gratification of that sense of guilt, even though he knew Isley wouldn't have testified against them without coercion. The rest of the stares he ignored.

Rhett stood in the doorway, and Collin was nearly convinced he was waiting on them. He and Izzy turned that way without a word. Collin itched to take her hand as they stepped into the shadow.

Leaning against the front of his desk, Rhett looked them over with a critical eye. Collin stood taller beneath his inspection, edging closer to Izzy as if he could shield her from their commander's gaze. He didn't say anything. But based on the look in his eye, Collin thought Rhett already knew what they'd decided.

"Give us until after the full moon," Collin said. "We have evidence that this cycle will be worse. We'll set our decision aside until Kedar is through it."

Rhett narrowed his eyes at Collin's words, at what they implied, and he turned to Izzy. Her arm brushed against his, and he turned to find her leaning against him with her head held high.

"We'll consider ourselves once Kedar is safe," she said steadily.

Cool, composed Izzy. There was no sign left of the turmoil she showed among the trees. Collin was sorry for it. But he couldn't deny that his heart warmed with pride to see how unflinchingly Izzy stared Rhett down.

"Very well," Rhett said.

Rather than dismiss them, Rhett leaned back and snatched a ink stained paper from his desk.

"The Keltern caravan was due to arrive in Kedar this afternoon. They sent a group of messengers north to say they were delayed and are currently camped south of Mount Talith. They won't come further north without an escort into our city."

Collin wondered what they'd seen to make them stop. The moon folk's warning not to go near the mountain rang in Collin's head.

"We can't afford for this caravan to turn around," Rhett said gravely. "Not with the harvest we took in. The Watch is sending thirty men. I'm sending eight. You two will lead the company."

"When do we leave?" Collin asked, far more blithely than he felt. Apparently, their disgrace was over.

"Midday," Rhett said. "The moon sets early tonight, which will make it possible for you to travel through the night. With all hope you can reach the caravan before midnight. The Watch Commander is sending his swiftest. They should keep up with your pace well enough."

Thirty-eight armored soldiers running past the mountain. They would draw attention. But on a moonless night, they had a hope of escaping resistance. Collin turned his head, sharing a look with Izzy. They asked each other the same, silent question. Collin saw his own answer mirrored in her eyes.

"We'll be ready," Izzy said.

"Good."

Rhett crossed his arms over his chest, watching them for another heavy moment.

"I don't need to warn you to keep your distance. I will offer a time of grace to make your decision, but in the meantime you *will* follow proper conduct."

Collin ground his teeth together but nodded.

"Who else are you sending?" Izzy asked.

Rhett snatched another paper from his desk and listed off the contents. "Isley, Kyne, Raith, Liam, Claret, and Mercer."

Mercer. Collin fought to keep his expression steady as Rhett spoke that name. Rhett was gauging Collin's response, and he wondered if Mercer's presence was merely another test. But a test for who? That Collin would give up thoughts of revenge for the sake of the task ahead of them? Or that Mercer would follow orders from those he hated? Either way, Collin didn't look forward to the days ahead.

"Report to the courtyard in an hour," Rhett said.

Collin and Izzy bowed in unison and left. Izzy marched away without hesitation, but Collin followed and grabbed her elbow to stop her. She twisted around, lifting her eyes to his. They were soft with apology, a regretful smile twisting her lips as she pulled away.

She turned her back on him, and something untamed deep in his soul awoke. Panic filled him, demanding that he couldn't let her out of his sight. If he did, if something happened, if someone *touched* her...

He almost took a step toward her, but stumbled backwards instead. Uncontrolled thoughts couldn't be followed. Collin knew that, and yet watching her walk away nearly defeated him. He stared until her blonde braid disappeared inside, heart pounding, before turning away.

Mercer stood across from him, leaning against the wall with a smirk. Collin forced his eyes away, walking resolutely toward his own barracks. But as he passed Mercer, he caught his low whisper.

"Missing time alone with your lover?"

Collin twisted, a surge of heat banishing all reason. He had Mercer pinned to the wall, his hand wrapped around the rat's throat, before he could blink. The snarl that passed between his teeth was guttural and savage. Mercer flinched.

It wasn't until Collin's head was inches from Mercer's that he realized his intention: the heat flooding his blood was telling him to rip Mercer's throat out. End the threat once and for all, taste the blood between his teeth. The bloodlust was so foreign that it snapped Collin back to his senses. He stared down at Mercer's wide eyes as horror washed through him like a cold, autumn storm. Collin released his throat.

Isley appeared beside him, tugging at Collin's arm. It took a moment for his chatter to coalesce into actual words in Collin's mind.

"Collin, I was hoping to talk to you. This is my first mission away from Kedar, and Berke isn't here to answer my questions."

Mercer didn't react, still staring up at Collin in utter terror. He could see Mercer's pulse thrumming in his throat, and another low snarl built in the back of Collin's mouth. He stumbled backwards, letting Isley pull him away. Whatever had overtaken him was still there, subdued but not silenced. It was *inside* him. Collin turned away from Mercer's prey-like fear, concentrating on Isley's nervous chatter as they walked into the barracks.

The next time the moon folk blessed him with their presence, Collin had questions they were going to answer.

CHAPTER FIFTEEN

Izzy

Izzy walked silently, matching the slow pace of the draft horses beside her. She'd been assured by the drivers that they were moving at the fastest sustainable pace their horses could manage, but still they crawled.

Scanning the forest on her right, Izzy's eyes fell on Collin ahead of her. And despite her determined efforts, her eyes lingered. This entire affair would've been easier to tolerate if she didn't have Rhett's warning ringing through her head.

Something was troubling Collin. But out here, surrounded by watchful eyes and every moment on their guard, she couldn't get him alone to make him tell her. Especially with Mercer watching their every move so closely.

Izzy sighed and forced her eyes back to the trees. She was careful not to look toward the caravan, not wanting to know which eyes were staring at her in mingled awe and fear. She was too aware of them already, even after three and a half days of slowly walking alongside them. They hadn't been attacked by so much as an angry squirrel, and Izzy had begun to hope that they would make it to Kedar in peace. Until this morning.

The forest seemed empty of all but the most ordinary signs of life, and yet Izzy didn't relax. Something was different, and she and Collin weren't the only ones to notice. No one was talking more than necessary, not even the children safe in the backs of their covered carts. The horses were restless. Their drivers were even more so.

"Birch grove."

Collin's whisper floated back to her on the faint breeze, and she glanced right without turning her head. The shadows shifted unnaturally. Coolness washed over her, tasting curiously of relief as she loosened her sword in its scabbard beneath the cover of her cloak. At least the poisonous anticipation was over.

The horses plodded along as usual, and Izzy kept her focus on that shifting movement all along the caravan. She hoped others had noticed what she and Collin had. If not...well, they were all trained to react quickly.

The first goblin stepped from the shadows. He'd hardly entered the sunlight when Collin's voice rang out.

"To arms!"

Izzy tossed her cloak over her shoulders, drawing her sword and dagger. A goblin leaped from the trees, falling on her raised sword. She shoved him off and turned to the two others rushing toward her.

She settled into the battle easily, keeping her back to the wagons with their frantic horses and only slightly calmer drivers. Her focus was razor sharp, her heartbeat a steady tempo as she guarded her short stretch of wagons. She couldn't see any Red Coaks other than Collin, spread out as they were between watchmen, but she heard Claret shouting for the merchants to remain calm and hide in their wagons. Behind her, a cry she thought belonged to Isley split the air. Swallowing back the dread summoned by that pained shout, she kept fighting.

"Izzy."

She turned, immediately seeing the troll smashing through the trees, stony fists swinging to clear wood and person alike from its path. She sprang forward, a step behind Collin as they rushed to help.

Collin slid into the troll's path, slicing open the tender skin beneath his arm and dodging the creature's infuriated blows with easy agility. Meanwhile, Izzy shoved a goblin from her path and climbed a rock. The superior height allowed her to leap onto the troll's back, driving her silver-gilt dagger through his neck, just beneath the skull.

The troll fell forward. Izzy leaped free, landing in a crouch with her back exposed. Collin was there in a heartbeat. Fighting back to back, Izzy's heart and mind sung with the familiar dance. Soon enough the air around them was open, goblins giving them a wide berth to avoid their blood-drenched blades. She and Collin didn't allow them the luxury.

A pained curse drew Izzy's gaze, and she found Mercer backed against a wagon wheel, desperately fending off three goblins.

"Of course," Collin growled, already running to his defense.

But a woman leaped from the wagon above his head, taking the head off one of the goblins with her sword. Two others were dead at her feet before Collin or Izzy could reach them, and then she turned to begin fighting the rest. Another man from the caravan fought further down the line, wielding a great sword that the goblins obviously didn't know how to fight against. It took less than a breath for Izzy to see that they could handle themselves. She spun and followed Collin to another troll tearing the roof off one of the carts.

Izzy felt the shift before she saw any difference. The air was purer, and she was suddenly aware of the thick, gibbous moon hanging in the sunlit sky. The goblins' raucous battle cries faded into the screams of retreat. No moonlight shone beneath that bright sun, but its effect was clear as the winter stars. Goblins fell back, shading their eyes as they hadn't a moment before. The troll before Izzy melted into pale ash, and Izzy saw its fate joined by each goblin or troll who took a step toward the caravan or its defenders.

Izzy and Collin kept fighting, stepping beyond the protective line to harry any enemy who was still within reach. But they only pursued the goblins as far as the tree line. Just south of them, Izzy saw goblins avoiding a grove of maple and recognized a few of their moon folk acquaintances calmly overseeing the chaos.

Izzy paused beside Collin, nodding when the moon folk met her gaze. But movement caught her eye, and as she turned her head she spotted a watchman raising a crossbow toward the moon folk.

"No," she barked, lunging toward the man.

She knocked the crossbow from his hands, the bolt slamming into the dirt just below the moon folks' feet.

"Stand down," she ordered fiercely, looking around lest any other watchmen have similar ideas.

She saw no other crossbows. The watchman standing before her took up most of her vision, looming over her with chest-heaving fury.

"You're defending them?" he asked in a growl.

"They just saved our lives," Izzy replied, going toe to toe with the man.

"How can you be sure they didn't incite the attack in the first place?"

"Why would they order goblins to attack us and then kill them as they fled?"

"I didn't see them do anything but watch."

Izzy paused. Had the man truly not felt their work, all silver dust and taste of moonlight? She let none of her confusion show on her face as she stepped even closer, forcing the watchman to retreat.

"The moon folk *did* aid us, and anyone who tries attacking them will answer to me and Collin."

The watchman was still furious. But he didn't challenge her. Izzy looked over the length of the caravan to be sure everyone was listening, and her eyes caught on Collin. He had his back to her, walking toward the tree line where the moon folk had disappeared. She took a automatic step toward him, intending to follow, but a rumbling, furious voice drew her attention away.

"Red Cloak."

Izzy turned to see the captain of the Watch standing before her, a head taller than her and twice as wide.

"You have no authority over my men," he said.

She looked him over again, his gore crusted armor and deep scowl. She recognized him. She respected him. But this was one situation where she had no intention of bending.

"This isn't Kedar, Captain," Izzy said in a steady, low tone Dal said gave him the shivers. "This domain is ruled by a different code. If you want your men to make it back to our city, you'll listen to *our* guidance."

The captain huffed, but Izzy talked over him.

"The moon folk you saw today have proven to be our allies on more than one occasion, and we will *not* respond to their aid with violence. Now I suggest you see to your wounded so we can get moving. We don't want to be out here after sunset."

The captain's anger hadn't abated, but with a final glare he turned away and began barking orders. Izzy's eyes caught on Isley toward the end of the caravan, holding his arm gingerly to his stomach, and she started toward him. But two voices at her back caught her attention and made her slow.

"That's the first time in decades I've seen them interfere in a fight."

"This business with Kedar must be more serious than we thought."

Izzy faced a moment of indecision, but ultimately twisted on her heel. The speakers were two men up on a wagon, and Izzy approached them determinedly. They watched her approach with apprehension.

"Can you tell me what you know of the moon folk?" she asked.

The men looked at each other. Izzy took a breath and tried to steady her voice.

"Those who aided us today have come a few times, but I know little of their kind or why they might be here. Please...can you tell me anything?"

"We aren't experts," the nearer man said, white brows low over his deep-set eyes. "The elves in the south interact with humans a little more than in these parts, trading or coming to our festivals. But we don't understand their actions any more than you do."

Izzy leaned back on her heel, disappointment a bitter taste in her mouth.

"I will say," the other man ventured. "Don't be too hard on the big fellow. Only those with elven blood can sense their workings. He could no more tell you what the moon folk just did than he could name the stars."

Everything quieted around her. Or perhaps her own heart drowned it out. All Izzy knew is that something inside her now crawled, slowly and resisting every step, toward a conclusion she couldn't bring herself to name. *Only those with their blood...*

"Do you have elven blood?" she heard herself say, as if through a thick veil. Her lips stumbled over the unfamiliar word.

He shook his head and jerked his thumb toward his companion. Izzy's eyes turned to the white haired man, who's brows were even lower over his eyes now.

"A grandfather half a dozen generations back was half elven," he said. "My strain isn't strong enough for anything more than seeing their workings and keeping me up on bright moon nights."

"It's obvious you and your fellow have more in you."

Obvious, was it?

Someone called her name. Izzy turned toward the voice automatically, barely remembering to thank the men as she walked toward Claret. She stood over Isley and Raith with a frown, a smear of blood on her cheek.

"Isley has a broken arm, and Raith's hand is torn up," she announced as Izzy drew near.

Isley gave Izzy a wan smile when he glanced at him, a thin sheen of sweat covering his pale face. Raith only shrugged when she turned to him. His left hand was bound tightly in cloth that was already turning red.

"We need to tend them as best we can and keep them toward the center," Izzy said.

"Just don't stick me in a wagon," Raith said. "I can walk fine."

"Me either," Isley said. His voice was weaker than Izzy wanted. She stared at him with a growing frown. If he was going into shock, they may *have* to stick him in a wagon.

A new presence drew Izzy's attention, and she turned to see two of the caravanners standing before her. It was the man and women who fought beside them.

"Anything we can do to help for the rest of the journey?" the man asked.

Izzy looked them both over. She'd noticed them before today and knew they kept to themselves. *They've proven themselves trustworthy enough.*

"Two of our own are out of the fight," Izzy said. "Can you take their place along the line?"

"Gladly," the woman said, flashing a toothy grin with a savage edge.

They turned away and walked toward the gap with an easy stride, making Izzy wonder just who they were. But that was a question for a later time. Claret was kneeling beside Isley, preparing to splint the bone. Izzy forced herself to kneel as well, to set aside the turmoil threatening to drown her.

She had plenty of practice with that, didn't she? Forcing all her problems and fears down, down, down where she could almost forget about them. But not this one...this she couldn't afford to forget. Nor, she suspected, could she avoid it much longer.

Collin

Collin stomped through the forest, grinding his teeth as rageful heat swept through him. Something had changed. He'd been ignoring it for days, that itch deep inside him like a half-healed wound. But it had doubled in strength as soon as the moon folk showed up. As soon as his attention was drawn to the fat moon looming over them. It had been all he could do to let the goblins retreat rather than hunt them down to the bloody end.

"Aibek," Collin called, forcing his way through the underbrush. "We need to talk."

He swatted away another maple branch and spotted the moon folk a short distance ahead. They stood in place: not disappearing, but not coming back toward him. Collin marched forward, jaw set, until he stood just before him. He drove his sword into the muddy ground.

"Enough with your cryptic, horse-dung answers. Am I marked?"

Aibek's eyes flashed with the first glimpse of anger Collin had seen in him. It wasn't a sight he'd soon forget.

"Watch yourself," Aibek said lowly. "I will not accept impertinence."

That fire blazing within him roared higher. Collin stepped forward, until he was within reach of Aibek and his few followers.

"I don't have the luxury of wandering where I choose, deciding who I bother to protect and who I destroy. *Tell* me. Am I marked?"

Aibek stared at Collin, his gaze cold and ancient. He turned his head and nodded to Silaine, who stepped forward and raised her hand to Collin's chest. He fought not to flinch back, to seize her wrist and force her away from him. Instead he watched her face. Her eyes were closed, and soon her lips twisted in a frown. Collin's heart plummeted.

"You are set to go through the rite," she murmured.

She released him, and Collin stumbled backwards. He hadn't really thought it could be true, had he? He'd suspected...he'd feared.

But he'd still hoped Aibek would tell him he was wrong. Now he swore the ground had disappeared from beneath his feet.

Aibek's face was set in a pitying look Collin would normally do anything to get rid of. But now...what could he say?"

"Can you take it away?" he asked. He hardly recognized his own voice.

Aibek shook his head, and Collin huffed. Of course he couldn't.

"A dormant spell like this is more difficult to remove," Silaine explained. "Particularly since it's closely entwined with who you were *created* to be."

"You mean I was born with that monster inside me?"

Even as he spoke the words his soul rebelled against the idea. Why would the Almighty create him to kill? Then again, he killed plenty with his own hands.

"Not a monster," Aibek said. "Not as we think of it."

"Then what would you call it?"

"Werewolves have played a noble role in our history, and your own. The Red Cloaks were founded as an order of werewolves sworn to protect Kedar."

"You can't be serious," Collin interjected. "The Red Cloaks?"

Aibek nodded slowly, warily. "It wasn't until a century ago that your order became primarily *human*. The actions that led to the change are still felt bitterly among my people."

Collin said nothing. If it were any other day, he'd ask a dozen questions that would likely go unanswered. But the revelation meant little now.

"What Artyom has done," Aibek continued slowly, "is awake the dormant blood within you and tie his own black sorcery into it, so that when the full moon completes the rite the surge of energy will power his curse and give your mind up to madness."

Madness. The sight of the wolf snarling, his bright eyes focused on Izzy, flooded his mind. Yes, that was madness. Aibek's mention of dormant blood stuck in his mind.

"I thought I was fully human," Collin said quietly.

"You are not," Aibek said slowly. "The blood of our people runs through you quite strongly for Kedar's folk. I imagine that is why your commander chose you for the order."

How or why Collin was brought into the order hardly mattered now. Nothing mattered, nothing except how to keep Izzy out of this.

He could ask Aibek to kill him. Collin dismissed the thought as soon as it came. If death was his fate, this wasn't how he wanted to meet it. He had to see Izzy again. He had to explain...or at least tell her he loved her one last time. Besides, he doubted Aibek would agree to it.

"Do I have any chance to escape this?" Collin asked. Not because he thought it was possible, but because Izzy would kill him herself if she found out he hadn't even tried.

"I cannot tell you how to break this curse," Aibek said. "What I can say is that every curse has its weakness. And who you were created to be is always stronger than what others attempt to shape you into."

Collin laughed, the caustic sound sticking in his throat. "You do love being mysterious, don't you?"

"Don't give into despair," Silaine said with a fierceness that drew Collin out of his own head. "Despair, betrayal, anger...all these will twist his curse deeper into your soul."

If he was doomed already, Collin didn't see much point in fighting it.

"I have one request to ask of you," Collin said, staring blankly at the trees as a thought slowly churned.

Aibek looked apprehensive. "We are still limited..."

"If Izzy comes out here alone, watch out for her," Collin interrupted. "Surely there's nothing binding you against that."

Aibek fell silent.

"I'm going to do what I can to make sure she comes out of this alive," Collin said. "After I'm gone she might be...reckless. Just...don't let her take on the world, alright?"

He didn't know why he was asking these people. He'd be better off asking Alair, Dal, Andred...Eldon. But he didn't know if he'd get a chance to. And there was some selfish, twisted part of himself that couldn't stand the thought of any of them taking his place once he was gone.

"We will do all we can," Aibek said.

Collin nodded. "Thank you."

He turned away then, not able to stand their sorrowful looks any longer. He grabbed his sword on his way past, numbly wiping the blade clean and sheathing it. Every step he took he could feel that itching, burning heat beneath his skin.

He was such a fool! Had he really thought he was safe? Of course this was Artyom's revenge. Of course he was as vulnerable as any other man who'd woken up with the wolf curse carved into his skin. He didn't need to ask anyone who his foil would be.

Collin thought he understood Artyom's full revenge against Rhett, now. Forcing doomed couple after doomed couple to play out the tragedy of Rhett's daughter and her lover. And what a fitting finale to take Rhett's chosen apprentices just when Kedar would need them most.

Bright sunlight marked the tree line, and Collin carefully schooled his expression so no one would guess what he'd just learned. By the time he emerged he was impassive as steel.

Everything had been set to rights while he'd been gone, the fallen goblins dragged from the road to allow the horses and carts to pass. Izzy met him at the road's edge.

"What did they say?"

Collin stared into her haunted eyes. Had she guessed already?

"It can wait until we're in Kedar," he said, not caring that it was a coward's choice. He couldn't do this here, not with so many people watching. Not when he couldn't so much as take her hand in his.

Izzy bit her lip in that stubborn look that said she wanted to argue. A different sort of heat burned a hole through his heart. Oh how he wanted to kiss her, here and now without a care who would see. But, as with everything else, he held back. And Izzy nodded in silence.

"Collin."

Collin turned to see the leader of the caravan standing on his wagon, staring at them.

"We're ready when you are."

"We're ready," Izzy called.

Collin took a deep breath. "Let's get moving. We have a few hours left, yet."

Izzy

Izzy rocked on her heels, gripping her dagger's hilt until its design was imprinted on her palm. It took every scrap of patience in her not to prod on the caravan slowly entering through Kedar's battered gates.

It wasn't the fading sunlight filling her with such urgency, nor the gibbous moon growing brighter by the moment. It was the knowledge that she should've had all along eating at her every reassurance. She had to *act*. But there was nothing to do, nothing but demand an answer and pray she was wrong.

Collin hadn't looked at her since he returned to the caravan. It wasn't as if they'd had time to talk. They'd had their hands full on the journey: reassuring the fearful, urging everyone faster, watching for further attacks from the shadows that loomed too deep as they passed by the mountain.

Some of the sense of impending doom eased once they left the shadow of Mount Talith, but that hardly set people at ease.

Izzy pressed forward, slipping into the city between two wagons. Collin was ahead of her. But rather than catch up with him, she darted down the first side street they passed. Let Collin sort things out in the square. She had her own questions to ask.

She was tempted to turn toward the scribes and their library, to search for her answers among the dusty scrolls she barely skimmed over thinking they meant nothing to her. But no...she would go to Rhett.

He was in the courtyard, observing the recruits going through their training exercises with Eldon. When he turned and saw her coming, a wary edge entered his eyes.

"The caravan?" he asked.

"We were attacked beside Mount Talith this afternoon, sustaining injuries but no losses. The moon folk drove away our enemies."

Rhett frowned. She wasn't sure if the cause was her brisk tone or mention of the moon folk, but Izzy didn't wait to find out.

"Are we fully human?" Izzy asked.

Rhett tensed, and with a glance at the recruits began walking toward his study. "Why would you think differently?"

"Collin and I see the moon folk working, twisting moonlight to their will. Two men in the caravan claim that only those with elven blood can see their work. Is that true?"

He didn't turn, didn't answer. But Izzy saw his shoulders stiffen. Izzy followed Rhett with the fatalistic step of someone walking to execution, silent as he slowly turned and leaned against his desk.

"Yes, it is true."

Izzy leaned backward, hands clenching into fists as her heart beat against her ribcage. How...how had she been so wrong? Her last hope crumbled to dust at her feet, but even so she found herself speaking.

"Why, besides historical precedent? Because the moonlight strengthens us as much as our enemies?"

"Yes," Rhett said more slowly. He was staring more intently at her now. "What brought on these questions?"

She stared at him, dread filling her chest and lodging in her throat with a silent scream. She couldn't tell him. Not yet. Because if she told him that she and Collin would be marked on the marrow, he would send them to the tower that night. And that she couldn't accept.

"I'm tired of secrets," she said.

It wasn't a lie, but he didn't believe her. That was obvious enough from his frown and the way he leaned toward her.

There was a time when she would've confided in him. There was a time she would've sought his guidance even before Eldon's. That time was long past.

"Am I dismissed?" she asked. "I have someone I need to talk to."

Rhett didn't answer right away, and for a moment she feared he would demand she explain instead. But he flicked his hand toward the door. Izzy wasted no time in leaving.

Izzy moved as if lodged in a dream, out of the compound and back through the city streets. She found Collin on the edge of the square where the caravan was already busy unpacking their wares.

"Where did you go?"

Izzy ignored him, grabbing his arm and dragging him away. She didn't search for some hidden place where they'd be safe. She only went until the streets were empty and dragged him into the first shadowed corner she saw.

She spun to face him, backing him against a wall.

"You were right," she said. "We should leave. Now."

"Izzy," Collin said, leaning closer.

"We can head north. There's plenty of empty land between us and the next kingdom, plenty of time to figure things out."

"Izzy."

"Just the two of us, Collin. Together."

"*Izzy*," Collin said emphatically, cupping her face in his hand.

Izzy fell silent, her breath spent. And Collin shook his head.

"You know we can't," he said, his thumb brushing lightly across the skin beneath her eye.

"We *can*," she said, voicing cracking. "We can leave now and never look back."

"It's too late for that. Running won't stop this."

"We'll find the moon folk. We'll beg..."

"They can't stop it." Collin offered her a wry, broken smile. "I already asked."

Her last hope faded into smoke, but her heart didn't give up. She leaned into him, searching for any idea, any wild plan that would prevent the curse from taking them too. Resignation weighed down Collin's expression.

"I will walk into that tower," he said quietly. "Doing anything else will put too many people in danger."

Izzy went on her toes, her voice dipping to a growl. "I won't let anyone kill you."

Collin stared at her, eyes soft. It gave Izzy the sense that he was drinking in one last glimpse of her...that he'd given up.

"And I won't let you anywhere near that place," Collin replied softly. "I will not hurt you."

Those words dislodged something within her. To be torn away from him, for Collin to say he didn't want her at his side...it was too much. She pulled out of his arms and fled into the deepening twilight.

CHAPTER SIXTEEN

Collin

Stumbling into the washroom, Collin leaned over the basin and splashed icy water across his face. He wasn't the first one up, but he was alone in the long, narrow room. Dawn was barely a hint outside the window. Izzy would be waiting for him. He should already be out there, taking every moment he could before the inevitable took place. Some unreasonable voice in his head suggested that as long as he delayed, nothing would change. Not until he stepped out that door and had to meet Izzy's heartbroken gaze.

He paused with water dripping off his nose, eyes locked on his reflection. His hand shook as pulled the edge of his shirt away and twisted his head to look. There it was, stained into his skin: the wolf mark. He gripped the edge of the basin to keep from swaying.

He knew it would be there. *He knew.* And yet seeing it...

He tied his collar closed to hide it from sight as he stumbled back toward his bunk. Everything in him longed to forget it was there, go about his morning until the search came. But he couldn't. He couldn't spar with Izzy, couldn't eat breakfast and bicker with their friends. He had to catch Rhett *now*, before the search began, and convince him to keep Izzy out of this. She couldn't enter that tower with him.

He was fastening the top of his boot when he heard a commotion outside. Dread twisted his stomach in on itself as he ran for the door.

A small crowd was gathered in the courtyard, with Rhett and Izzy at its center. Izzy wore her thin-strapped camisole...the wolf mark stark against her skin.

"No," he growled, lunging forward.

Dal and Alair grabbed his arms, forcing him to a standstill.

"Slow down," Dal said. "If you..."

"Of course I'm marked," Collin snarled, tugging against their restraint. "Who else?"

He ignored the way his friends flinched. His eyes were locked on Izzy. She wasn't looking at him, her jaw set as she stared resolutely at the paving stones.

He knew what she'd done. Where Collin planned to tell Rhett privately so he could keep her *out* of everyone's view, Izzy had confronted Rhett in front of everyone to tie his hands. He had no choice.

Except Rhett did have a choice. He had the only choice.

"Let me closer," he said, turning his eyes to Dal.

He hesitated. Collin snapped.

"I'm not the wolf *yet. Let me closer.*"

Alair released him, then Dal. Collin sprinted for Izzy with both men on his heels. Collin ignored the stunned faces he passed, sweeping Izzy into his arms with no regard for those watching. His heart calmed to have her close, regardless of the storm raging everywhere else. And for a single heartbeat, as she leaned against him, everything was right.

Collin lifted his eyes to Rhett and found an executioner staring back. No friend, no second father. Just their commander.

"I'll enter the tower willingly," he said, glad his voice was steady.

"And you can shoot me down yourself, if you want. But keep Izzy out of it."

Izzy ripped herself away from his embrace, her eyes a raging fire. Collin forced himself to focus on Rhett.

"I'm the only one who has to die. Don't let Artyom win again. Keep Izzy *away* from me."

"That is *my* choice," Izzy said, in a voice choked with rage.

Rhett glanced at Izzy once, and Collin thought he saw something break through for that instant. But there was no sign of it in his voice.

"Izzy will have the same choice as every foil before her."

Heart sinking, Collin turned to Izzy. There were no words he could bring himself to say, not now. But silently he pled with her to stay away, to save herself and let him go.

"I'm not leaving Collin to die," she said, her eyes fixed on him with the intensity of the sun. "We'll go together."

There was an age-old weariness in Rhett's words.

"So be it. Take them into holding."

Dal and Alair took hold of him again, and Collin didn't resist this time. Nor did he look at either of them as they led him toward the arch. Izzy was marched ahead of him, and Collin stared at her unbrushed hair hanging in a messy braid down her back.

Others gathered around them both as they entered the streets. Collin wasn't sure if it was to guard against their escape or to shield them from the stares of those they passed.

The Tower of the Cursed was separated from any private dwellings, and the day of each wolf moon featured the same morbid parade of the marked. Collin had always avoided it. He didn't know if the attention they gathered along their path was typical or reserved solely for them. They were an oddity, after all. No Red Cloak had been taken by the curse before.

He didn't look at those they passed, didn't want to know if they watched with pity or triumph. The red cloaks so many of them feared and despised subjected to the curse they fought. Did they see it as an ironic justice? Did they mourn at all for their loss?

Izzy hated this more than he did, that he knew. If she wore her cloak she'd have the hood up, edges wrapped carefully around herself. He could see the tense line of her shoulders even here.

Collin desperately wished they could spend their last few hours together in peace. What did vows mean now that they were doomed? Perhaps if they were alone he could convince her to...

To what, leave him? She wouldn't. She'd sworn nothing would separate them, and apparently she included death in that oath. He wanted to be angry with her. He wasn't. After all, he'd do the same. Of course they would face this end together, just like every other milestone of their lives. If there wasn't a twisted arena laying at the end of their path, the inevitability of one of them killing the other, he might be glad for it.

It was a relief to reach the tower, for the lack of onlookers if nothing else. He'd drunk his fill of humiliation. Dal and Alair led him to one of the rooms around the outside, cells that were larger than Collin had guessed from his previous glimpses.

Collin stepped forward, stretching his shoulders as Alair and Dal released him. It wasn't until he turned that he realized Dal and Alair entered with him, as had Berke. Viron locked the cell behind them, and all three of his friends stared back at him as if bracing for an argument. Collin only crossed the cell and dropped onto the hard wooden bench.

"What are you doing?" he asked, leaning back against the cold stone.

Alair sat beside him. "Keeping you company. There's no way we're going to let you spend the day alone, stewing in your thoughts."

Collin laughed, though the helplessness of the sound made him cringe.

"What if Rhett orders you back?"

"We'll march to the wall at sunset like good little soldiers," Dal said. "But before then, Rhett can rot for all we care."

He glanced at the barred door with that, as if afraid Rhett would catch his words. A smile crossed Collin's mouth in spite of himself.

"What about Izzy?" he asked. "She shouldn't be alone, either."

"Eldon's got Izzy," Berke said, crossing his arms over his chest. "He's the only one she'll allow near her, I suspect. Except you."

"Except me," Collin echoed, resting his head against the stone. The ceiling was as dark and solid as the rest. He knew the center of the tower was open to the sky...open to the moon. Collin lifted his head to fix each of his friends with a hard look.

"Be honest with me. How much did you know about Izzy and me?"

Dal grimaced and glanced at Berke.

"We tried to *know* as little as possible," Alair said. "But it was fairly obvious something was going on between you two."

"It predated your arrival at the order," Berke said. "We could tell ourselves that since nothing had changed, nothing was a problem."

"And if we'd told you the full of it?"

"Rhett wouldn't have heard it from us," Dal said. This time he didn't glance at the bars. "He wouldn't have had anything on you for that whipping, either, if we'd gotten to Mercer soon enough."

"Was he smug this morning?" Collin asked.

"Not for long," Berke rumbled.

Another smile flickered across his face, this one darker. But that twisted satisfaction didn't last long.

"Tonight will be worse than we've faced before. There will be greater numbers, greater power backing them...Artyom means to defeat Kedar tonight."

"We'll make sure to pass that along," Alair said. "Kedar won't fall while we still breathe."

Collin knew that. His fear was that they *wouldn't* be breathing by the time the moon set. This was the first time since he'd entered the Red Cloaks that there was truly *nothing* he could do to help them.

No...even if he was on the wall, he would *be* the danger. Dread was a dark weight pressing on his chest until he struggled to breathe.

"Promise you'll take care of her," he said desperately. "If she survives this...she isn't as tough as she acts."

"We know that," Berke said gently. "We also know her well enough to guess that she doesn't intend to leave this tower without you."

No, she didn't. But Collin had to believe she would. If he didn't...

"You never know," Alair said with false brightness. "The two of you might walk free yet."

Collin laughed again. "Maybe we will."

Dal slapped his back. "You're not dead yet. No situation is hopeless until you give up."

Izzy

IZZY ENTERED the cell with her shoulders back and stared at the blank wall. She knew some lingered. Andred had stayed close to her the entire torturous walk over, Tay and Farren guarding her back. Izzy was grateful for the glares the three women inflicted on everyone who stopped to stare. But she couldn't bring herself to face Andred, to thank her...or to ask her to stay.

Visitors were allowed. Izzy knew that much. Most of their friends had turned into the cell where Collin was. Alair had turned back and caught her gaze, as if asking if he should follow her, but Izzy had shaken her head. Collin needed their company more than she did. And now she stared at the stone, waiting for Andred to slip away.

She didn't leave, not until Eldon came. Then Izzy listened to her near-silent footsteps disappear as the door closed behind Eldon. But she still didn't turn around. Her vision blurred, the wall a few paces from her a wash of pointless gray.

"I won't kill him."

Izzy's own voice surprised her, rough and threaded through with the grief she was fighting to keep locked away.

"I know," Eldon said.

"No one else is going to kill him either, not while I'm still breathing."

Izzy clamped her lips shut, her heart pounding in her throat. There was pain *everywhere*, from her aching cold fingers to the deep, shattering agony in her chest. Eldon shuffled toward her, and she clenched her hands into fists at her sides. If he said *anything* about duty, about not wanting to lose both of them, Izzy would kick him out. She didn't care if it meant she'd spend the long hours alone.

But when his hand gently touched her shoulder, only two words passed his lips.

"Little Star."

She wanted to be angry, to rant and rave and claim this was partially his doing. If he and Rhett hadn't supported that one vow, she and Collin wouldn't have fled to the forest. If they'd told her and Collin the truth from the beginning, perhaps they would've been more cautious. If a hundred tiny details had been different, perhaps it wouldn't be *them* walking into that cold, bloodstained tower tonight.

But none of the accusations running through her head made it to her lips. Instead she turned, burying her head in Eldon's shoulder as her tears finally broke loose. Izzy wept like a child. She needed *someone* to hold her right now. If it couldn't be Collin, Eldon was the closest to family she had.

Izzy had no idea what she should do when night fell. She only knew what she couldn't live with.

What can I do? She prayed silently, begging the Almighty to listen. *Give me a way to save him. Please!* She knew they weren't stronger than this curse. But she couldn't, she *wouldn't*, give up.

Izzy leaned her head against the cold stone at her back. The bench was hard and worn, the stone even more so, but Izzy didn't care. Watching the ceiling was better than staring at the weapons leaning against the wall. The afternoon sun was shining through the grate at the door with all it's piercing inevitability.

Eldon had left a while ago. Abby and Maizy had heard...they'd come to see Izzy and Collin both. She'd been glad when Eldon took them home; seeing Maizy's child-like grief reopened every wound she'd spent the hours covering up.

Dal had come afterward, checking on her at Collin's request. His awkward teasing had dragged a smile to her lips, but it didn't last once he left. Her request to the guards to see Collin herself had fallen on deaf ears. She didn't know the watchmen guarding her cell, and if they knew her it didn't make them inclined to extend any sort of lenience.

"Give us some privacy."

Every fiber in Izzy's body tensed at the sound of that voice, at the screech of the door as it was opened to allow Rhett's entrance. The guards' muted footsteps grew further and further away as Izzy kept her gaze solidly on the stone above her head. Despite her resolve to ignore his presence, Izzy's mouth loosened first.

"Are you going to say that it's our fault? That if we'd guarded our hearts better we wouldn't be in this situation?"

There was no response. Izzy stared at the blank wall for a moment longer before the silence was too much. She twisted, planting her feet on the ground as she focused her gaze on Rhett. He stood in the center of the cell, shoulders bowed and gaze on Izzy's feet. When he finally lifted his eyes... Izzy's breath caught. It was the gaze of a broken man, not the fierce commander she knew.

"This is my doing."

"Do you intend to explain *why*?"

Rhett took a slow, shuddering breath.

"My choices caused my daughter's death. And now yours."

"What choices?" Izzy asked harshly. "*How* did Tahlia die?"

Rhett looked away before speaking. "I caught Tahlia and Iah running away together. In my anger, I tried taking her back by force. Iah shifted at the sight, killing Tahlia when she stepped between us. He went mad. And I killed him."

The dreadful story, told so succinctly in Rhett's carefully masked tone, made Izzy feel sick. He wasn't exaggerating. It *was* his choice. His choice not to accept his daughter's decision, to force his will upon her and Iah. His choice to inflict the same control over her and Collin.

"And if you could go back?" Izzy asked.

"It doesn't bear thinking about."

Disappointment threatened to choke her, though she wasn't sure what she'd hoped he would say. Did she want him to apologize for holding them to the same vow that drove his own daughter from the order?

Izzy didn't know what else to say. Except as she stared at Rhett, as she wondered what Tahlia and Iah would tell her now, new determination leant strength to her limbs. She straightened, taking a steadying breath.

"Give me something to try," she said. "Anything that could make a difference."

Rhett was slow to speak, and the new determined glint to his eyes struck new fear in her heart. Would he try to save her at Collin's expense? Rewrite the ending by taking *everything* from her?

"I'll be dead before anyone lays a hand on him," she growled. "So give me an idea how to save him. You know more about this than anyone."

"If I had any idea how to break this curse, I would've tried it years ago."

"I'm not looking for simple answers. I'm looking for *any* scrap of hope that we won't be dead by sunrise."

Rhett shook his head. But when he spoke again his voice was quiet, coaxing.

"I know you and Collin like my own children. He would have you end his suffering rather than risk causing you harm."

Izzy was on her feet before she was aware of it, head pounding as fury rippled out from her chest.

"No," she said, voice shaking.

"You know it's true."

"*You* have no say in this, Commander Rhett. My vows say nothing of my choice tonight."

"Izzy..."

"Goodbye."

The word broke from Izzy's lips. Rhett fell silent, a stricken look on his face. Izzy forced herself to keep speaking.

"I pray I'll see you after tonight, but if I don't...I want you to know that I am grateful for the home you gave us among the Red Cloaks."

Rhett stared at her. There was more Izzy wanted to tell him, so much more. But she couldn't bring herself to say it. As Rhett stared at her, she suspected the same was true for him. He lifted his hand as if to reach for her, only to drop it back to his side.

He left without a word.

CHAPTER SEVENTEEN

Izzy

Izzy hugged her knees to her chest. Frantic energy pulsed through her limbs, demanding she get up and *move*, but she stayed where she was. She couldn't get Rhett's voice out of her head. *He'd rather you end his suffering...*

That was only true because he believed death was his only posible fate. Izzy wouldn't accept that. She leaned her head back too quickly, skull striking stone with a sharp ache that spread across her head. How did she find hope in this hopeless curse?

Almighty, I beg you...help me find an end to this evil. Not just for our sakes, but for the sakes of every victim. For the sake of those who come after us.

Izzy didn't receive a discernible answer. No sudden idea or slowing of time. But she kept praying as her thoughts churned and churned searching for any hint of what might save them.

Crimson caught her attention from the side of her vision.

"It's time to enter the tower."

Izzy turned to meet Hendrick's gaze. He was often the choice to guard the tower on Wolf Moons, and as he stared at her now she thought she understood why. She didn't think she saw any pity or mercy in his gaze. He wouldn't hesitate to kill either of them if he believed it necessary.

Could she trust him not to interfere? He'd spoken in their defense when Mercer brought his accusation. He'd also advocated for their punishment.

Izzy stood and approached the door, her eyes flicking to the sunlight still staining the stones. They had a while yet before the moonlight would envelop the world...time she could spend with Collin.

The doors to the tower were thick and plated with steel, requiring two men to open and shut. Izzy walked through them with a steady gait that hid the uneven beat of her heart.

Where she stood was already in shadow, sunlight crawling up the wall above her head. She followed the wall all the way to the circular scrap of sky far above her. The tower stretched higher than the city wall, and as worn and chipped as they were perhaps she could scale those stones. But she wouldn't. Not unless she needed to buy herself time.

"Izzy."

Izzy turned, her eyes meeting Collin's gaze as he entered the tower. She barely caught a glimpse of their friends at his back, Hendrick's grim expression as the doors swung shut. She was running for his arms.

She collided with him, throwing her arms around his neck, and for a moment nothing else existed. His arms wrapped around her back, clinging to her with a familiar desperation. Izzy stared over his shoulder at the closed door, the side of her head pressed against his as they breathed and held on tight. If only it was so simple as never letting go of him.

"You have to leave," Collin whispered hoarsely.

"No," Izzy growled, tightening her arms. "I'm staying right here."

"Izzy." Her name was a groan, his arms gripping her like he

wasn't sure whether to hold her tighter or rip her away. "I don't want to hurt you."

"I'm not abandoning you. And I am *not* killing you."

"Instead, you'll stand around and let me kill *you*."

She shook her head fiercely. No. She would never inflict that on him. But neither would she end his life, no matter what he became. Even if they were loose in the city and lives were at stake, she wasn't sure she'd be able to stop him. The thought terrified her. It also fueled her fierce and desperate faith that there *was* a way to conquer this.

She finally stood why so many of the foils chose to enter the tower, even knowing it would bring their death. How could she not *try*?

Izzy pulled back, and Collin's arms tightened around her for a short moment before loosening. Letting her step away if she wanted to. But Izzy only backed away enough to look him in the eyes, to take his face in her hands so he couldn't turn away.

"Neither of us is dying tonight."

Collin laughed brokenly. "I wish I shared your optimism."

She did too. Seeing the pain in his eyes, the wild edge like a caged animal, broke something inside her. His lips parted.

"Izzy, I..."

"Kiss me."

Collin paused, his eyebrows quirking down. "Is this really the time?"

He glanced up at the sky, seeking out how much sun they had left. Izzy dragged his face back down.

"Collin. Will you *finally* kiss me?"

He didn't argue again.

Perhaps Collin's kiss was awkward. It was certainly unpracticed. But no one was watching, and Izzy didn't care. It tasted of a thousand days spent together but apart, and thousand silent promises and stolen moments. A thousand beautiful dreams crushed to dust and moonbeams. Izzy would've dwelt in that moment forever.

Collin broke away, and for a long moment they stood like that, breathless in each other's arms. Izzy didn't open her eyes as Collin rested his head against hers. Her thoughts were scattered.

They were wise to avoid this before. Because if Collin had kissed her like that in the woods, she was sure everyone would've read it written across her face when they returned. Perhaps the lashes would've been worth it if they could've had the life they'd dreamed of for so long. But it was far too late for that.

"Try," Izzy said. "Promise me you'll *try*..."

Her voice broke, and she buried her face in his shoulder. His arms tightened around her, his voice quiet as he replied.

"I promise."

THE SUN WAS ALMOST GONE. Izzy could feel the moonlight now, as the world descended into shadow and twilight. It had risen hours ago, but as long as the sun drowned out its light the curse wouldn't take hold. It wasn't until moonlight enveloped the world unchallenged that their time would run out. Collin still insisted on putting the width of the tower between them some time ago.

Izzy couldn't take her eyes away from Collin, though she'd run out of words. Now they were both trapped in this agonizing wait, eyes locked on each other as they drank in what might be their last sight of one another. Izzy hadn't ceased praying since she'd crossed the threshold of the tower. Even she was growing weary of her repeated plea, but she couldn't stop. She couldn't give up.

Collin tensed as the last scrap of sunlight fled.

"Izzy," he said. "Please."

She didn't move. There was something in the air, a sensation that reminded her of the moon folk. But it soured on her tongue. She watched Collin silently fight against the curse digging into his flesh, helplessness eating away at her heart. There was nothing she could do to stop this, to make it easier.

A gasp slipped from her lips when she felt the same taste of moon and shadow dig into *her* flesh. It wrapped around her heart, strangling her as the two sides fought for dominance. She couldn't say which won. Strength flooded her limbs, but with it came a sense of abject vulnerability that made her claw at the stone behind her back. She had to run, to hide, to do anything to escape. But their time was up.

The change was quick, far quicker than Izzy was prepared for. One moment Collin stood across from her, silently begging her to climb the walls and flee. The next a wolf stood in his place.

Izzy stood frozen, lips parted in mute shock. She'd known what would happen, but that didn't mean she was prepared. *Collin...* A vice closed down around her chest, making each breath labored as she stared at the creature before her. *Almighty, save us.*

He shook his large head, nose pointed to the ground, and Izzy held her breath. Terror gripped her, and her hand automatically reached for her sword. But bile rose in her throat as her hands wrapped around leather and steel, stomach twisting as shame filled her every fiber. *This is Collin. This is* Collin. She needed to remember that just as much as he did. Finger by finger, she released her sword hilt.

Izzy had never seen a natural wolf, but she'd been told werewolves were always bigger. She would've sworn Collin was even larger yet. When he finally raised his head, it was higher than her own. She pressed herself against the tower wall, rough stone digging into her skin.

Maybe I should *run.*

Izzy crushed that thought mercilessly. She would not run from him. Even from a practical standpoint, only prey ran. And she wouldn't act like prey.

Her lungs screamed, and Izzy dragged in a breath. It was ragged and loud, and the wolf's head whipped around to face her. Amber eyes, a shade lighter than Collin's true eyes, pierced her through.

"Collin," she whispered.

The wolf took a step forward.

Not the wolf. *Collin.* Collin took a step forward, eyes glowing in the darkness. He lowered his head, and alarms rang in Izzy's mind. It was a hunting stance.

"Collin, I love you," she said, louder this time.

Was it her imagination that he paused? It was too quick for her to be sure, but Izzy remembered Thane. She remembered how his love's voice brought confusion, if not clarity. She had to keep talking.

"Collin I know you can hear me, no matter what chains Artyom locked you in."

Izzy stepped away from the wall. She wasn't sure if it was a sign of trust or a defensive measure; if it came to a fight, she couldn't afford to be pinned against the wall.

"I'm not going anywhere," she said, as she and the wolf slowly approached one another. "And I'm not going to treat you like a moonstruck animal. You're still Collin, I'm still Izzy. If this...if this was inside us all along, then *nothing has changed.*"

The wolf had stopped, but any hope that he was listening quickly melted away. He lowered his front half toward the ground, preparing to pounce. Izzy tensed, even as she continued speaking whatever words came to mind. When he sprang, she was ready.

Izzy dropped, sliding beneath Collin and spinning to face him as he collided with the ground. She lunged to the side, barely escaping the snapping jaws aiming to tear out her throat. Her heart thrummed in her chest, panic fighting to take hold of her limbs, to overrule her mind. She needed to draw her weapon, to *fight back.* But even as Collin lunged for her again, a bestial snarl ripping through the air when she evaded him, she kept her hands *empty.* And she kept talking.

"I've loved you since you dumped that bowl of caterpillars over

Mariel's head," she said, ducking his snapping jaws and sprinting to put some space between them.

The tower was so much smaller now. How long could she evade him?

"Or since you helped me save that kitten the miller wanted to drown."

She spun to face him, seeking which way to flee next.

"Whichever came first, I knew then and there I wanted to spend my life with you."

The wolf was still. Was he hesitating? Was he listening?

It was all the distraction he needed. He leaped, and this time Izzy didn't move fast enough. He knocked her against the wall, jaws latching onto the arm she raised between him and her throat. Teeth tore through leather and flesh, agony splitting through Izzy and drawing a cry from her lips. She grabbed his ear, jerking it down. He released her arm. But he came again for her throat, and Izzy barely managed to hold his muzzle away from her flesh.

Tears dripped down her cheeks as she fought with him. This was her last chance, her last desperate attempt. If she failed...she prayed Collin never knew how this ended. A low growl rumbled up his throat, his struggling against her grip slowing. Her arms trembled as she held on, her eyes meeting the predator's gaze staring down at her.

"I am yours Collin, now and forever. I *trust you*."

Now the wolf stilled. And though every thread of caution inside her was pulled taut, though her training warned her it was another feint, she loosened her grip. Slowly, ever so slowly, she raised empty hands to the side of her head.

"I trust you," she whispered. "I will always trust you."

The wolf drew closer, and a small gasp escaped her lips. *Please, Almighty, let him hear me. Please let it be enough.* Because it was all she had.

His nose pressed against the side of her neck, his teeth hidden away. She stretched shaking hands to grasp the thick fur along his neck.

The air changed, like a new breeze blowing through, and it was *Collin* standing there, his head pressed against her shoulder as his entire body trembled. Her hands rested on feverish skin, and hot tears ran down his face onto her shoulder. Izzy laughed breathlessly.

"I knew you could do it."

Collin groaned her name, lifting his head. And as their eyes met, Izzy's mouth spread in a trembling smile. She could hardly breathe for the heat raging in her chest. He was *alive*. The curse hadn't conquered them. She thought her heart might break free of her chest as Collin raised his hand and carefully brushed a tear from her cheek, his fingers trembling as they touched her skin.

The creak of the heavy door cut through her surreal relief. Izzy slipped away from Collin, drawing her sword as she stood between him and the three figures stepping into the tower.

"You won't touch him," she snarled.

Adrenaline was white hot in her veins, erasing the tearing pain from her arm as she held the sword. The front figure raised his hands.

"I'm not here to hurt anyone."

Eldon. He wouldn't lie. Another figure stepped forward, and Izzy twisted to face him. But he only tossed a set of clothes over her shoulder. Collin muttered a thanks, and Izzy's face blazed. In the heady relief she hadn't thought...she was careful not to turn around, focusing her attention on Eldon instead.

"Did Rhett order you to watch?"

"I'm here of my own will," Eldon replied. "You're the stubbornest pair I've known...I'd hoped you would make it through."

Izzy couldn't consider that, not yet. She couldn't afford more tears. She turned toward the other two, Hendrick and Sabriel if she had to guess.

"And you two?" she asked harshly.

"We have orders that no wolf is to leave the tower alive," Hendrick said.

Izzy tensed, but Hendrick continued.

"But since I don't see a wolf, I don't believe that order still stands."

"That's good of you," Collin said drily, his voice close to Izzy's back.

She huffed, keeping her sword raised even as Collin slipped an arm around her back to rest on her hip. She wasn't taking chances. She was *not* going to risk losing him again.

"You have to get out of here," Eldon said. "Even if Rhett accepts that the curse is broken, the city won't."

"If there *is* a city after tonight," Sabriel added.

As if summoned by Sabriel's words, Izzy heard the sounds of battle. It surrounded them, cries and clashing weapons echoing off the towering stonework. How could she hear it in such detail? It should've been muffled, distant... Izzy shook her head.

"They're in the city?" Collin asked.

"It doesn't matter," Eldon said. "We'll see to it. You need to get as far from Kedar as you can before the sun rises. I brought supplies that will last you until Horrheim."

Izzy twisted, meeting Collin's shadowed eyes. They were still that amber shade, eerie as they reflected the moonlight. But familiar as they silently conversed.

"We aren't fleeing," Collin said slowly. "Not yet, at least."

Sabriel replied, "You can't fight on the wall. Everyone knows you're marked. If anyone recognized you..."

"Calm down, Sabriel," Collin said. "I know we're as good as exiled. We're going to fight this war at the source."

The following silence only punctuated the sounds of battle raging around them. Izzy smelled smoke.

"You shouldn't." It was Eldon, quiet and pained. "You've already escaped death once tonight. Please, take the blessing you've been given and *go*."

Izzy turned to him. Curiously, his offer held little temptation. Her voice was sure as she responded.

"You know that isn't who we are."

Eldon turned to Collin, as if expecting him to see reason.

"Did you happen to bring me any weapons?" Collin asked.

Resignation overtook Eldon's plea, and he turned toward the door. "Everything is outside."

Sabriel fell in step beside Izzy and Collin as they followed Eldon.

"If I asked how you did it..."

"I'm not sure," Collin replied shortly.

"Right."

They were two steps out of the tower when Hendrick began handing Collin weapons. While Collin strapped them in place, Izzy knelt to look inside the two packs leaning against the wall. A lump rose in her throat as she took in everything Eldon had prepared. When she looked up at him, unable to voice her thanks, he smiled wanly.

Turning to Collin, Eldon drew a dagger from beneath his cloak. It was longer than Izzy's but bore an opal in its hilt that identified the two daggers as a matched set.

"A gift from Maizy," Eldon said thickly. "From all of us."

"Thank you," Collin said as he took the dagger, strapping it into place beside his others.

"You'll need these."

Izzy stood, turning to find Sabriel holding their cloaks out to them.

"We aren't Red Cloaks anymore," she said, and in spite of everything grief accompanied the words.

"You're always Red Cloaks," Eldon countered. "And these are yours no matter where you go."

Izzy took her cloak without further argument, its fabric chilled from the night air. As it settled over her shoulders something inside her fell back into place. It was strange how a mere symbol could mean so much, but it did. She turned to Collin and saw it mirrored in his eyes. Holding her breath, she nodded.

Together, they shouldered their small packs and turned to face Eldon, Hendrick, and Sabriel. For a moment no one moved or spoke. Then Eldon took a small step forward. But he didn't touch them, didn't embrace them as he would've before.

"May the Almighty protect you and give you the strength to defeat this evil," he said.

Collin's voice was warm as he said, "Thank you. We pray the same for the rest of Kedar's protectors."

Izzy stared at Eldon, wishing she knew what to say. Even if they survived a fight with Artyom, she knew they couldn't come back here.

"I hope we see you again," she whispered. It was the most honest farewell she could offer.

Eldon nodded, and she and Collin turned away as one. They'd only made it two steps before she grabbed his hand, rebellion against every chain that bound them raging through her blood. And he held on tight. Together they ran into the shadows.

CHAPTER
EIGHTEEN

Collin

Escaping the city proved almost as difficult as breaking the curse. Collin kept Izzy close, their fingers interwoven as they searched for a path through the scattered fights that blocked every path out of the city. It wasn't just keeping unseen: running past those fights without offering any help, leaving their friends and allies to fight alone...

But no true victory could be won here, not with Artyom still alive. That's what he repeated to himself as they turned a blind eye to the battle they should've been fighting. He knew Izzy struggled too... every time they passed Red Cloaks and watchmen fighting trolls and goblins in the streets her hand tensed around his. But they kept running.

He saw everything. His eyes pierced the darkness like never before, and Collin tried not to think about why as they navigated Kedar. And that wasn't the only sense that had sharpened: he smelled the smoke and blood coating the city, heard every pained cry and call of temporary victory, felt Izzy's presence at his side like miniature lightning strikes running up his arm. The wolf was still snapping to escape.

Izzy had said nothing about her arm as they readied themselves to escape. He prayed the wound wasn't serious. But the memory of her pain, of her blood on his tongue...*that* he feared he would never escape. He'd nearly killed her. And yet here she was, holding his hand and trusting him to lead them through a strange and deadly battlefield.

"I am yours, Collin, now and forever."

Those were the words that woke him up. He couldn't repeat what she'd said before, only that her voice had struck a chord deep inside, beyond the snarling bloodlust that encompassed his entire being. But those words, that promise...*that* broke through. Almost too late.

"I will always trust you."

She shouldn't. Collin knew she shouldn't have placed that much trust in him, not as weak as he was. But she had, and Collin clung to that gift as a lifeline. If she trusted him with her life even now, then he would trust that she would draw him out if the wolf took over again. And it *wanted* to take over.

He couldn't think about that now, couldn't afford to ask himself what he *was* or what to do about it. Defeating Artyom was his focus now. If the rite he'd just passed through helped them do it...he wouldn't think about it.

The northern gate was in sight. They left the alley, rounding the edges of a fierce fight. They were mostly ignored. But a familiar voice made Collin slow, twisting his head to see Dal leading an attack against an ogre with fire dripping from his hands. He stopped, looking back at Dal and the small force he had gathered around him.

Izzy tugged at his hand, pulling him on. *Keep them alive,* he prayed as he and Izzy leaped over splintered wood and bloodied corpses into the gray field beyond. Little of the horde was outside, at least on this side of the city. One glance to either side showed a shifting mass along the wall to the east and west. They were too focused on the city to bother with the two cloaked figures running for the trees.

"Any idea how to find him?" Izzy asked quietly as they ran.

"It'll be simple to sniff him out."

Collin glanced over, taking in Izzy's furrowed brows. They'd both picked up their pace by silent agreement when they reached open ground, breathing deep from the clean air.

"Can you feel it?" he asked.

Moonlight surrounded them here, washing over him like cool autumn rain. Already he felt...refreshed. Especially after the bitterness in the city, the air poisoned by more than smoke. He hadn't realized how much it dug into his skin until they'd left it behind. And now he could feel the trail of that poisoned shadow deeper in the trees ahead.

"I...do," Izzy said, mystified.

Collin slowed when they reached the trees, though he could see every rock and tree that interrupted their path, even the fallen leaves washed gray by what light filtered through the branches above.

"We can move faster," Izzy said quietly. "I can see."

Collin slowed, turning to Izzy and taking in the fearful look to her eyes. She could see. She could taste the thin thread of sorcery connecting the cloud over Kedar to its maker. Which meant...

It isn't just me.

A shard of relief pierced through his focus, countered by a grief that weighed heavy in his chest. He wasn't the only one who'd changed with the moon's rising. As Collin stared down at Izzy he knew neither of them were sure how to handle it. And yet he couldn't help but be glad that even in this they were united.

He elbowed her, forcing a grin to his lips.

"I'm glad I'm not the only one," he said. "You know I get tired of waiting for you to catch up."

Her eyes narrowed, and she kicked his shin. Collin gave into temptation and dipped his head, pressing a kiss to her lips. He didn't think he'd ever grow tired of the freedom to actually *kiss* her, though he prayed they would have plenty of years for it to become common place. The look of surprise on Izzy's face, perhaps even regret that he pulled away so quickly, filled his heart until it was near bursting.

Later. He would have time to express his love later. If they survived.

But Collin couldn't consider that they wouldn't survive, not after everything they'd overcome that night. Not knowing what would happen if Artyom continued his war of vengeance. He forced his focus back to the task at hand, running toward the bitter shadows further ahead.

Artyom wasn't in the deep forest like Collin expected. They came across him before Collin was prepared, stopping a dozen paces from the sorcerer. Artyom was staring at a raised piece of ground covered in moldering leaves.

"I'm disappointed," he said. "I'd hoped Rhett would come for me himself. But he's never been one for direct conflict, has he?"

Collin still held Izzy's hand, his fingers playing over the hilt of Eldon's gift beneath the cover of his cloak. He couldn't afford to draw it yet. Artyom continued as Collin and Izzy took a cautious step forward.

"Always making his plans from the shadows and sending others to do his work. I'm the same, of course. But at least I don't send children to get themselves killed doing my bidding."

"Do you see us as children?" Collin asked with genuine curiosity.

Artyom glanced their way, and Collin took from his shrewd look that he noticed how they were edging closer to him.

"You were children the first time you stumbled across my cottage. Children playing at a game they couldn't imagine the scope of. That's why I spared you, initially. I never liked harming children."

Izzy's hand tensed in his own, and he knew she was gritting her teeth against the accusations rising in his mind as well. There were children in Kedar that he'd already harmed, many of them.

"I suppose I even grew fond of you over the years," Artyom said, and Collin bit back a scoff. "You're so persistent. Just like Iah."

He glanced at the ground when he said that, and Collin wondered if this was where Iah was killed.

"Was he your son?" Collin asked.

They'd closed nearly half the distance between them, now. Collin wasn't sure how much closer Artyom would allow them. If they could keep him waxing on about the past...

"Grandson," Artyom corrected. "Though he had as little sense as my son. It's almost fitting that Iah was killed for the woman he loved, rather than his heritage. Just like his foolish father."

Collin didn't want to listen to Artyom's story, but they needed more time. Confronting him head on would likely end the same way it had last time. They couldn't afford to let Artyom disappear again.

Or would it? Artyom was maintaining a powerful spell. Collin could smell it surrounding the man, funneled up into the sky to rain down on Kedar and the horde. Perhaps that was distraction enough. And if not...perhaps breaking his concentration would give Kedar a fighting chance.

"I know you've come to kill me," Artyom said. "And after what I've done to you, it's fair really. But my work isn't done."

He offered an indulgent smile in their direction, and a snarl rose from Collin's chest. He barely managed to bite it back, though he didn't hide his sneer. Artyom's expression didn't falter.

"As an apology for making you the object of my revenge, I'll offer you the chance Iah never had. You can walk away now, and I will swear never to touch the lives of you or your family again."

Collin stopped, and Artyom turned to face them directly. His eyes were too bright as he examined them, manic. His voice was smooth and quiet as he spoke.

"You've already conquered so much. Walk away and begin a new life. Kedar gave up on you, the Red Cloaks betrayed you...why not leave it behind? It isn't as if you can return. Walk away and *forget*."

Collin looked at Izzy, and for a moment he allowed Artyom's honeyed words to wash over him. He could almost hear the smile in Artyom's voice as Collin stared down at Izzy.

Then Collin moved. In a single movement, he'd drawn his knife and flicked it at Artyom's chest. The silver gilt blade pierced through whatever protections he'd hedged around himself, but a jerk of his arm caused the knife to pierce through Artyom's bicep, rather than his heart. Izzy threw two more, smaller, knives. But those fell to the ground at Artyom's feet as he stumbled back, looking down at his arm in shock.

"The Red Cloaks *are* our family," Izzy said.

Collin smiled at her fierce words. They'd refused Eldon's plea. No amount of persuasive sorcery dripping from his lips could make them take his offer.

They lunged forward, intending to finish Artyom now while the shock was fresh. But the ground between them rumbled, roots breaking through the soil and writhing in the air. Collin and Izzy barely pulled back in time to avoid them.

Beyond the blockade, Artyom drew the dagger from his arm slowly, dropping it into the leaves.

"I suppose your names will join the many others who've died by my hand."

Cracking ripped through the air as two trees ripped more roots from the soil, their branches twisting into strange and broken limbs. Collin glimpsed obsidian set deep into their trunks, around eye level, before the golems were near enough to be a problem.

He and Izzy leaped apart to avoid an oak smashing club like branches on the ground where they'd stood. Golden leaves fell like thick rain, obscuring his sight as he ducked and leaped to avoid the thrashing trees. Above the groaning wood, he heard Artyom.

"Not to worry, I won't interfere with your game. I have plenty to do already."

"How considerate of you," Collin said in a half snarl, gritting his teeth to fight back the heat rising up his throat.

If only they'd brought an ax. Collin drew a dagger that was thick and sturdy, hacking at anything that came within arm's reach. As he fought his way toward the thick trunks, Izzy stayed back and danced between the two golems. It was a dangerous place to be, caught between the two of them, especially since she must be drained from fighting...him.

Collin shook his head and kept going. His dagger stuck in the next branch he attacked, and when the tree shifted it lifted him off the ground. Several curses ran through Collin's mind as he scrambled for a foothold. He found a grip just as the golem shook his knife free. Thick branches were twisting around him, forming a cage to crush him in the center, but Collin slipped through before they could close and hit the ground in a roll. He came up on his feet near Izzy.

"Your turn," he said, straightening.

She flashed him a dry look before leaping into the chaos of limb and leaf. Collin whispered a prayer for her safety as he drew another dagger, stepping into the dance of slashing, ducking, and lunging out of reach.

Collin glanced toward Artyom and realized he was watching them fight, bushy gray eyebrows low over his eyes. Concerned his golems wouldn't be enough to defeat them, was he? Collin could help that worry along.

Collin flashed a toothy grin at Artyom. "These hold up better than clay, I'll give you that."

A deep groan filled the air as the smaller tree toppled over in a crunch of broken branches. Izzy leaped free, landing a few steps from Collin as he ducked a swipe from the larger oak.

"Or not," he said, glancing again at Artyom.

He felt rather than saw Artyom's retribution. A fraction of soured moonlight pulled back from Kedar, centering over *them*. He glanced at Izzy with a grim smile that she already matched before he turned back to his taunting.

He nearly had his head knocked off trying to search for Artyom and turned his attention to the remaining golem. It was faster now, powered by more than whatever spell sat in the obsidian. He was glad they only had one to contend with as a stray branch ripped across his exposed skin. Golden leaves continued to rain down and Collin wondered how the branches weren't bare yet.

Still, with both of them fighting the same enemy, Collin had enough breath to speak.

"You'd probably say I should thank you for cursing us," Collin said. "Now that *your* twist is gone, our newly awakened heritage makes this sort of thing a lot easier. Don't you agree, Izzy?"

"Easier than most of what we do," she said, leaping over a low sweeping root and grabbing hold of a branch that carried her into the air, closer to the main trunk.

"But I don't feel like thanking you," Collin continued.

From within the tree, Izzy snorted at his casual statement. A genuine grin pulled at his lips, even as he severed branches trying to lift him from the ground by his hair. He lunged in between two woody limbs and stabbed the tip of his dagger into the trunk.

He missed the stone, and barely had enough time to yank the blade loose before ducking behind the trunk. A thick branch slammed against the trunk where he'd stood. Collin didn't have time to look for Artyom, but he thought the air held more malice than before.

"Maybe if you were as grandfatherly as you try to sound, I'd feel differently."

Stepping around the trunk, slamming his dagger into the stone. Obsidian shattered. Collin ran to escape the toppling tree.

"Then again, maybe not," he said as he ducked a now-limp branch falling toward the ground.

Collin emerged near Izzy, who appeared unharmed other than a ratty braid and a cut on her cheek. They twisted to face Artyom as one. The sorcerer stood with one hand gripping his wounded arm, glaring at them between the bare and broken branches of his fallen golems.

"What other witticisms do you have to offer?" he asked in a hiss. "Do you believe I'm so easily distracted?"

Collin shrugged. "It seems to be working."

He didn't think Artyom was lending much aid to the horde at the moment. The air around them was thick with rot and shadow, skeletal hands searching for a grip on his throat. And while Collin was fiercely glad they'd managed to distract him from Kedar, he wondered if now they'd be able to reach him.

Moonlight broke through the clouds, bathing the clearing in light, and Collin tensed. What would Artyom use *this* for? Artyom stood taller beneath the light, towering over Collin and Izzy with a fresh, wild grin.

But even as dread tangled in his chest, Collin realized he also was standing taller. He felt...renewed. As if the light surrounding them offered nourishment straight to his soul. The sensation of being strangled by mist faded. He breathed deep and rolled his shoulders, glancing at Izzy with a grin of his own. Aibek was right, cryptic or not. Artyom wasn't the only one who benefited from the full moon.

Collin drew his sword in unison with Izzy. Artyom watched them closely, and Collin knew they couldn't count on surprising him with any move they might make. He took another breath, plotting their course.

"Almighty, guide our hands," he prayed.

"Lend us strength to end this evil," Izzy continued.

They attacked as one. Collin leaped through the fallen tree, reaching Artyom first with the intension of battering him hard while Izzy went around. But Artyom sidestepped his sword with unexpected speed, thrusting a hand at Collin's chest with a single, hissed word.

Collin flew backward, skidding through the leaves until he hit a tree. His sword fell from his hand, his chest crushed by an invisible weight. But his eyes were clear as Artyom grabbed Izzy around the throat, his other hand holding her wrist to keep her from sliding her dagger up through his ribs. The look of pure hatred on his face spoke more clearly than words.

Heat ignited in his heart, washing through him like a wildfire as his body ripped itself apart and reassembled in a heartbeat. He was on four paws before he could blink, a wild snarl ripped from his throat. But his mind was icy clear as he lunged for Artyom.

He snapped at Artyom's arm first, forcing him to release Izzy. Then Collin went for his throat.

One, bloody moment and it was over. But Collin stood over Artyom's corpse a moment longer, a low snarl crawling up his throat as he waited for any sign that he'd missed his mark, that the sorcerer still lived. Only when he saw the life fade from Artyom's pale eyes did he lift his head.

Collin gingerly stepped over the body, his movements clumsy without bloodlust overruling his actions. He wanted to gag at the blood that coated his teeth. But he ignored it, searching for Izzy.

She stood a few steps away, her dagger still in her hand though she held it at her side. Fear flickered in her eyes, but was it fear of or *for* him? Collin didn't move. He was himself, the snarling beast submissive to his will, but Izzy had little way to know that.

Inwardly, he searched for the part of himself that knew how to activate the shift, to return to the form Izzy didn't have to fear. It was harder than before.

"Collin," she whispered, and her voice struck a cord that reverberated down to his very soul. He followed its path, holding tight.

He took one step toward her before he was a man again.

His cloak settled around his shoulders, making him suddenly aware that it was the only scrap of clothing he still wore. He stopped short, watching Izzy's face turn red as she turned away. She tossed his pack toward him without turning around, and Collin wasted no time in digging out new clothes.

He also washed the blood from his mouth, grimacing when the taste lingered. So did the snarling thing in his chest, begging to be used again. It would never leave him, now. The thought brought a wave of helplessness.

He hadn't asked for this. *Izzy* hadn't asked for this. Aibek claimed this was who he was created to be, but how was he supposed to move forward when he had little idea who he was anymore? He glanced up at Izzy's back, the leaves and twigs sticking out of the tangle that could hardly be called a braid anymore. He would let her decide. After all that he'd put her through that night, she was the one who should determine how they moved forward.

Almighty, guide us, he prayed. They couldn't go back. They would have to figure it out together.

Once decent, Collin approached Izzy slowly. She didn't turn around, though he knew she was aware of his proximity. Slowly, he set a hand on her shoulder.

She twisted around and threw herself into his arms. Sweet, drowning relief washed over him as he wrapped her in his arms, running his hand over her head, her back...

"Are you hurt?" he asked.

"No," she said. "Are you?"

"Healthier than ever."

Perhaps that was a lie. His ribs felt like he'd been stepped on by a draft horse, but it was easy to ignore with Izzy in his arms. She pulled back far enough that Collin could see her skeptical look. She prodded his ribs, and he couldn't hide a wince.

"Mostly healthy," he corrected. "Nothing that won't heal with time."

"Good."

Collin lowered his head, but Izzy pressed her fingertips to his lips to stop him. Confusion flooded his mind, until he saw the grimace on her face.

"I rinsed my mouth," he said, smiling against her fingers.

Again, that skeptical look. But she slowly lowered her fingers. Collin wasted no time capturing her lips with his.

CHAPTER NINETEEN

Izzy

Izzy held tight to Collin's hand, the breeze blowing her hair back as she looked out on Kedar. The destruction of the night was easily visible in the torn earth and bodies from the horde being piled in the fallow fields. But the walls still stood, and a flurry of activity surrounded the gates. They were preparing for the next attack. Izzy prayed it wouldn't come now that Artyom was dead.

They wore their cloaks, and Izzy knew they were easily visible from the wall. She'd thought she'd seen a flurry of activity shortly after they'd arrived at the edge of the trees, people pointing and shouting. But even with her eerily sharpened senses, she couldn't make out what they said.

"Here they come," Collin said, as crimson-clad figures emerged from the broken gate. Izzy stepped closer to Collin, hoping and dreading their arrival. Who came out to greet them? Who had survived the night?

Rhett was the first she recognized as he led the small group. The way he marched across the open ground, the stern set to his face...it was hard to mistake. Not long after Izzy recognized Dal and Alair walking behind him, and Andred. But not Eldon. Panic gripped her.

"He's probably with Abby and Maizy," Collin murmured. "They wouldn't have gone to him."

Izzy forced herself to nod, taking a slow breath in an attempt to calm her nerves. He was right.

Rhett stopped a distance away, holding up a hand for the others to stop with him. His gaze was hard and calculating as he looked them over, and it made Izzy feel small. She turned her eyes to Dal, Alair, and Andred, wondering if they would also look at Collin and Izzy with suspicion. But they were all smiling, relief softening even Andred's features. Dal lifted his hand in a wave, while Alair glanced from her and Collin's clasped hands back to their faces and winked.

"We wanted you to know that Artyom is dead," Collin said to Rhett. "There will be no more werewolves. We can't say the same for the horde, but they won't have a sorcerer's backing now."

Rhett continued to stare at them without speaking. Izzy swallowed before adding her own piece of their final report.

"The curse is gone, but the abilities it awoke within us remain. Collin is still a werewolf."

"But his hold on my will is broken." Those words came out in a near snarl, his hand gripping Izzy's tighter. "We're a danger only to our enemies."

"I can't risk Kedar," Rhett said, the words falling like stones. "They won't accept that you aren't a threat."

"We aren't asking to come back," Collin said.

Their friends' faces fell at that, and Izzy struggled to swallow back the grief of that truth. But her voice was steady when she spoke.

"We just...wanted everyone to know we survived. That we did our duty...we protected Kedar."

"But we also want to ask," Collin said slowly, "if you will release us from our vows. We're getting married either way, but if we can't expect your blessing we at least don't want to betray our oaths."

Alair let out a quiet whoop of joy with this news, but Andred elbowed him with a sharp look at Rhett. Izzy thought Dal's face might split in half with the width of his smile, and she grinned back. But that smile faded.

"Where's Eldon?" she asked.

"He's fine," Dal said soothingly. "He resigned this morning."

"Hendrick and Sabriel are locked up for letting you two loose," Andred added, watching Rhett carefully.

But Rhett still didn't speak. Nor did he look away from Collin and Izzy, cloaked with clasped hands.

"How did you two survive?" Alair asked.

"The same way we do everything," Collin replied with a laugh. "Together."

Dal rolled his eyes at that. After a moment of heavy silence, Collin took a step backward. Izzy followed, though their farewell felt incomplete.

"We'll leave now," Collin said. "May the Almighty guide and shield you."

"We'll send word once we find somewhere to settle," Izzy added, desperate for any connection to Kedar, however tenuous.

"You better," Alair said, with a smile Izzy couldn't help but answer.

"Stick around a while and we'll bring you some new boots," Dal added, his eyes on Collin's bare feet.

"I'd appreciate that," Collin said.

"We might even convince Eldon to come out here."

Izzy leaned into Collin, hope painful in her chest.

"Meet us on the north road," Collin said. "We won't be far."

"Will do."

Collin took another step backwards, and this time they kept moving. In some ways this had gone far better than Izzy had dared to hope. But it was still difficult to leave, even with the promise of seeing their friends once more. Her eyes went to Rhett, his gaze heavy as they slowly retreated.

"I release you from your vows," he said, his voice heavy with...

could it be grief? "And...you have my blessing, whatever that might be worth to you."

Her smile was all the thanks she could bring herself to offer, a light freedom filling her chest to overflowing.

"Don't cut your foot on a pinecone," Alair called, as they began to turn around.

"Don't be late," Collin called over his shoulder.

They didn't pause again after that, retreating into the trees where they were shielded from sight.

Their journey to the northern road was quiet. Though Izzy and Collin both watched their surroundings closely, Izzy wasn't wary of attack. The horde had fled after Artyom's death, and what little sign she and Collin had found indicated that they'd run far and long.

The tension in Izzy's limbs didn't last long, even if the turmoil of Rhett's mixed farewell lingered as a heavy weight in her chest. The morning air was crisp, and the sound of leaves tossed by the gentle breeze settled inside her with a comforting warmth. Scraps of mist and frost turned the forest floor silver, but her cloak blocked out the chill. It was a morning too peaceful to be real. Watching the autumn world around her, she could almost forget the evil and bloodshed these trees witnessed during the night.

Were they truly leaving this? The woods that had been their sanctuary, their home?

Collin's hand tightened around her own, and as she turned to look at him her heart settled. *He* was her home.

They'd hardly reached the northern road when the sound of hooves greeted them in the distance. Izzy and Collin stayed on the edge of the road, ready to melt into the shadows if it was strangers approaching. But the faces that greeted them as they rounded the bend were all familiar.

Alair was the first off his horse, coming straight for Izzy and lifting her off the ground in his exuberance.

"You two have the resilience of an alley cat," Dal said, throwing an arm around Collin's neck to drag him down to his level.

"And the sense of one, too," Berke said, dropping to the ground. "You escape one death just to run to another? Being titled guardians doesn't mean you save the entire moon-cursed city on your own!"

"Always ones for the showy task," Alair laughed, finally setting Izzy back on her feet.

"Enough from you," came Eldon's voice as he shoved aside Dal and Alair.

Izzy caught one glimpse of red rimmed eyes before Eldon threw his arms around both of them, embracing them with a fierceness Izzy hadn't experienced since she was a child. She held on just as tightly.

"Thank the Almighty," he breathed.

Izzy closed her eyes to hold back the tears that burned within them. But when he stepped back, she still had to wipe moisture from her cheeks. Dal shoved a pair of boots into Collin's arms.

"Put those on before you get frostbite. How did you walk all the way here with bare feet?"

"It's not as if I had a choice," Collin said, sitting on a rock to slip on the gifted boots.

Andred appeared beside Berke, a sack in her hands. Though her smile wasn't wide, the earnest relief in her eyes was enough to bring a fresh ache to Izzy's heart.

"We brought what Eldon missed," she said.

"He didn't find your savings," Alair said. "So we slipped it in with a few other...parting gifts."

Izzy raised her eyebrows as she peeked within the bag. A small flask of oil, a kit for repairing their armor, and a crumpled paper were all she saw.

"We made a list of where all to send word so Rhett doesn't have a say in who knows about it," Andred said. "He may have pardoned you unofficially, but none of us want to take chances."

"Thank you," Izzy said thickly.

"Tears on our Iron Girl?" Dal said. "Better get it together, or we might think you'll miss us."

Izzy glared at Dal before stepping forward to drag him into an embrace. His laughter didn't fully disguise his own emotion as he wrapped his arms around her, gently patting her back. When she stepped away, Collin was at her side, already wrapping an arm around her waist.

"Stay in contact," Eldon said. "Changes are coming for Kedar. It may be that years will allow the memory to fade...you may not need to stay away forever."

Izzy didn't have much hope of being welcomed in Kedar again. She knew how fear and pain lingered. But she smiled at Eldon, praying that he was right...that this farewell wasn't final.

"We will," Collin said. "If Kedar ever needs us..."

"You've done more than Kedar should've ever demanded of you," Eldon said heatedly. Seeing the fire in his eyes, Izzy wondered if he truly meant what *Rhett* should've demanded from them. But she wouldn't ask.

Alair elbowed Collin. "Let us take some of the glory for a change."

"And you aren't the only ones willing to aid a friend," Berke said. "If you ever need us, we'll come."

That promise, more than any other word spoken that morning, made Izzy wish desperately that they didn't have to go. She looked at Eldon and found him staring at her with a sad smile.

"Don't allow your past to determine your future," he said. "You are free of any vows made to Kedar or her leaders. Don't let them bind you."

"We don't plan to," Collin said, his hand tightening around Izzy's waist.

"But don't forget us," Alair said.

Izzy smiled. "Do you believe we're so faithless?"

Silence overtook them, no one wanting to begin the separation that they all feared would be indefinite. But they couldn't stand there forever. Izzy and Collin stepped back as one, though as they did a chasm opened in Izzy's chest. Their friends watched them, sorrow tugging at their eyes. But they let them go.

They each shouldered their packs, their friends' gifts safely stowed within. And as with Rhett, they didn't immediately turn to face their path. But this time it was for an entirely different reason. Izzy stared at their friends, their family, memorizing each face with a prayer that she'd see them again.

"The Almighty keep you," Collin murmured.

Their friends all bowed deeply, fists raised to their hearts in silent homage. Izzy turned away before she lost all will to continue. And though neither of them was ready to leave Kedar behind, though each step away from their friends tore against her heart, her eyes looked to the horizon. To the future shrouded in mist and moonlight that awaited them.

She never had to leave Collin's side again. That gave Izzy the strength to keep walking.

Izzy stood with her back to the wall, surveying the celebration that filled the streets around them. A bright gibbous moon shone above them, though its light was disguised by the hundreds of torches and candles lighting the town. How long had it been since she'd seen people celebrate with such *joy*?

Of course, her own joy had more to do with Collin's arm around her waist than the music. It was still strange showing affection in full view, not having to hide every touch or resist the desire to step into his arms.

They'd been staying in Horrheim for a few days, ever since the local minister married them. And every moment since taking those vows, vows she meant with every fiber of her soul, had been better than she'd imagined.

"How about the sea?" Collin asked, quiet in spite of the cacophony surrounding them. Izzy still heard him clearly.

"Tempting," she replied. "I don't want to go across it, though."

"Where's your sense of adventure?"

Izzy glared up at him. He only grinned.

The only shadow hanging over them now was where to go. Izzy didn't want to stay this close to Kedar, nor did Collin. To be a few days travel away and forbidden to return...it was too much. Better to begin a new life entirely, take their chance to explore the world they'd only heard stories of. If only their freedom didn't feel so much like exile.

"I want a purpose," Izzy said, tucking herself deeper against Collin's side and ignoring the indulgent looks of older women sitting nearby.

Horrheim was smaller than Kedar, and everyone seemed to recognize them as the newlywed strangers. Oddly enough, Izzy didn't mind their attention. At least, not as long as she had Collin beside her.

"Yes," Collin said. His voice was heavy, and Izzy knew what he was thinking.

They'd talked a few times about what their new conditions meant for the future. Izzy had assured him in every way she knew how that she would stand by them, that they would find a place where they could live in the open. But she knew he was still struggling. Some adjustments would take time.

The question in his eyes dwelt in her mind as well. Could they find a place that didn't see werewolves as something to *fear*? Could they find a place and a purpose when they'd be unknown, untested... untrusted? But the alternative...

Izzy didn't want to wander aimlessly. And the idea of settling down somewhere, anonymous and idle, twisted her stomach into knots. They'd spent so many years *protecting* people. She wasn't sure she was ready to give that up.

"It doesn't hurt to wander a while," Collin said. "We'll look for where we're needed."

"Alright," she said.

Now Collin looked down at her, likely hearing the doubt in her voice. Before them, the song ended with a round of applause and laughter. Collin stepped away from the wall.

"Come on," he said, tugging her toward the dancing. "Let's see if we can dance *without* weapons for a change."

Izzy shook her head but followed him into the crowd. She glanced up as they took their places, staring at the bright moon. Her worries drained away as the first notes of music trembled in the air.

Collin

"We can travel west and see how far we get," Collin said coaxingly. "You know I've always wanted to see the coast."

Izzy shot him a glare, her finger still resting against the rough map carved into the board before them.

"And you know that winter isn't far away. Where would we stay between here and there?"

"I'm sure there are plenty of small villages that don't make it onto a map like this."

He gestured to the weathered wood. The map stood beside the town's announcement board, which bore a few weathered scraps of bark and parchment offering animals for sale or asking for workers on the nearby farms. Collin wasn't sure how much they could trust the map at all, but it was the best they had. Eldon had been too generous when he filled their packs, and their friends had brought their stocked up wages when they'd met them on the road. But they still didn't have enough to spend a small fortune on a decent map of their own.

"But will those villagers want strangers intruding when food will already be scarce?"

Collin caught her unspoken concern. After a week in Horrheim,

Collin knew it would be difficult to hide his...condition. Especially somewhere small.

He beat back the lingering sense of vulnerability, of loss. Izzy had accepted the entirety of who he was just as she always had, but not everyone would be so trusting. He didn't want to be a monster villagers hunted to protect their children. Which meant they had to find somewhere large enough that they could melt into the crowds.

"Fine," Collin sighed. "North it is."

Izzy didn't respond. She was looking off to their right, and when Collin followed her gaze he spotted the couple immediately. They looked familiar in a vague way he couldn't place. And they were staring straight at them.

"They were with the caravan," Izzy whispered.

"They saved Mercer's hide," Collin said with sudden clarity.

"Yes."

Collin didn't have time to ask what Izzy knew about them other than that they could fight. The couple stopped a few paces from them with welcoming smiles that Collin returned cautiously.

"Collin and Izzy, is it?" the man said.

"Yes," Collin replied. "I'm afraid I never caught your names."

A wry smile flashed across the woman's face, there and gone in a heartbeat. "He's Fremont, and I'm Risha."

"We're glad we've run into you," Fremont said. "We'd hoped to see you in Kedar, but learned too late that you'd...left."

That hesitation told Collin that they knew he and Izzy had a rough departure. But how much else did they know? And *why* would they seek them out?

"We wanted to see the world outside of Kedar," Collin said easily.

"And freedom from restrictive rules?" Risha asked, her eyes fixed on their clasped hands.

Collin's smile sharpened. "That too."

"We were impressed with your skills when we fought south of Kedar," Fremont said. "It isn't often we find people skilled in fighting dark magic."

"The Red Cloaks are all trained," Izzy said.

"But we hear few are as proficient as you two."

Collin didn't answer, nor did Izzy. He wanted to know what these two were hinting at.

"We wondered if you'd be interested in continuing your line of work outside of Kedar," Fremont said. "We know our employer would be interested to meet you."

Collin didn't have to turn to Izzy. The tightening of her hand, the way she shifted her cloak to make it easier to draw one of her knives...she was intrigued, but cautious. So was he.

"We might be interested," Collin said slowly. "But we don't follow blindly."

They both grinned.

"That's just what we're looking for."

"Who is your employer?" Izzy asked, a subtle challenge in her voice.

The pair looked immensely pleased at that question, but it was a mischievous sort of pleasure that set Collin a little more at ease. There was no malice in their expressions. Fremont's smile turned secretive.

"Have you ever heard of Nyxwood?"

WANT MORE OF IZZY AND COLLIN?

If you want to know how Izzy and Collin first met Eldon and Rhett, **sign up for my newsletter!**
You'll receive the Wolf Heart short story "Potential," as well as...

- "Dreams and Vows," a bonus story from Memories of Salt and Stone,
- A journey into the mind of a storyteller with too many stories to tell,
- The story of the Blood-born Champion and the Stuttering Songbird who follows him,
- And an Ashton Legacies short story following the events of *Aderes in Karkhana*

My newsletter will give you updates on my author adventures, recommendations from my bookshelf, and glimpses of the wonder saturating the world around us.

ALSO BY MAEGAN M. SIMPSON

CHANGED HEARTS COLLECTION

Stone Heart

LEGENDS OF EMYR

Memories of Salt and Stone

Memories of Sea and Sky

Memories of Blood and Bone

Memories of Truth and Terror

THE AGONIZOMAI SERIES:

Frosted Fire

Born in Darkness

Broken Healer

Menacing Whispers

Winds of Wrath

Shrouded Hope

Heir Eternal

ASHTON LEGACIES:

Aderes in Karkhana

Viggo in Orlin

SECRETS OF THE NATIONAL PARKS SERIES:

Shadow of Memory

Dragon's Flight

Midnight's Wings

About the Author

Maegan M. Simpson accepts many titles, including Daydreamer, Mountain Girl, and Indie Author of 16 books. She believes that God created our world full of beauty and wonder, even in the broken pieces, and endeavors to capture that wonder in her writing.

Maegan's life so far has been full of adventures, whether it's finishing college, taming dragons (alright, they're cats), or devouring every book she can get her hands on. When she's not exploring fantasy lands or searching for faeries in the shadows, Maegan lives in rural New Mexico with her family. There, she enjoys gardening, painting, and exploring the mountains she calls home.

For more books and updates visit https://maeganmsimpson.com/

www.ingramcontent.com/pod-product-compliance
Lightning Source LLC
Chambersburg PA
CBHW020458310726
48979CB00016B/2713/J

9781966420002